享受學習英語的樂趣！

　　中國人學英文最大的困難，就是開不了口說，很多人學了英文幾十年，還是不會說，這是全世界非英語系的國家，學英文共同遭遇的困難，全世界的人類，不知道浪費了多少時間、生命、多少金錢在這上面。編者十多年前就開始研究，閱讀了四十多本長篇小說，試著汲取書中的佳句，編寫語言教材，通通都失敗，其中發明了「三句一組、一次說三句」的英語會話方式，雖然對英語會話有立即的效果，但總不能每天對著牆壁講話，太痛苦了吧！

背了幾篇演講稿，勝過在美國待十幾年！

　　「演講式英語」解決了一切的困難，**不需要外國人，自己就可以背，背完就可以演講**。到美國東學一句、西學一句，太慢了，只要背熟幾篇演講稿，就遠超過在美國待十幾年。自「演講式英語」開班以來，班上有小孩子、有遠從美國來的華僑，也有從屏東、高雄坐飛機來上課的，由此可知「演講式英語」的魔力。

說好英語，是一項藝

　　一般演講稿句子太長，不適合非
誦，而且演講的內容非日常生活用語，
會忘記。「**演講式英語**」句子短，簡潔有

說的話組成，特別平易近人，只要背了 20 篇，英文程度可想而知，同學可以從 20 篇中，混合組成無數篇英語演講，利用這些精心挑選的句子，說出來的話之美、之藝術，遠超過一般美國人。

「演講式英語」是語言學習的革命

　　「演講式英語」的發明，是語言學習的革命，將來所有的語言教科書，都將被淘汰，**那些讀了沒有效果的東西，長**

期摧殘人類的生命，真奇怪！現在科技如此進步，唯有「語言學習法」還是和百年前一樣。「劉毅英文家教班」成立四十年來，讓同學一年考得比一年好，現在的榜單簡直無人能比，同學分數之高，別人都不敢相信。可是，他們都沒有享受到，學習英文的樂趣，如果，讓他們從高一開始，背 20 篇演講稿，那到了高三，不管什麼考試，不管什麼演講啦、托福啦，都能得心應手。

會演講，自然會寫英文作文

這些演講稿，我們花了很多年的時間才完成，每個句子精挑細選，務必是美國人日常生活說的話，編者自己都先試背過，背完後一個月，再背一遍，背不下來的再改正，一切以容易背為原則，前前後後經過無數位中外人士的實驗，我可以肯定的說，**這些演講稿，同學可以背下來**，並且終身受用。「演講式英語」也可說是萬用作文，背完不僅立刻會說英文，也可增加字彙，演講中的句子，也可用在作文中。

背演講是學習英語發音最自然的方法

「演講式英語」的錄製方式，真不簡單，首先，我們**排除萬難**，找了一對美國男女，**男生的聲音很有磁性，女生的聲音像天使**，非常好聽。在演講班有位小朋友，五歲半，她跟著練習，一個月後，英語發音竟然和美國人一樣，所以越小學英文越好。

背完的同學，只要常掃瞄錄音 QR 碼，常常聽，就不會忘記，懶的同學，跟著美籍老師反覆唸，自然就會背，ABC 還不會的孩子，只要常常聽錄音，自然就會。**小孩子最好用自然學習的方法，不要強迫他**。有人說，小孩應該學兒童美語，像河馬 hippo，犀牛 rhino 等等，事實上，孩子每天都接觸大人、接觸電視，而且很快就會長大，這些大概一輩子都用不到。可是，背「**演講式英語**」，從十歲到九十歲都用得到。

你也可以成爲一個英文演講高手！

學英文，最簡單的方法就是「背」。要背，就要背最好的東西。「演講式英語」的內容，都實際在班上使用過，效果奇佳，爆發力非常強。經過許多英文老師的見證，「演講式英語」有下列好處：

1. 馬上開口説英文：只要你掃瞄錄音 QR 碼，開口跟著美籍老師唸，很容易就能琅琅上口，你會發現，用英文演講，比用中文演講還要容易，因爲大部份的人都聽不懂，你只要隨便説，別人就會很佩服你。

2. 隨時隨地可以練習：很多人認爲，學英文最大的困難，是沒有練習英語的環境、沒有外國人可以交談，但是，你只要背了「演講式英語」，你會發現，你每天説英文的時間，比説中文的時間多，你不需要外國老師，自己就可以學，有了要參加演講比賽的目標，背起來非常的快。

3. 聽説讀寫樣樣行：只要背了演講稿，你就可以説出優美的英語，會説了，自然聽得懂別人説什麼，會説英文，自然可以將它寫出來；會寫了，當然會讀。演講稿背多了，閱讀英文雜誌、看起英文報紙來，會覺得非常親切、不會陌生。

4. 培養自信，就從演講開始：每次背完一篇演講稿，就可以上台演練，面對群眾演講，是一種難得的經驗，在教室裡面，每個同學都有要上台演講的衝動，一旦上台，有了同學的鼓勵，更加對英文有興趣。能夠上台用英文演講，還怕不敢跟外國人説話嗎？背過的好東西講出來，當然有自信。

5. 背一篇，就是一篇：英文像是大海，範圍無限大，東學一點、西學一點，學得模模糊糊，學了多少，忘了

多少，背演講稿，實實在在，背一篇就是一篇，背得愈多，不僅英文能力增加，知識也隨之增加，無論和中國人或外國人交談，都頭頭是道。

6. 自言自語有益健康：根據心理學家研究，每天自言自語有助於健康。自言自語背英文演講稿，妙極了！你不會煩惱、不會寂寞，會覺得人生真美好，每天只要不斷地背英文，一天有精神，身體愈來愈好！

7. 演講可以改變個性：用英文演講，能改變自己的個性，會變得活潑又美麗。例如：演講班有一位學生，原本在學校學期末，老師寫的評語是「個性內向害羞」，在她上了一期演講班後，表現優異，在台上，可以大聲背出英文，所有人都為她喝采，她覺得很光榮，個性就改變了，由內向變得外向，每天見到老師、同學都笑咪咪，後來，她居然被老師選為班長。

英文演講稿，背多了當然會忘記，想要不忘記，最簡單的方法，就是教別人，一個人可以教，兩個人也可以教，一百人也可以教，教別人「演講式英語」，最大的受益者就是自己。老師看到同學原本不會開口說英文，原本對英文沒興趣，當學生能夠上台侃侃而談，用英文演講，老師就會感受到很有成就感，會愈教愈起勁。

「演講式英語」源自「劉毅演講式英語①②冊」，原來版面大、紙張厚，不容易攜帶。精編後，去掉不需要的頁數，縮小成 25 開，紙張改成 60 磅以下，讀者拿起來輕鬆，旅行時可隨身攜帶。

劉 毅

CONTENTS

1. Self-introduction
自我介紹

1

Ladies and gentlemen:	各位先生，各位女士：
It's great to be here!	很高興來到這裏！
I'd like to introduce myself.	我想要介紹我自己。
My name is Pat.	我的名字叫派特。
I'm a student.	我是個學生。
I come from Taiwan.	我是台灣人。
I'm an outgoing person.	我很外向。
I love to meet people.	我喜歡接觸人群。
Meeting people is my forte.	和別人接觸是我的專長。
I'm very frugal.	我非常節省。
Money doesn't burn a hole in my pocket.	我不會亂花錢。
But I like to be generous with my friends.	但是我喜歡對朋友慷慨。

** ————————————

self-introduction〔ˌsɛlfˌɪntrə'dʌkʃən〕*n.* 自我介紹
introduce〔ˌɪntrə'djus〕*v.* 介紹　　Pat〔pæt〕*n.* 派特
outgoing〔'aʊtˌgoɪŋ〕*adj.* 外向的　　meet〔mit〕*n.* 認識；和～接觸
forte〔fort, for'te〕*n.* 專長　　frugal〔'frugl̩〕*adj.* 節省的
money burns a hole in one's pocket 某人亂花錢
generous〔'dʒɛnərəs〕*adj.* 慷慨的；大方的

1

I have many hobbies.　　　　　我有很多嗜好。
I enjoy many things.　　　　　我喜歡做的事很多。
I like reading, exercising,　　　我喜歡閱讀、運動，和旅行。
　and traveling.

Traveling is my life.　　　　　旅行是我的最愛。
I love to travel.　　　　　　　我愛旅行。
I'm not a stick in the mud.　　我不喜歡老是待在一個地方不動。

I'm always on the go.　　　　　我總是到處走動。
I'm always on the move.　　　　我總是動個不停。
I would never let the grass　　我絕不會待在一個地方不動。
　grow under my feet.

I'm a rolling stone.　　　　　我很好動。
I can't keep still.　　　　　　我無法靜止不動。
I can't stay in one place too long.　我不能在一個地方待太久。

I want to see the world.　　　我想看看這個世界。
I want to see the unseen.　　　我想去看沒看過的東西。
I want to do what's never　　　我想做以前沒做過的事。
　been done before.

** ————————————————

stick〔stɪk〕*n.* 棍子　　mud〔mʌd〕*n.* 泥土
stick in the mud 不常走動的人；喜歡待在一個地方的人
on the go ①不斷地走動；②忙個不停
on the move 在走動；在動個不停　　grass〔græs〕*n.* 草
let the grass grow under *one's feet* 某人待在一個地方不動
rolling stone 好動的人　　still〔stɪl〕*adj.* 靜止的；不動的
unseen〔ʌnˈsin〕*n.* 沒看過的東西

1

My ambition is to be a great
English teacher.
Teaching English is my passion.
Mastering English is my goal.

I won't accept mediocrity.
I want to grow.
I want to improve all aspects
of my life, physically,
spiritually, and academically.

I'm willing to work hard.
I'm willing to pay the price.
I'm prepared to go the distance,
through thick and thin, in
good times or bad, under
any circumstances.

我的志願是成爲一個很棒的
英文老師。
敎英文是我的愛好。
學好英文是我的目標。

我不能接受普普通通。
我要成長。
我要改進我人生的各個層面，
在身體、心靈和學術方面。

我願意努力工作。
我願意付出代價。
我準備要堅持到底，在任何
情況下，無論甘苦，無論情
況是好是壞。

** ───────────

ambition〔æm'bɪʃən〕*n.* 志願；野心
passion〔'pæʃən〕*n.* 愛好；熱情　　master〔'mæstɚ〕*v.* 精通
mediocrity〔ˌmidɪ'ɑkrətɪ〕*n.* 平庸；普通
aspect〔'æspɛkt〕*n.* 方面　　spiritually〔'spɪrɪtʃʊəlɪ〕*adv.* 心靈上
academically〔ˌækə'dɛmɪkəlɪ〕*adv.* 學術上
willing〔'wɪlɪŋ〕*adj.* 願意的　　***go the distance*** 堅持到底
through thick and thin 不顧甘苦
in good times or bad 不畏艱難；不論是好是壞
under any circumstances 在任何情況下

1

I work like a madman.	我拼命工作。
I work like a maniac.	我瘋狂地工作。
I'm relentless in the pursuit of my goal.	我持續不斷地追求我的目標。
I have some drawbacks.	我有一些缺點。
First, I'm always changing my mind.	第一，我老是改變心意。
This is something I want to work on.	這是我想要努力改進的。
Second, I have a bad sense of direction.	第二，我方向感很差。
I often get lost.	我常常迷路。
When I'm with another person, I always let him guide me.	當我和另一個人在一起時，我總是會讓他來帶著我走。
Third, I'm a forgetful person.	第三，我很健忘。
I often misplace things.	我常常忘記把東西擺在哪裏。
I'm the type of person who is always losing things.	我是那種老是會掉東西的人。

** —————————————

madman〔'mædmən〕*n.* 瘋子　maniac〔'menɪ,æk〕*n.* 瘋子
relentless〔rɪ'lɛntlɪs〕*adj.* 不間斷的；持續的；不屈不撓的
drawback〔'drɔ,bæk〕*n.* 缺點　*change one's mind* 改變心意
work on 努力　*a sense of direction* 方向感　*get lost* 迷路
guide〔gaɪd〕*v.* 引導　forgetful〔fɚ'gɛtfəl〕*adj.* 健忘的
misplace〔mɪs'ples〕*v.* 忘了把～擺在哪裏　type〔taɪp〕*n.* 類型

1

What is worse, I'm not very smart.　　更糟的是，我不是很聰明。
My IQ is very low.　　我的智商很低。
I can only do one thing at a time.　　我一次只能做一件事。

I can only pay attention to what's　　我只能注意重要的事。
　important.
When I want to do something,　　當我要做某件事的時候，我
　I want to do it well.　　就要把事情做好。
I hate to do it halfway.　　我討厭半途而廢。

I have my good qualities.　　我有我的優點。
Number one: I'm a team player.　　第一，我很有團隊精神。
I'm a person of responsibility.　　我是個有責任感的人。

I seldom complain.　　我很少抱怨。
I seldom lose my temper.　　我很少發脾氣。
I'm a person of action.　　我是會做事的人。

Number two: I'm optimistic.　　第二，我很樂觀。
I'm happy-go-lucky.　　我很樂天。
I always look on the bright side　　我總是看事情的光明面。
　of things.

** ————————————————

　what is worse 更糟的是　　*IQ* 智商 (= *intelligence quotient*)
　at a time 一次　　*pay attention to* 注意
　halfway〔'hæf͵we〕*adv.* 不徹底地　　quality〔'kwɑlətɪ〕*n.* 特質
　good quality 優點　　*team player* 有團隊精神的人
　lose one's temper 發脾氣　　*a person of action* 行動家
　optimistic〔͵ɑptə'mɪstɪk〕*adj.* 樂觀的
　happy-go-lucky〔'hæpɪgo͵lʌkɪ〕*adj.* 樂天的；隨遇而安的

I have a big heart.	我心胸寬大。
I hold no grudges.	我不會懷恨在心。
I always let bygones be bygones.	我總是既往不咎。
Number three: I'm very thoughtful.	第三，我非常體貼。
I'm very considerate.	我很善解人意。
I'm a person who cares about others.	我很關心別人。
My motto is: Play hard, study hard, and work hard.	我的座右銘是：盡情玩樂、用功讀書，努力工作。
I do as much as I can every day.	我每一天都盡力而為。
I don't waste any time.	我不浪費任何時間。
God only gives us a certain period of time.	上帝只給我們某一段時間。
He wants us to make the best use of it.	他要我們做最好的利用。
He wants us to enjoy it.	他要我們過得快樂。

** ————————————————

have a big heart 心胸寬大　　hold〔hold〕*v.*（心中）懷著
grudge〔grʌdʒ〕*n.* 怨恨
bygones〔'baɪ,gɔnz〕*n. pl.* 過去的事（注意發音，重音不要唸錯）
Let bygones be bygones.【諺】既往不咎。
thoughtful〔'θɔtfəl〕*adj.* 體貼的
considerate〔kən'sɪdərɪt〕*adj.* 體貼的　　***care about*** 關心
motto〔'mato〕*n.* 座右銘　　certain〔'sɝtn̩〕*adj.* 某一
period〔'pɪrɪəd〕*n.* 一段（時間）　　***make the best use of*** 善用

1

Enjoy life while you're still young.	趁年輕，享受人生。
Don't miss any opportunities.	不要錯過任何機會。
Don't pass up any good chances.	不要放棄任何好機會。

Life is short.	人生是短暫的。
Life is sweet.	人生是甜美的。
Life is precious.	人生是珍貴的。

Go for broke.	全力以赴。
Live for the moment.	為此刻而活。
I live my life like there is no tomorrow.	我要好好生活，就當做沒有明天。

Live it up.	盡情享受人生。
Try new things.	嘗試新事物。
Eat, drink, and be merry, for tomorrow may never come.	盡情吃、喝、玩樂，因為明天可能永遠不會來。

**

miss〔mɪs〕v. 錯過　　opportunity〔͵ɑpɚ'tjunətɪ〕n. 機會
pass up ①放棄（＝*give up*）　②拒絕（＝*reject*）
precious〔'prɛʃəs〕*adj.* 珍貴的　　broke〔brok〕*adj.* 破產的
go for broke 全力以赴；孤注一擲
moment〔'momənt〕*n.* 時刻
Live it up. 盡情享受人生。（＝*Enjoy life to the full.*）
merry〔'mɛrɪ〕*adj.* 快樂的（＝*happy*）

1

I don't care if I live a long or short life.

我不在乎活多久。

To me, quality is more important than quantity.

對我而言,質比量更重要。

I want to live each day as my last.

我想要把每一天當作是最後一天。

Yesterday is history.

昨天是歷史。

Tomorrow is a mystery.

明天是個謎。

Today is a present.

今天是個禮物。

My philosophy of life is:

我的人生哲學是:

I will try to help the people around me.

我會儘量幫助我周圍的人。

The closer they are to me, the more I like them.

愈是跟我親近的人,我就愈喜歡他們。

People are a good investment.

人是一種很好的投資。

Helping people is an investment in heaven.

幫助別人,就是把錢投資在天上。

This kind of investment will earn high interest.

這種投資,會有很高的利息。

※※ ――――――――――――――――

quality (´kwɑlətɪ) *n.* 品質　　quantity (´kwɑntətɪ) *n.* 量
mystery (´mɪstrɪ) *n.* 謎　　present (´prɛznt) *n.* 禮物;現在
philosophy (fə´lɑsəfɪ) *n.* 哲學
investment (ɪn´vɛstmənt) *n.* 投資
heaven (´hɛvən) *n.* 天堂;天空　　earn (ɜn) *v.* 獲得
interest (´ɪntrɪst) *n.* 利息

1

Love and be loved.　　　　　　愛人者，人恆愛之。
Live and let live.　　　　　　　相互幫助，共存共榮。
If the people around me are　　　如果周圍的人快樂，我也會很
　happy, I'm happy.　　　　　　快樂。

I like making friends with　　　我喜歡交朋友。
　people.
I hope we'll become good　　　希望我們能成為好朋友。
　friends.
I'm looking forward to seeing　我期待很快能再見到大家。
　you again soon.

Please feel free to call me.　　　請不要拘束，儘管打電話給我。
I'm open 24/7.　　　　　　　　我任何時間都可以。
I never close.　　　　　　　　　我從不打烊。

Thank you.　　　　　　　　　　謝謝。
God bless you!　　　　　　　　祝福大家！
Have a great day.　　　　　　　再見。

** ————————————————

Live and let live. 【諺】自己活，也讓別人活；相互幫助，共存共榮。
make friends with 和～交朋友
look forward to + *V-ing* 期待　　*feel free* 不要拘束
24/7 任何時間（唸成 twenty-four seven）
be open 24/7 是指一個禮拜的七天中，二十四小時都不休息，即
　「全年無休；從不打烊」。

【背景説明】

1

這篇自我介紹太重要了！你用的機會太多了。

1. Ladies and gentlemen: (各位先生，各位女士：)

    演講時，美國人都先說：Ladies and gentlemen，如果只看到女士，只說 Ladies，如果只看到男士，說：Gentlemen，看到小孩也在，就可以說：Ladies and gentlemen, boys and girls。

2. It's great to be here! (很高興來到這裏！)

    這句話美國人常說，也可說成 I'm happy to be here. 或是 I'm pleased to be here.

3. *I'd like to* introduce myself. (我想要介紹我自己。)

    這裏的 I'd like to = I would like to = I want to
    I'd like to 和 I like to 不同，I'd like to 是「我要」，
    I like 是「我喜歡」。

4. 如果是比較不正式的自我介紹，例如參加美國旅行團，叫各人作自我介紹，通常是導遊叫大家站在一起，作自我介紹，你就可以直接說：My name is Pat.
    I'm a student.
    I come from Taiwan.

    即使只是這三句話，就是一個簡單的自我介紹。

5. **Pat** (派特)

    > 這個名字，男女皆可用，是男生名字 Patrick (派屈克)、女生名字 Patricia (派翠西亞) 的暱稱，皆含有出身高貴的意思。你如果沒有英文名字，不妨用這個名字。

1

6. I come from Taiwan. (我是台灣人。)

= *I am from Taiwan.*

> 用現在式動詞，表示過去如此，現在如此，未來也如此，是
> 不變的事實，所以表示「我是台灣人。」若要告訴別人「我從
> 台灣過來的」，要用過去式，要說 *I came from Taiwan.*

7. 現在，唸 **100** 遍：*Ladies and gentlemen:*
> *It's great to be here.*
> *I'd like to introduce myself.*

> 你會發現你已經完美地說出三句開場白了。

8. Meeting people is my forte.

> forte 這個字，來自法文 forté，這個字的發音很特別，
> 根據 K.K.音標發音字典，forte 應該唸成〔fort, fort〕，
> 而在 Encarta World English Dictionary 上，則唸成
> 〔fort, for'te〕，但是現今美國人，大多唸成〔for'te〕，
> 我們應根據美國人最新的唸法。

9. Traveling is my life.

> 字面的意思是「旅行是我的生命」，引申爲「旅行是我的最愛。」
> 下面的句子美國人也常用：

> > Traveling is my love. (旅行是我的愛好。)
> > Traveling is my passion. (旅行是我的愛好。)
> > Traveling is my interest. (旅行是我的興趣。)

10. I am not a *stick in the mud.*

> (我不喜歡老是待在一個地方不動。)

> > *stick in the mud* 字面的意思是陷入泥沼中的棍子，不能
> > 移動或移動得很慢，引申爲「老古板；守舊的人」，或引
> > 申爲「不常走動的人；喜歡待在一個地方的人」。

1

11. I would never let the grass grow under my feet.

這句話字面的意思是「我不會讓草在我腳下生長」，引申為「我不會待在一個地方不動；我好動。」

這句話有幽默的語氣。

12. I am a *rolling stone*. (我很好動。)

rolling stone 原指「經常改變地址或職業的人」，在此表示「好動的人」。源自諺語：A rolling stone gathers no moss. (滾石不生苔。)

13. Teaching English is my passion.

很多人被 passion 這個字害死了。在字典上，passion 這個字大多當「激情；熱情」解，事實上，passion 這個字，最常用的意思是「愛好」(a strong liking)。

Teaching English is my passion. 意思就是「教英文是我的愛好。」這句話的語氣比 Teaching English is my interest. (教英文是我的興趣。) 強烈。

14. Mastering English is my goal.

字面的意思是「精通英文是我的目標」，也就是「把英文學好是我的目標。」

> Mastering English is my goal.
> = Learning English well is my goal.

15. I want to improve⁄all aspects of my life,⁄physically, ⁄spiritually, ⁄and academically.

這句話很長，但是美國人常說，美國小孩寫作文也常用。中國人說「德、智、體」，中國人強調品德第一，美國人強調身體第一 (physically)。難怪美國人一般說來身體強壯。

美國小孩子從小所接受的教導就是 You have to take care of yourself *physically*, *spiritually* and *academically*.
（你要好好地照顧你的身心和學業。）

16. I'*m prepared* to go the distance.（我準備要堅持到底。）

    I'm prepared 雖然是被動形式，但意義卻是主動，此種用法是為了強調。

17. I'*m always changing* my mind.（我老是改變心意。）

    現在進行式與 always 連用，可表示說話者認為不良的習慣。

    注意：在這篇演講稿中，有很多這種用法。

18. My IQ is very low.

    I can only do one thing at a time.

    > 這是美國人的幽默。美國人常常喜歡嘲笑自己，來取悅他人。
    > 美國人常常自嘲說：
    >
    > My IQ is very low.（我的智商很低。）
    > I'm stupid.（我是笨蛋。）
    > I'm dumb.（我很笨。）
    >
    > 例如，迷路了，美國人就會自言自語說這些話。
    > 很多美國人喜歡一件事沒做好，就想做另一件事，他們的
    > 父母常教導他們：
    >
    > Do one thing at a time.（一次只做一件事。）
    > *Doing things one at a time* is the only way
    > 　 to do things.
    > 　（一次做一件事情，是做事情唯一的方法。）
    > Take one step at a time.（一步一腳印。）

1

19. I have my good qualities.

「優點」的説法有：① good quality ② good point ③ strength

20. I'm a person of action.

如果照字典的翻法，a person of action 是「行動家」，這句話如果你翻成「我是行動家」，不是一般人所講的語言，所以不容易被接受，正確的翻法應該是「我是會做事的人。」表示我不是光説不練的人。

21. I'm happy-go-lucky.

happy-go-lucky 英文解釋是 taking things as they come，就是「隨遇而安；聽天由命；無憂無慮」的意思。

22. Go for broke. (全力以赴；孤注一擲。)

表示去做某事，若做不成，金錢、名譽都將破產。源自賭博，將所有的錢孤注一擲。這句話是慣用句，broke 是形容詞，做介詞 for 的受詞，似乎不可能，所以，要當作慣用句來背。

23. Yesterday is history.
Tomorrow is a mystery.
Today is a present.

關鍵在 present 這個字，是雙關語，表示「現在」也表示「禮物」。這三句話的重點是在，我們能有今天，就是上帝給我們的禮物。這三句話的意思是「昨天已經成歷史了，已經沒有了。明天是神祕的，還不知道有沒有。今天就是禮物，是最重要的。」這是美國人的文化，強調活在當下的急迫性。

在這篇演講稿中，有很多這種觀念，像 Go for broke.
Live for the moment. I live my life like there is no
tomorrow. 都是美國人的思想，你跟美國人講這類的話，他們會覺得很興奮、很親切。

1

24. People *are* a good investment. (人是一種很好的投資。)

> 動詞 are 和主詞 People 一致，和補語 a good investment
> 無關。這個觀念很多文法書都弄錯了。

25. Love and be loved.
    Live and let live.

> Love and be loved. 是 Love and you shall be loved.
> 的省略。Live and let live. 是 Live and let others live.
> 的省略。這兩句話的意思就是「愛人者，人恆愛之。自己活，
> 也要讓別人活。」

26. I'm open 24/7.

> 唸成 I'm open twenty-four seven.
>
> 便利商店 7-11 有一個故事，這種便利商店原本是從早上
> 7:00 開到晚上 11:00，所以稱作 7-11。
>
> 有一天，有家店的門鎖壞了，不得不繼續營業，結果他們
> 發現，夜裏生意好得出奇，於是他們便改成 24 小時營業，
> 原本想把名字改爲 24-7，但因爲大家已經習慣 7-11 這個名
> 稱了，所以改不過來。
>
> I'm open 24/7. 就表示 I'm open 24 hours 7 days a week.
> 表示「我全年無休。」

27. God bless you! (祝福大家！)

> 通常有人打噴嚏時，美國人會回應這句話：God bless you.
> 意思是「上帝祝福你。」有一個傳說是在古歐洲的時候，流
> 行一種可怕的病——瘟疫，得了這種病會一直打噴嚏，只要
> 打噴嚏就代表這個人活不久了，於是教宗便宣佈，只要有
> 人打噴嚏，就要祝福這個人，所以聽到有人打噴嚏，就會
> 回應這句話，現在可引申爲祝福的話。

1

【作文範例】

1. My Hobbies

I have many hobbies. I enjoy many things. I like reading, exercising, and traveling. Traveling is my life. I love to travel. I am not a stick in the mud. I am always on the go. I am always on the move. I would never let the grass grow under my feet. I am a rolling stone. I can't keep still. I can't stay in one place too long. I want to see the world. I want to see the unseen. I want to do what's never been done before.

Sometimes I like to go to the park just to be alone. I consider the park my favorite retreat. I can sit on a bench and read without anyone bothering me. I can also stroll around the park to give my eyes a rest. Walking in the park is my favorite exercise.

2. My Ambition

My ambition is to be a great English teacher. Teaching English is my passion. Mastering English is my goal.

I won't accept mediocrity. I want to grow. I want to improve all aspects of my life, physically, spiritually, and academically. I am willing to work hard. I am willing to

1

pay the price. I am prepared to go the distance, through thick and thin, in good times or bad, under any circumstances. I work like a mad man. I work like a maniac. I am relentless in the pursuit of my goal.

3. My Good Qualities and Drawbacks

I have some good qualities. Number one: I am a team player. I am a responsible person. I seldom complain. I seldom lose my temper. I am a person of action. I can get the job done. *Number two:* I am optimistic. I am happy-go-lucky. I always look on the bright side of things. I have a big heart. I hold no grudges. I always let bygones be bygones. *Number three:* I am very thoughtful. I am very considerate. I am a person who cares about others.

I have my drawbacks. First, I am always changing my mind. This is something I want to work on. *Second,* I have a bad sense of direction. I often get lost. When I am with another person, I always let him guide me. *Third,* I am a forgetful person. I often misplace things. I am the type of person who is always losing things. *What is worse,* I am not very smart. My IQ is very low. I can only do one thing at a time. I can only pay attention to what's important. When I want to do it, I want to do it well. I hate to do it halfway.

4. My Motto

My motto is "Play hard, study hard, and work hard." I do as much as I can every day. I don't waste any time. God only gives us a certain period of time. He wants us to make the best use of it. He wants us to enjoy it. We should enjoy life while we are still young. Don't miss any opportunities. Don't pass up any good chances. Life is short. Life is sweet. Life is precious.

Go for broke. Live for the moment. I live my life like there is no tomorrow. Live it up. Try new things. Eat, drink, and be merry, for tomorrow may never come. I don't care if I live a long or short life. To me, quality is more important than quantity. I want to live each day as my last. Yesterday is history. Tomorrow is a mystery. Today is a present.

5. My Philosophy of Life

My philosophy of life is, "I should try to help the people around me. The closer they are to me, the more I like them." I am convinced that people are a good investment. Helping people is an investment in heaven. This kind of investment will earn high interest.

Love and be loved. Live and let live. If I am eating steak, I will at least let my friends have a bite. If the people around me are happy, I'm happy. In this way, as years go by, I will have more and more friends. I am sure I will never be lonely. I will be a merry old man.

2. *How to Master English*
如何學好英文

2

Ladies and gentlemen:	各位先生，各位女士：
It's an honor to be here.	很榮幸來到這裏。
I'm anxious to share a secret.	我急著想要告訴你們一個秘密。
English is everywhere.	英文很重要。
English is a key to success.	英文是成功的秘訣。
We must master it.	我們必須把英文學好。
So many people study English.	有很多人在學英文。
So few can speak it well.	但很少人可以說得很好。
What is the problem here?	到底是什麼問題呢？
People study the wrong material.	我們在研讀錯誤的教材。
People use the wrong methods.	我們在使用錯誤的方法。
We are wasting our time.	我們在浪費時間。
I've researched every method.	我已經研究了每一種方法。
I've tried them all from A to Z.	我徹底地試過所有的方法。
Old methods are not useful.	老方法沒有用。

** ——————————————————

honor (ˋɑnɚ) *n.* 榮幸　　anxious (ˋæŋkʃəs) *adj.* 渴望的
be anxious to V. 急著想～　　share (ʃɛr) *v.* 分享
master (ˋmæstɚ) *v.* 精通　　material (məˋtɪrɪəl) *n.* 教材
waste (west) *v.* 浪費　　research (ˋrisɝtʃ) *v.* 研究
from A to Z 徹底地 (= *thoroughly*)

2

Traditional methods are too limited.	傳統的方法效果十分有限。
They teach only one sentence for each idea.	他們一個觀念只教一個句子。
If we forget it, we're out of luck.	如果我們忘了，我們就完了。
We learn "Situational Dialogues," like going to the post office, or visiting the doctor.	我們學的是「情境對話」，像是去郵局或看醫生的對話。
Do we have any chance to use them?	我們有機會使用這些情境對話嗎？
The answer is "No."	答案是「沒有。」
We can't go to the post office every day to practice English.	我們不能每天到郵局練習英文。
We can't expect people to talk based on the situational dialogues.	我們不能期待別人用情境對話爲基礎和我們說話。
If we don't use them, how can we remember them?	如果我們不使用這些對話，我們如何記住它們呢？

**　** ———————————————

traditional〔trə'dıʃənḷ〕 *adj.* 傳統的
limited〔'lımıtıd〕 *adj.* 有限的　　***out of luck*** 完了
situational〔ˌsıtʃʊ'eʃənḷ〕 *adj.* 情境的
Situational Dialogues 情境對話
visit〔'vızıt〕 *v.* 看（醫生）(＝*see*)　　***be based on*** 以～爲基礎

Luckily, *now we have invented a shortcut.*	幸好，現在我們發明了一個捷徑。
We have found a new method of learning English.	我們找到一個學習英文的新方法。
I'd like to introduce a specially designed speech draft.	我要介紹一個特別設計的演講稿。
In this draft, three sentences are one unit.	在這篇演講稿中，三個句子為一組。
Each unit connects with another.	一組接著一組。
They are all linked together like a chain.	就像一條鏈子環環相扣。
The content is common and simple.	內容既常用又簡單。
It's made up of everyday American speech.	它是由日常生活美語所組成。
By using the material in the speech, you can speak great English.	藉著使用這篇演講教材，你可以說出很棒的英文。

**

luckily (ˈlʌkɪlɪ) *adv.* 幸運地   invent (ɪnˈvɛnt) *v.* 發明
shortcut (ˈʃɔrtˌkʌt) *n.* 捷徑   specially (ˈspɛʃəlɪ) *adv.* 特別地
designed (dɪˈzaɪnd) *adj.* 設計好的   draft (dræft) *n.* 草稿
unit (ˈjunɪt) *n.* 單位   *connect with* 連結
link (lɪŋk) *v.* 連結   chain (tʃen) *n.* 鏈子
content (ˈkɑntɛnt) *n.* 內容
common (ˈkɑmən) *adj.* 常用的；實用的
be made up of 由～組成

2

By memorizing one speech, you will start to speak English.

背好一篇演講，你將會開始說英文。

By memorizing ten speeches, you will become fluent in English.

背好十篇演講，你的英文會變得流利。

By memorizing twenty, you will speak better than native English speakers.

背好二十篇，你會比土生土長的外國人說得還要好。

The reason for that is you have been trained to speak well.

理由是你已經被訓練說好英文。

The sentences you speak have been carefully selected.

你所說的句子，都是經過仔細的挑選。

Memorizing the speeches has the following benefits:

背誦演講稿有下列好處：

Number one: You can practice alone.

第一，你可以獨自練習。

You can speak to yourselves.

你可以對自己說話。

You don't need a conversation partner.

你不需要練習對話的對象。

** ——————————

fluent ('fluənt) *adj.* 流利的   native ('netɪv) *adj.* 本土的
benefit ('bɛnəfɪt) *n.* 好處   alone (ə'lon) *adv.* 獨自地
partner ('pɑrtnə) *n.* 伙伴

2

Number two: Whenever you feel lonely or depressed, you can practice a speech.

第二，當你感到寂寞或沮喪時，你可以練習演講。

Did you notice that monks chant scriptures over and over?

你有沒有注意到和尚都是一再反覆地唸經嗎？

Reciting the speech again and again can give you peace of mind.

重覆不停地背誦演講可以使你心靈平靜。

Number three: Since the speeches are carefully designed, they are easy to remember.

第三，因爲這些演講是精心設計過的，很容易記下來。

Anyone can learn them.

人人都能夠學習它們。

Anyone can remember them.

人人都能夠記住它們。

With them, you can easily learn to speak English in threes.

用這些演講稿，你可以很容易學會說三句一組的英文。

Speak three sentences in a row.

連續說三個句子。

Then, you can say one sentence after another nonstop like you're making a speech.

然後，你就會不停地一句接一句，就像在發表一篇演講。

** ───────────────

lonely〔'lonlɪ〕*adj.* 寂寞的   depressed〔dɪ'prɛst〕*adj.* 沮喪的
monk〔mʌŋk〕*n.* 和尚   chant〔tʃænt〕*v.* 唸經
scripture〔'skrɪptʃɚ〕*n.* 經典
over and over 一再反覆地（= *again and again*）
recite〔rɪ'saɪt〕*v.* 背誦   ***peace of mind*** 心靈平靜
in threes 三句爲一組   ***in a row*** 連續
nonstop〔'nɑn'stɑp〕*adv.* 不停地

Number four: The speeches inspire.　　　第四，演講可以鼓舞人心。
The speeches are great for learning.　　　演講對學習很有幫助。
They build confidence and　　　　　　演講可以同時建立你的自
　　language skills at the same time.　　　信及語言能力。

Ladies and gentlemen, with the　　　各位先生，各位女士，演
　　speeches you will excel.　　　　　　講可以使你勝過他人。
Practice and memorize the speeches.　　要多練習，多背演講。
There is no better way.　　　　　　　沒有更好的方法。

Don't wait.　　　　　　　　　　　　不要等待。
Don't hesitate.　　　　　　　　　　不要猶豫。
Now is the time to change the way　　現在是你改變學習英文方
　　you learn English.　　　　　　　法的時候。

But, *remember*, *to speak English*　　但是，記得，英文要說得
　　fluently requires four more　　　流利，還需要四件事。
　　things:
First, practice, practice, practice.　　首先，要不斷練習。
Repetition is the key.　　　　　　　重覆背誦是關鍵。

** ────────────────

inspire〔ɪn'spaɪr〕*v.* 鼓舞人心
build〔bɪld〕*v.* 建立　　confidence〔'kɑnfədəns〕*n.* 自信
skill〔skɪl〕*n.* 技能；能力　　*at the same time* 同時
excel〔ɪk'sɛl〕*v.* 勝過他人　　hesitate〔'hɛzə,tet〕*v.* 猶豫
require〔rɪ'kwaɪr〕*v.* 需要　　repetition〔,rɛpɪ'tɪʃən〕*n.* 重覆背誦

Speak up.	大膽說。
Speak loudly.	大聲說。
Right or wrong, always be heard.	不管說對或說錯,你都要讓別人聽到你的聲音。
Be confident.	要有自信。
Be fearless.	要有勇氣。
You must make mistakes to improve.	你必須在錯誤中求進步。
Speaking English is most important.	說英文絕對重要。
Make conversation your priority.	會話第一優先。
Writing, reading, and listening will follow.	接下來才是寫作、閱讀,和聽力。
Second, teach others English.	第二,教別人英文。
Help them and you help yourselves.	幫助別人,就是幫助自己。
You will improve too.	你也會跟著進步。
Teaching is the best motivation for memorizing the speech.	教別人英文是背好演講的最大動力。
You will never get sick and tired of teaching the speech.	教演講不會讓你感到厭煩。
The more you teach, the more articulate you will be.	教得越多,你的口才就會越好。

** ————————————————

speak up 大膽說　　confident〔ˈkɑnfədənt〕*adj.* 自信的
fearless〔ˈfɪrlɪs〕*adj.* 勇敢的　　improve〔ɪmˈpruv〕*v.* 改善;進步
priority〔praɪˈɔrətɪ〕*n.* 優先的事　　motivation〔ˌmotəˈveʃən〕*n.* 動力
get sick and tired of 對~感到厭煩
articulate〔ɑrˈtɪkjəlɪt〕*adj.* 口才好的

2

Third, try like hell.	第三，拼命努力。
Immerse yourselves.	專心投入。
Eat, drink and sleep English.	時時刻刻想著英文。
Go nuts.	爲英文瘋狂。
Go bananas.	爲英文發瘋。
Be an English maniac.	做一個英文狂人。
Be a sponge.	像一個海綿。
Soak English up.	吸收英文。
Seek every opportunity to speak.	尋找每個說英文的機會。
Fourth, enjoy English!	第四，要喜愛英文！
Make English your love.	讓英文成爲你的最愛。
Make learning and progress fun.	讓學習及進步成爲一件有趣的事。
Put English first.	以英文爲第一。
You need to have passion.	你需要有熱情。
English requires commitment.	英文需要專注。
To sum up, memorizing the speeches is the way to go.	總之，背演講是唯一的方法。
So many students say they don't have the chance to practice English.	很多學生說他們沒有機會可以練習英文。
Wrong!	錯！

** ——————————

try like hell 拼命努力　　immerse〔ɪˋmɝs〕v. 專心於
eat, drink and sleep 時時刻刻想著…　　***go nuts*** 發瘋
go bananas 發瘋　　maniac〔ˋmenɪˏæk〕n. 瘋子
sponge〔spʌndʒ〕n. 海綿　　***soak up*** 吸收
progress〔ˋprɑgrɛs〕n. 進步　　passion〔ˋpæʃən〕n. 愛好
commitment〔kəˋmɪtmənt〕n. 專心；專注　　***to sum up*** 總之

2

With the speeches, the chance
　is everywhere.　　　　　　　這些演講，讓機會隨處
　　　　　　　　　　　　　　　可見。
The initiative is with you.　　主動權在於你自己。
The ball is in your court.　　一切由你決定。

Practice, speak, and talk.　　多練習，多講，多說。
Practice until you get fluent.　練習直到你說得流利爲止。
Speak and talk until you become　說到你的聲音變得沙啞。
　hoarse.

Your confidence will soar.　　你的自信會增加。
Your progress will amaze everyone.　你的進步會讓每個人吃驚。
You won't want to stop speaking　你不會想要停止說英文。
　English.

Let's roll.　　　　　　　　　我們開始吧。
Take action now.　　　　　　現在開始行動。
English is waiting for you.　　英文在等著你。

Thanks very much.　　　　　非常感謝。
It's always a pleasure.　　　十分榮幸。
Have a lovely day.　　　　　再見。

** ————

initiative〔ɪ'nɪʃɪ,etɪv〕*n.* 主動權　　court〔kort〕*n.* 球場
hoarse〔hors〕*adj.* 聲音沙啞的　　soar〔sor〕*v.* 提高
amaze〔ə'mez〕*v.* 使…吃驚　　***Let's roll.*** 我們開始吧。
take action 開始行動　　pleasure〔'plɛʒɚ〕*n.* 榮幸
lovely〔'lʌvlɪ〕*adj.* 愉快的

2

【背景說明】

　　　　這篇演講稿中的內容太珍貴了，你將學會真正說好英文的訣竅。

1. I'm anxious to *share* a secret.
   （我急著想要告訴你們一個秘密。）

> 一般中國人只會說 I'm anxious to *share* a secret *with you*.
> 但是美國人可以把 *with you* 省略。美國人很喜歡用 share
> 這個字表示與人分享。
>
> 如：I'd like to *share* a story.
>
> 當然也可以說 I'd like to tell a story.
>
> 當句子短的時候，接 with *sb.* 的情況比較多。
>
> 如：I'd like to *share* my ideas *with* you.

2. I've tried them all *from A to Z*.
   = I've tried them all *thoroughly*.
   （我徹底地試過所有的方式。）

　　美國人很喜歡用 *from A to Z* 這個片語來加強語氣。

　　如：I've been to all the hotels *from A to Z*.
　　　　（所有的飯店我都去過了。）

　　　　He knows this book *from A to Z*.
　　　　（他熟讀了這本書。）

　　　　He knows Taipei *from A to Z*.
　　　　（他對台北市很了解。）

3. If we forget it, we're *out of luck*.

（如果我們忘了，我們就完了。）

> 當某人走投無路時，代表好運氣全用完了。out of luck 字面的意思是「沒運氣了」，引申為「倒楣透了；完了」。

>> We are *out of luck*.（我們完了；我們慘了。）
>> = We are *through*.
>> = We are *done for*.

4. The speeches inspire.

> inspire〔ɪn'spaɪr〕*v.* 鼓舞人心；給予靈感

> 在這句話中，inspire 是不及物動詞，作「鼓舞人心」解（ = *give inspiration*)。

5. Speak up.

> 你如果看到同學不敢開口說英文，你就可以說：

>> Speak up.（大聲說出來。）
>> Speak loudly.（大聲說。）
>> Don't be afraid to make mistakes.（不要害怕說錯。）
>> (speak up = speak out)

> Speak up. 有兩個意思：
> ① speak out「說出來」② speak loudly「大聲說」。

6. *Right or wrong*, always be heard.

（不管對錯，你都會被聽到。）

> *right or wrong* 是副詞片語，「不管對錯」的意思，是 *whether it is right or wrong* 的省略。
>
> 如：I intend to do this, *right or wrong*.
> （我打算做這件事情，不管對或錯。）

2

7. Teaching is the best motivation for memorizing the speech.
（教書是背演講最好的動力。）

和美國人在一起，一天到晚聽他們講 motivate 和 motivation
這兩個字，我們要好好研究一下。

No matter what you do, motivation is the key.
（無論你做什麼事，動機就是關鍵。）

I was motivated by your speech.
（你的話鼓舞了我。）

8. You will never get sick and tired of teaching the speech.

美國人喜歡說 sick and tired of，但是要注意這個成語的
發音，要唸成 sick'n'tired of〔ˈsɪkn̩ˈtaɪrdəv〕，這是一般
美國人的習慣說法。

例：*I'm sick and tired of* hamburgers.
（我對漢堡感到厭煩了。）

I'm sick and tired of the rain.
（這場雨使我感到厭煩。）

副詞子句

9. *The more you teach*, the more articulate you *will* be.
　　　　　　　　　　主要子句

the…the〜是相關修飾詞，第二個 the…所引導的是主要
子句，所以才用 shall，will 表示未來。（詳見文法寶典 p.504）

10. Try like hell. （拼命努力。）

字面的意思是「像在地獄裡面一樣嘗試。」所謂嘗試，就是
努力，表示「拼命努力。」

2

11. Immerse yourselves. (專心投入。)
    = Commit yourselves.
    = Be committed

    美國人說 immerse yourselves，但他們不說
    be immersed (誤)

    > 如： ***Immerse yourselves*** in your studies. (專心讀書。)
    > = ***Commit yourselves*** to your studies.
    > = ***Be committed*** to your studies.

12. Eat, drink and sleep English. (時時刻刻想著英文。)
    = Think about English all the time.

    > 如： Eat, drink and sleep reading. (時時刻刻都在閱讀。)
    > = Read all the time.

13. Go nuts.
    = Go bananas. (發瘋。)

    Go nuts. Go bananas. 也許是猴子看到堅果或香蕉會發瘋。

    說成： Go nuts for English.
    = Go bananas for English.
    = Go crazy for English.

14. Be an English maniac. (為英文瘋狂。)

    maniac 是「瘋子」的意思，引申為「～的癖好者」。

    > 如： He is a fishing maniac. (他很喜歡釣魚。)

15. 美國人喜歡說 Be a sponge. 在美國人小時候，父母常常教
    導他們說： ***Be a sponge.*** (要像海綿一樣。)
    Soak it all up. (全部都吸收。)
    Soak up every drop. (滴水不漏的吸收。)

    你要常說 ***Be a sponge.*** Soak English up. 說起來才像美
    國本土的人，這是美國的文化。

2

16. Make <u>English</u> your <u>love</u>.（讓英文成為你的最愛。）
    受詞   受詞補語

你也可以說：

Make English your constant companion.
（讓英文常常陪伴你。）
Don't leave home without it.
（英文永遠與你同在。）

17. English requires *commitment*.（學英文需要專心。）
= English requires dedication.

在這裏 require = need，字面的意思是「英文需要承諾」，也就是「英文需要專注；英文需要你全心投入。」美國人非常喜歡使用 commit 或 commitment 這兩個字，在字典上 commit 的解釋不清楚，要從字根分析，才知道它真正的意思。

$$\frac{\text{com} \mid \text{mit}}{\textit{together} \mid \textit{let go}}$$ 字根上是「讓他帶著一起走」，就是「委託」，別人委託你帶東西，你見財起意，就會犯罪、犯法，所以 commit 有「犯~」的意思。commitment 是 commit 的名詞，它主要的意思是「委託、承諾、保證」。

如： My number one *commitment* is to my family.
= My biggest responsibility is my family.
（我決心照顧我的家庭。）

18. The initiative is with you.（主動權在你。）
= You take the initiative.

美國人也常說 The ball is in your court. 字面的意思是「球在你的球場裏。」表示「由你做決定。」

有一位美國年輕人，喜歡到處交女朋友，看到美貌的女生，就把名片給她，這位年輕人跟我說：The ball is in her court. 意思是由她決定，是否會打電話給他。

19. Your confidence will soar.

> soar 的主要意思是「高飛；翱翔」，這句話字面的意思是
> 「你的信心會飛得很高」，引申為「你的信心將會大大增加。」

20. Let's roll.

> 自從 911 事件後，在美國最熱門的 T-shirt 上面寫的字
> 就是 Let's roll! 由於在飛機上有個乘客，決定要跟劫
> 機者一拼，就大喊，"Let's roll!"（我們行動吧！）

> 凡是要開始做什麼事的時候，你就可以說：
> > Let's rock.
> > Let's roll.
> > Let's rock and roll.【應唸成 rock′n′roll】

> 這三句話都表示「開始吧。」從前使用在搖滾舞會中，表
> 示「我們開始跳舞吧」，現在也可用在各方面，表示「我們
> 開始吧。」這三句話可以一起講，有一點幽默的語氣。

21. Have a lovely day.
> = Have a great day.
> = Have a wonderful day.
> = Have a super day.
> = Have a good one.
> = Have a great one.

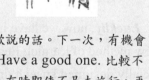

> 這都是美國人再見的時候，喜歡說的話。下一次，有機會
> 跟美國人說再見的時候，要說 Have a good one. 比較不
> 這麼老套，自己英文才會進步。有時即使不是去旅行，再
> 見的時候，美國人也說：
> > Have a good trip.
> > Have a nice trip.
> > Have a safe trip.

【作文範例】

1. How to Master English

2

English is everywhere. English is the key to success. Those who speak it well have an advantage. To have a competitive edge over other people, we must master English.

So many people study English and so few can speak it well. What is the problem here? It is that people study the wrong material. They use the wrong methods. They are wasting their time. I've researched every method. I've tried them all from A to Z. Old methods are not useful. Traditional methods are too limited. They teach only one sentence for each idea. If we forget it, we are out of luck.

We learn "Situational Dialogues," like going to the post office or visiting the doctor. Do we have any chance to use them? The answer is "No." We can't go to the post office every day to practice English. We can't expect people to talk based on the situational dialogues. If we don't use them, how can we remember them?

Luckily, now we have invented a shortcut. We have found a new method of learning English. I'd like to introduce a specially designed speech draft. In this draft, three sentences are one unit. Each unit connects with another. They are all linked together like a chain. The content is common and simple. It's made up of everyday American speech. By using the material in the speech, we can speak great English.

By memorizing one speech, we will start to speak English. By memorizing ten speeches, we will become fluent in English. By memorizing twenty, we will speak better than native English speakers. The reason for that is the students have been trained to speak well and the sentences spoken have been carefully selected.

Memorizing the speeches has the following benefits. *Number one:* We can practice alone. We can speak to ourselves. We don't need conversation partners. *Number two:* Whenever we feel lonely or depressed, we can practice a speech. We always see monks chanting scriptures over and over. Reciting the speech again and again can give us peace of mind. *Number three:* Since the speeches are carefully designed, they are easy to remember. Anyone can learn them. Anyone can remember them. With them, we can easily learn to speak English in threes. We can speak three sentences in a row. Then, we can say one sentence after another nonstop like we are making a speech. *Number four:* The speeches inspire. The speeches are great for learning. They build confidence and language skill at the same time.

With these speeches we will excel. We must practice and memorize the speeches. There is no better way. Let's not wait. Let's not hesitate. Now is the time to change the way we learn English. But we must remember, *to speak English fluently requires four more things. First,* we must practice, practice, and practice. Repetition is the key to learning languages. We need to speak up. We need to speak loudly. Whether right or

2

wrong, we must always be heard. We have to be confident in ourselves. We have to be fearless. We must make mistakes to improve. Speaking English is most important. We must make conversation the priority. Writing, reading, and listening will follow.

Second, we can teach others English. When we help them, we help ourselves. We will improve too. Teaching is the best motivation for memorizing the speech. We will never get sick and tired of teaching the speech. The more we teach, the more articulate we will be. *Third*, we need to try like hell. We need to immerse ourselves. We have to eat, drink, and sleep English. We must become a sponge and soak up English. We have to seek every opportunity to speak. *Fourth*, we must enjoy English! We must make English our love. We must make learning and progress fun. English needs to be first. We need to have passion. English requires commitment.

To sum up, memorizing the speeches is the way to go. So many students say they don't have the chance to practice English. That is so wrong! With the speeches, the chances are everywhere. The initiative is with us. The ball is in our court. Let's practice, speak, and talk. Let's practice until we get fluent. We should speak and talk until we become hoarse. Our confidence level will soar. Our progress will amaze everyone. We won't want to stop speaking English. Let's roll and take action now. English is waiting for us.

2. A New Shortcut to Speaking Fluent English

Have you ever thought about this problem? We have all studied English for a long time, but it seems to me that almost no one can speak English well. Through relentless research of over two years, I have found we've been heading in the wrong direction, studying the wrong material, and using the wrong method in learning spoken English.

Nowadays, most materials we use come from so-called "Situational Dialogues," like going to the post office, visiting the doctor, or being at the airport. Do we have any chance to use these outside the class right away? The answer is no. We can't go to the post office to practice English day after day. We can't beg the people we meet to ask questions exactly according to the dialogues we've learned. If we study situational dialogues, but we seldom have the chance to use them, how can we remember them after some time, when we're really in those situations, and really need to use those words?

Everybody can say, "Good morning," and "How are you?" because they are used over and over. *Therefore*, all the material we learn must be usable every day; otherwise, sooner or later, we will forget it.

There are a lot of things you can say daily. For instance, you need to eat at least three meals a day. Before eating, you're certainly hungry. You must grab the chance to speak to anybody who is with you. If there is nobody around, talk to the wall, or simply talk to yourself, saying as follows:

> I'm hungry.
> I'm hungry as hell.
> I'm hungry as a wolf.

When the food is on the table, you can yell:

> Let's eat.
> Let's dig in.
> Let's pig out.

While you're eating, whether the food is tasty or not, it's time for you to practice English again. You can say another three sentences, such as:

> It's delicious.
> It tastes great.
> It's out of this world.

Likewise, when you finish eating, you can say:

> I'm full.
> I'm stuffed.
> I can't eat another bite.

The above twelve sample sentences I've just given you can be used at least three times a day. You'll never forget the words you often use, just like you've never forgot "Good morning," and "How are you?"

If you really want to become proficient English speakers, this is Rule Number One. You must only choose the material you can say every day, because if you don't use it, you will lose it.

Even if the material you learn can be used daily, suppose you can't remember, then what can you do? We have spent much time and effort, and finally worked out a new approach to make sure that you can remember these English sentences easily.

It's common knowledge that human short-term memory skills are limited. Almost nobody can memorize more than nine consecutive digits. Let's take the number 411213111 for example. Can you easily remember those nine digits? Of course not. Most people can't. But, if you break them up into three groups, like 411-213-111, then they're already easier to remember. If you further rearrange the numbers into 211-311-411, then they will become almost impossible to forget.

You can use the same method when studying English. Instead of trying to recite set dialogues that are difficult to remember, you should study a group of three sentences that have been carefully arranged, just like the number 211-311-411. They must be easy to remember, hard to forget, and fun to learn.

In the beginning stage, you may study just one set of sentences, which we call a triple. You should start by saying a group of three sentences. When you feel comfortable saying the first triple, then you should learn another one. Before long, you will be able to say many sentences without a pause. For example, we already know "I'm hungry. I'm hungry as hell. I'm hungry as a wolf." Building on that triple, you can continue with:

> I'm starved.
> I'm starving.
> I'm starving to death.
>
> My stomach is empty.
> My stomach is growling.
> I could eat like a horse.

As you memorize these triples, you should make sure that you thoroughly understand each word, as well as the grammar involved in each sentence. When you have the slightest doubt about the sentence you are learning, you must always straighten out that misgiving, before you go on to a new sentence. For example, referring to one of the above triples you just heard, you should know whether there is any difference between "I'm starved," and "I'm starving." When you figure out that the word "starve" is just like the verbs "graduate," "determine," "marry," and "prepare," etc., whose active and passive forms have the same meaning, you have not only learned something else, but more importantly, you can say those sentences without a bit of doubt, without any hesitation, and in full confidence.

As time passes, our memory skills will inevitably deteriorate. The younger we are, the better our memory skills are. Make no mistake about it. We are all under the pressure of time. If you really want to speak English well, you can't wait any longer. Now is the time!

To speak English fluently requires three things: practicing, speaking, and talking. Practice until you get perfect. Speak until you become hoarse. Talk! Talk! Talk English!

> Commit yourself.
> Dedicate yourself.
> Totally focus on your goal.
>
> Never give up.
> Never give in.
> Never say never.

2

You must continuously think about, review, and practice English, anytime and anywhere, whether you are walking, eating, or even dreaming. Learning English is not a part-time job. You must put your heart and soul into it. You must make English your passion.

With the speeches, you can easily learn to speak three sentences in a row. Whenever you have the chance, *you must open your mouth* and say as many sentences as possible. Too many students say they don't have the chance to practice English. Wrong! With the triples in these speeches, the chance is everywhere. The initiative is with you. The ball is in your court. When you can say more than six sentences, one after another nonstop, your English skills will surprise everyone around you. They will be amazed, flabbergasted, and speechless at your English speaking ability. Your confidence will soar. You will feel proud of yourself. You won't want to stop speaking English.

3. Award Ceremony Speech: Thank You All So Much
得獎感言

3

Dear distinguished guests,	各位親愛的貴賓，
ladies and gentlemen,	各位先生，各位女士，
all my classmates and friends:	我所有的同學和朋友們：
I'm so surprised.	我真是驚訝。
I can hardly believe it.	我很難相信。
I don't know what to say.	我不知道該說什麼。
My dream came true.	我的夢想成真。
My prayers have been answered.	我的禱告有了回應。
I thank God for my very good luck.	感謝上帝給我如此好運。
First, *thank you all*.	首先，感謝大家。
I appreciate *this* so much.	我非常感激。
I will treasure *this* moment for a long time.	我會一直珍惜這個時刻。

** ——————————————————

distinguished〔dɪ'stɪŋgwɪʃ〕*adj.* 傑出的；高貴的
distinguished guests 貴賓　　hardly〔'hɑrdlɪ〕*adv.* 幾乎不
come true 實現　　prayer〔prɛr〕*n.* 禱告
appreciate〔ə'priʃɪˌet〕*v.* 感激　　treasure〔'trɛʒɚ〕*v.* 珍惜

It feels just great.	感覺真好。
It's like I'm floating on air.	我就像飄浮在空中一般。
I don't want this feeling to end.	我不想失去這種感覺。
I am honored.	我很榮幸。
It's a great privilege.	這是一種難得的殊榮。
I really don't deserve it.	我真的不敢當。
Second, it was a great experience.	第二，這是個美好的經驗。
I had an awesome time.	我非常愉快。
I will never forget it.	我永遠不會忘記的。
I can't thank you enough.	感激不盡。
It gives me such joy.	我真是快樂。
It means a lot to me.	這對我很重要。
Third, we all did our best.	第三，我們全都盡力了。
We tried as hard as we could.	我們已經盡了全力。
WE ARE ALL WINNERS.	我們全都是優勝者。
I was fortunate.	我很幸運。
I really lucked out.	我真的運氣好。
I still can't believe I won.	我仍然不敢相信我贏了。

**

float〔flot〕*v.* 飄浮　　***floating on air*** 非常高興
honored〔'ɑnəd〕*adj.* 榮幸的　　privilege〔'prɪvḷɪdʒ〕*n.* 殊榮
deserve〔dɪ'zɝv〕*v.* 應得（賞罰）
awesome〔'ɔsəm〕*adj.* 很棒的（ = *wonderful* ）　　joy〔dʒɔɪ〕*n.* 快樂
winner〔'wɪnɚ〕*n.* 優勝者

Fourth, I'd like to thank my parents.	第四，我想要感謝我的父母。
My teachers were also great.	老師們也很好。
My friends gave me super support.	我的朋友給我很大的支持。
I couldn't have won this by myself.	我無法自己單獨贏得這個獎。
Trying alone, I would have lost.	只靠自己努力，我一定輸。
I know that for sure.	我非常確定。
Fifth, I've learned two valuable lessons.	第五，我學了兩個有價值的課程。
"Believe in your potential."	「相信自己的潛力。」
"Hard work really does pay off!"	「努力工作會有回報！」
This is my advice to everybody.	這是我對大家的忠告。
If I can win this, anyone can do it!	如果我能贏，任何人都可以！
That's the honest truth.	這是最明確的事實。
Tomorrow I will pinch myself.	明天我會捏捏我自己。
I want to make sure this is real.	我要確定這是真的。
I'll be afraid this was just a dream.	我怕這只是一場夢。
I'm glad I tried.	我真高興我努力過了。
I almost didn't.	我幾乎做不到。
I was too afraid.	我太害怕了。

3

** ———————————————————

super〔'supɚ〕*adj.* 非凡的；超級的　　fortunate〔'fɔrtʃənɪt〕*adj.* 幸運的
valuable〔'væljuəbḷ〕*adj.* 有價值的　　potential〔pə'tɛnʃəl〕*n.* 潛力
pay off 回報　　advice〔əd'vaɪs〕*n.* 忠告　　pinch〔pɪntʃ〕*v.* 捏

3

Now I'm a believer!	現在我相信了！
You must get in it to win it.	你必須投入，才會得獎。
This award strengthens my resolve.	這個獎金加強了我的決心。
Finally, prizes are material.	最後，獎賞只是有形的物質。
Awards come and go.	獎金來來去去。
But this memory will last forever.	但是這個回憶會永遠留存。
The competition was excellent.	這次競爭對手十分優秀。
I applaud everyone here.	我爲這裏的每個人喝采。
I was lucky today.	今天我很幸運。
A final thanks to the judges.	最後感謝評審。
I'm flattered to be selected.	被選上我受寵若驚。
You've made me very happy!	你們讓我很開心！
God bless.	祝福大家。
Good luck.	祝好運。
See you next time.	再見。

**

believer〔bɪ'livɚ〕n. 相信者　　award〔ə'wɔrd〕n. 獎賞；獎金；獎品
strengthen〔'strɛŋθən〕v. 加強　　resolve〔rɪ'zɑlv〕n. 決心
prize〔praɪz〕n. 獎賞；獎品；獎金　　material〔mə'tɪrɪəl〕n. 形式
memory〔'mɛmərɪ〕n. 回憶　　forever〔fɚ'ɛvɚ〕adv. 永遠地
competition〔,kɑmpə'tɪʃən〕n. 競爭；競爭對手【不可數】
　　(= the other competitors)
excellent〔'ɛkslənt〕adj. 優秀的　　applaud〔ə'plɔd〕v. 鼓掌；稱讚
final〔'faɪnl̩〕adj. 最後的　　judge〔dʒʌdʒ〕n. 評審
flattered〔'flætɚd〕adj. 受寵若驚的

【背景説明】

當你上台領獎，你該説些什麼呢？這篇演講稿提供了一切。當你要感謝別人的幫助，該説些什麼呢？這篇演講稿提供了非常多優美的句子。

1. Dear distinguished guests:

distinguish 這個字，主要意思是「區別」。
distinguished 字面的意思是「被區別的」，已經轉變爲完全的形容詞，意思是「卓越的；傑出的；高貴的；地位高的」，distinguished guests 意思就是「各位貴賓」。

2. 前面六句可以用在很多場合。當別人介紹一個美麗的女朋友給你，你就可以説這些話，來表示感謝了。

> I'm so surprised.
> I can hardly believe it.
> I don't know what to say.
>
> My dream came true.
> My prayers have been answered.
> I thank God for my very good luck.

3. I can hardly believe it.

美國人也常説成 I can't believe it.

4. I don't know what to say.

這句話可説是一個萬用句，在各種情況都可以用，如：

3

A: Wow, you're so wonderful! (哇，你眞棒！)
B: Really?! *I don't know what to say.*
　　(眞的嗎 ?! 我不知道該說什麼。)

A: Here is a little something for you.
　　(這是我要送給你的一點小東西。)
B: Wow, *I don't know what to say.*
　　(哇，我不知道該說什麼。)

A: I lost your car. (我把你的汽車弄丟了。)
B: *I don't know what to say.*
　　(我不知道該說什麼才好。)

5. My prayers have been answered.

這句話聽美國人講過太多遍了，當你有什麼好事情發生的時候，你就可以說這句話。

當你開車，一路上沒有紅燈的時候，你就可以說：

My prayers have been answered.

(我的禱告有回應了。)

考試考好了，你也可以說這句話。平均下來，每一個美國人，每天至少會講兩次以上，因爲美國人相信，禱告多了，就會有好運。這句話就相當於中國人說「我今天眞好運。」

今後，凡是你遇到一點順利的事情，如找到停車位、買到便宜的東西、碰到美女，你都要大聲說：My *prayers* have been answered. 這句話是慣用句，是固定用法，prayers 一定要用複數形式，句子也要用完成被動式。

prayer〔prɛr〕*n.* 祈禱；〔'preɚ〕*n.* 禱告者
pray〔pre〕*v.* 祈禱

句中的 prayers，是指「祈禱」，不是「祈禱者」。而 pray 只能當動詞，沒有名詞用法。

6. I ***thank God*** for my very good luck.

美國人碰到什麼好事都會說：Thank God!

比較下列各句的語氣：

> ***Thank God!***【一般語氣】
> I ***thank God!***【語氣稍強】
> I ***thank God*** for my good luck.【語氣強】
> I ***thank God*** for my very good luck.【語氣最強】

一般神有很多種神，像 sun god（太陽神），但是「上帝」
（God）只有一個，所以用大寫。

7. ***It feels*** just great.

在 It feels *just* great. 中，just 是副詞，修飾形容詞 great，
在這裏 just 等於 really。

just 當副詞用，根據前後句意，有不同意思，都是加強語氣：

> I feel ***just*** fine.（我感覺真好。）【just = really】
> It's ***just*** one o'clock.（剛好 1 點正。）【just = exactly】
> I'm ***just*** leaving.（我正好要走。）【just = nearly】
> I'm ***just*** kidding.（我只是開玩笑。）【just = only】
> He ***just*** left.（他剛走。）【just = a very short time ago】

問：為什麼 It feels just great. 不說 I feel just great. 呢？
答：當然可以說 I feel just great. 但是，It feels just great.
　　也可以。（詳見 p.146）

8. I am honored.
It's a great privilege.
I really don't deserve it.

當別人跟你說很好聽的話，或送你一些珍貴的東西，你都可
以說這三句話。

I'm honored. 字面的意思是「我受到了致敬。」引申爲「我很榮幸。」

It's a great privilege. 字面的意思是「它是個大的特權。」，引申爲「我很榮幸。」

這句話美國人常説。如：

> A: You can drive my car. (你可以開我的車。)
> B: *It's a great privilege.* (我很榮幸。)

你見到一個你很尊敬的人，你也可以説：

> *It's a great privilege* to meet you. (很榮幸認識你。)
> I really don't deserve it. (詳見 p.144 , 145)

9. I have an *awesome* time.

awesome〔'ɔsəm〕*adj.* 令人敬畏的

awesome 這個字來自 awe〔ɔ〕*n.* 敬畏，主要意思是「令人敬畏的」，引申爲「可怕的；令人嘆爲觀止的」，在句中的 awesome 等於 wonderful；impressive；excellent。

> I have an *awesome* time.
> = I have a wonderful time. (我非常愉快。)

美國小孩子看到龐然大物的卡車等奇怪的東西，就會大叫：

> *Awesome!* (眞棒！)

美國男人看到身材很好的美女，就會大叫：

> What an *awesome* body! (身材眞棒！)

看球賽的時候，見到很精彩的一幕時，你就可以説：

> That was an *awesome* play! (眞是精彩的一幕！)

10. I'm floating on air.

這句話字面的意思是「我飄浮在空氣上」，引申爲「我很快樂。」這種講法很多：

> I'm floating on air.
> = I'm walking on air.
> = I'm on cloud nine.

> = I'm on the top of the world.
> = I'm in seventh heaven.【有些英漢字典寫成 *the*
> *seventh heaven*，但美國人都不加 the，加 the 是表示具體。】
> = I'm very happy.

3

11. I can't thank you enough.

　　字面的意思是「我怎麼謝你都不夠」，表示「我非常感激。」
　　也可以說成 I can't thank you too much.

12. WE ARE ALL WINNERS.

　　大寫的意思，表示加強語氣。

13. I really *lucked out*.

　　luck out 有兩個相反的意思：

　　　① 運氣很好。

　　　　例如：I *lucked out*. (我運氣很好。) (= *I was lucky.*)

　　　② 倒楣 (諷刺的口吻)。當你錢包掉了，你就可以說：
　　　　Somebody stole my wallet.
　　　　I guess I really *lucked out*.
　　　　(有人偷了我的皮夾。我想我倒楣透了。)

14. I couldn't have won this *by myself*.

　　這是假設法的過去式，表示「與過去事實相反」。
　　by myself 是副詞片語，表示「假如靠我自己」。這句話
　　意思就是「光靠我自己的力量，我沒辦法得獎。」這句話
　　美國人也常說成 I couldn't have won this on my own.

中國人學英文，能夠講到假設法的過去式，很不簡單，
所以這句話你非要唸熟不可。一般美國人講話的時候，
把 I couldn't have 講成 I couldn'tve 你要說成
I couldn't have.... 才行。

3

15. *Trying alone*, I would have lost.

    Trying alone 在句中，等於 *If I had tried alone*。
    這句話的意思是「假如我孤軍奮鬥，我早就輸了。」

16. I know that for sure.

    不管你講什麼話，講完之後，都以講這句話，來加強語氣，
    也可以說成：I know it for sure.（我確實知道。）這是很多
    美國人的口頭禪。例如：

    > You can do it. *I know that for sure.*
    > （你可以辦到。我深信不疑。）
    > The weather is beautiful. *I know that for sure.*
    > （天氣很好。我確定。）
    > You will be here. *I know that for sure.*
    > （你會來這裏。我確信。）

17. Hard work really does *pay off*.（努力工作一定會有回報。）

    美國人太喜歡用 pay off 這兩個字了，pay off 在字典上
    有很多意思，他們常用的意思是「有收穫；有回報」，
    英文解釋是 bring in profit。

    例如：This trip really *paid off*.（這次旅行很有收穫。）
    Buying this car will *pay off*.（買這部車會有收穫。）
    Going to college will *pay off* in the future.
    （上大學在未來將會有收穫。）

    Hard work really *does* pay off.也可以說成：Hard work
    does really pay off.句中的 *does* 都是用來加強語氣。

18. That's the honest truth.

美國人很喜歡説：

That's true. (的確。)
That's the truth. (的確如此。)
That's the honest truth. (千眞萬確。)
That's the God honest truth. (我發誓那是眞的。)
That's the honest to God truth.
(我向上帝發誓，那是眞的。)

這五句話，是美國人常用的回答話，如：

A: This computer is fantastic! (這部電腦眞棒！)
B: That's true. (的確。)
　That's the truth. (的確如此。)
　⋮

19. I will pinch myself.

美國人的民族性，容易興奮，一點小事，他們就會很高興。
例如，當你送給他一個小禮物，他就會説：

I can't believe it. (我眞不敢相信。)
Pinch me. (捏我一下吧。)

他説 Pinch me. 的意思是「捏我一下；掐我一下。」聽者未
必眞的會去捏他一下，這也是美國人幽默的個性。

有好事情發生，你就可以説：

This is great. (眞棒！。)
I will pinch myself. (我要捏我自己一下。)

要把英文學好，就要了解美國的文化，也要學美國人平常
所説的句子，英文進步得才會快。

20. Now I'm a believer.

在字典上，believer 是作「信徒；相信者」解。
這句話的意思是「我現在相信了；現在我開竅了。」
I'm a believer. 後面也可加上 in，表示「我相信～」。

例：I'm a believer in fresh air as a cure for illness.
（我相信新鮮的空氣能夠治療疾病。）

I'm a believer in 比 I believe in 的語氣要強，原則上，
在英文裏，只要句子長，語氣就強，中文也是如此。

3

21. You must *get in* it to win it.

在句中，get in 等於 get involved in，字面意思是「牽涉
進去」，引申爲「投入」。不定詞片語 to win it 當副詞用，
表示結果，修飾 get。這句話的意思是「你必須投入才會得
獎。」也可説成：You must *get involved in* it to win it.

22. This award strengthens my resolve.

這句話可以説成 This award strengthens my determination.
也可以説成 This award increases my resolve.

resolve 這個字當名詞，一般中國人不會用，在這裏等於
determination。這句話的意思就是，「這個獎勵將增強我
的決心。」

23. Awards come and go.（獎金來來去去。）

美國人很喜歡説 come and go，表示「來來去去，會消失」。
如： Money comes and goes.（錢來來去去。）
Friends come and go.（朋友來來去去。）

24. I *applaud* everyone here.
applaud〔ə'plɔd〕*v.* 鼓掌；稱讚

這句話的意思是「我向在這裏的每一個人鼓掌。」也可以説
成：*I give everyone here a big hand*。

25. A final thanks to the judges.

thanks 這個字，永遠複數形，可表單複數，如：
Many thanks.（多謝。）
A final thanks to the judges.（最後感謝評審。）

【作文範例】

Accepting a Prize

At the end of every competition there can be only one winner. In a way, this is unfortunate because every participant deserves recognition for his efforts. That is particularly true in this case, where so many excellent students competed for the prize. It was with great surprise that I learned I was the winner. I feel so lucky and, of course, I am very happy. But more than the prize, I value the experience I have had. It was such a wonderful time that I will never forget it. *Furthermore*, I believe we are all winners because we all did our best. The only difference between us is that I was lucky.

After winning this award, I am thankful for several things. *First of all*, I am thankful for you, my competitors, because I really owe my victory to you. If you hadn't given me such strong competition, I would not have worked so hard. It was an honor to compete against you. I am also thankful for the support of my parents, teachers and friends. I couldn't have succeeded without it. *Finally*, I am thankful for the lessons I have learned. I learned to believe in myself and that hard work really does pay off. The material reward is wonderful, but it is these lessons that will last all my life.

3

【中文翻譯】

領　獎

　　每項比賽結束，都只能有一位優勝者。就某方面而言，這是很令人遺憾的，因為每位參賽者所付出的努力，都應該得到肯定。當許多優秀的學生爭奪獎項時，尤其如此。當我知道我獲勝時，我非常驚訝。我覺得很幸運，而且當然非常高興。但除了獎項之外，我更重視自己所得到的經驗。這是段很棒的時光，我永遠都不會忘記。此外，我認為我們都是優勝者，因為我們全都盡力了。唯一的差別在於，我比較幸運。

　　在贏得這個獎之後，我要感謝許多事情。首先，我感謝你們，各位競爭者，因為我的勝利，完全要歸功於你們。如果你們沒給我這麼強大的競爭壓力，我就不會這麼努力。能和各位競爭，我感到很榮幸。我也要感謝我的父母、老師，以及朋友的支持。沒有他們的支持，我是不可能成功的。最後，我要感謝我所學到的課程。我學會相信自己，還有努力真的會有收穫。有形的獎賞固然很棒，但這些教訓，卻能使我終身受用。

4. A Speech to Honor Parents
向父母致敬的演講

Ladies and gentlemen:	各位先生，各位女士：
I feel so lucky to be here.	我覺得很幸運能來到這裏。
All that I am today is because of my parents.	我今日所有的成就，都是我父母的功勞。
Dear Mom and Dad:	親愛的爸爸、媽媽：
You are my loving parents.	你們是深愛我的父母。
These words are from my heart.	這些是我心中的話。
From the day I was born,	自從我出生以來，
you did everything for me.	你們爲我做每件事。
How can I express my thanks?	我該如何表達我的感謝？
You fed me *when I was hungry*.	當我餓了，你們餵我吃東西。
You washed me *when I was dirty*.	當我髒了，你們幫我洗澡。
You nursed me *when I was sick*.	當我生病了，你們照顧我。

**

loving〔ˈlʌvɪŋ〕*adj.* 親愛的　　heart〔hɑrt〕*n.* 心
born〔bɔrn〕*adj.* 出生的　　express〔ɪkˈsprɛs〕*v.* 表達
thanks〔θæŋks〕*n.* 感謝　　feed〔fid〕*v.* 餵食
nurse〔nɝs〕*v.* 照顧

4

You *held* me *when I cried*.
You *helped* me *when I needed it*.
You gave me many happy childhood memories.

當我哭了，你們抱我。
當我需要幫忙的時候，你們協助我。
你們給了我許多快樂的童年回憶。

You always put me first.
You made me feel so special.
I couldn't have asked for more.

你們總是把我擺在第一位。
你們讓我感到如此的特別。
我已經不能再要求什麼了。

I *respect* the values you taught.
I *admire* the hard work you did.
I *thank* you for your sacrifice.

我尊重你們所教的價值觀。
我佩服你們的努力。
我感謝你們的犧牲。

You raised me well.
You tried so hard.
You did the best you could do.

你們把我教養得很好。
你們非常努力。
你們盡了最大的力量。

**────────────────────

hold〔hold〕v. 抱　　childhood〔'tʃaɪld,hʊd〕n. 童年時代
memory〔'mɛmərɪ〕n. 回憶　　*ask for* 要求
respect〔rɪ'spɛkt〕v. 尊重　　values〔'væljuz〕n. pl. 價值觀
admire〔əd'maɪr〕v. 讚賞；佩服
sacrifice〔'sækrə,faɪs〕n. 犧牲　　raise〔rez〕v. 養育

Today, *I will make you a promise.*	今天，我要給你們一個承諾。
Then, *I will make a toast.*	然後，我要向你們舉杯致敬。
Both are from my heart.	這都是發自我的內心。
I promise to make you proud of me.	我保證會讓你們以我為榮。
I promise to always respect and love you.	我保證要永遠尊重和愛你們。
Also, *I promise* to take care of you as long as I live.	我也保證會永遠地照顧你們。
Now, *everybody*, I propose a toast.	現在，各位，我提議大家來乾杯。
Let's raise our glasses together.	讓我們一起舉杯。
Let's drink to honor my parents.	讓我們舉杯向我的父母致敬。

4

** ————————————————————

promise (ˈprɑmɪs) *n.* 承諾　*v.* 保證
toast (tost) *n.* 乾杯；舉杯致敬
proud (praud) *adj.* 感到光榮的　　***take care of*** 照顧
as long as 只要　　propose (prəˈpoz) *v.* 提議
raise (rez) *v.* 舉起　　glass (glæs) *n.* 玻璃杯
drink (drɪŋk) *v.* 乾杯；舉杯祝賀　　honor (ˈɑnɚ) *v.* 向…致敬

4

My dear parents:	親愛的爸媽：
You light up my life.	你們照亮我的生命。
You mean the world to me.	你們是我的一切。
A toast.	乾杯。
Cheers.	乾杯。
Bottoms up.	乾杯。
To conclude our party I would like to recite the famous Irish blessing.	我想朗誦一段有名的愛爾蘭祝禱辭，來結束今天的聚會。
"May the road rise to meet you."	「願你心想事成。」
"May the wind be always at your back."	「願你一切順利。」
"May God hold you in the palm of His hand."	「願上帝時時庇佑你。」

** ————————————

light up 照亮　　mean〔min〕*v.* 意味著
mean the world to sb. 是某人的一切；是某人最重要的人
cheers〔tʃɪrz〕*n.* 乾杯；舉杯致敬　　*Bottoms up.* 乾杯。
conclude〔kən'klud〕*v.* 結束　　recite〔rɪ'saɪt〕*v.* 朗誦
famous〔'feməs〕*adj.* 有名的　　Irish〔'aɪrɪʃ〕*adj.* 愛爾蘭的
blessing〔'blɛsɪŋ〕*n.* 祝禱辭；祈神賜福
rise〔raɪz〕*v.* 出現　　meet〔mit〕*v.* 出現在…的面前
wind〔wɪnd〕*n.* 風　　palm〔pɑm〕*n.* 手掌心

【背景説明】

　　這篇演講太感人了！百善孝爲先，家中如果請客時，你就可以背這篇演講稿給他們聽，學會感謝是成功之道。

　　這篇演講可以用一輩子，不管年紀多大，只要你父母在，都可以發表演説。

4

1. ***I feel*** so lucky to be here. （我覺得很幸運能來到這裏。）
   = ***I feel*** very lucky to be here.

   　　美國人很喜歡用 feel 這個字，如見了面説：

   　　　　How do you ***feel***? （你覺得怎樣？）

   　　早上起來，覺得精神很好，可以説：

   　　　　I feel lucky today. （我今天很幸運。）

   　　當某人講的話，你不認同時，你可以説：

   　　　　I don't feel comfortable with what you said.

   　　　　（我不同意你說的話。）

2. All ***that I am today*** is because of my parents.
   （我今日所有的成就，都是我父母的功勞。）

   > 在句中，***All that I am*** today = ***What I am*** today。
   > ***that I am today*** 是形容詞子句，修飾 All，because of
   > 可代換成 due to（由於）。
   >
   > All that I am today／is because of my parents. 這句話字
   > 面的意思是「我今日所有的一切，都是因爲我的父母親。」引
   > 申爲「我今日所有的成就，都是我父母的功勞。」

這句話非常感人，背的時候，要有所停頓。背誦演講的時候，剛開始就有這麼長的句子，實在有點不對，但這句話太重要了。先大聲背 All that I am today，背十遍以上，再繼續背 is because of my parents。演講時，All that I am today 要大聲強調，is because of my parents 聲音要稍低，並且要感性。

3. Dear Mom and Dad:（親愛的爸爸、媽媽：）

在美國家庭裡，通常都以 Daddy, Dad, Pa 等來稱呼父親，Father 是較為恭敬的稱呼。而稱呼母親呢？通常用 Mommy, Mama, Ma, 或用 Mom，較鄭重時用 Mother。

中國人都說爸爸媽媽，而美國人則說 *Mom and Dad*。

4. You are my *loving* parents.

這句話的意思是「你們是深愛我的父母。」用 *loving* 這個字要小心，*loving* 是 showing love 的意思，如：

I am your *loving* child.（我是深愛你的小孩。）
You are my *loving* brother.（你是很愛我的哥哥。）
You are my *loving* son.（你是很愛我的兒子。）
You are my *loving* friend.（你是很愛我的朋友。）

loving 在字典上沒有解釋清楚，所以我們才舉很多的例子。

若要說「你是我親愛的朋友。」則用 You are my *beloved* friend. 或 You are my *dear* friend.

其實，*loving* 這個字很容易區別，在美國，兒子寫信給媽媽的時候，就常署名 your *loving* son（深愛妳的兒子）。

5. These words are *from my heart*.

（這些是發自我內心的話。）

這句話很感人，要特別記住 <u>from</u> my heart 中的 from，和
下一句的 ***From*** *the day* 的 From 連接，你背的時候就不會
忘了。

6. You did everything for me. （你們爲我做每件事。）
How can I express my thanks? （我該如何表達我的感謝？）

4

這兩句話很有用，可以天天掛在嘴上說，別人會很喜歡你。
注意 thanks 這個字，當作「感謝」時，永遠要用複數形式。

有些名詞永遠要用複數形式，如：belonging*s*（財產）、
rich*es*（財富）、goods（貨物）、earning*s*（所得）、
greeting*s*（問候）、wish*es*（祝福）。（詳見文法寶典 p.84）

7. You fed me *when I was hungry*.

（當我餓了，你們餵我吃東西。）
You washed me *when I was dirty*.

（當我髒了，你們幫我洗澡。）
You nursed me *when I was sick*.

（當我生病了，你們照顧我。）

這三句話有押韻，很好背。nurse 本身是名詞，是「護士」
的意思，當動詞用時，有「像護士般照顧」的意思。

8. You <u>held</u> me *when I cried*. （當我哭了，你們抱我。）
You <u>helped</u> me *when I needed it*.

（當我需要幫忙的時候，你們協助我。）

這兩句話也是押韻，一個是 held，一個是 helped。

9. You gave me many happy childhood memories.

（你們給我許多快樂的童年回憶。）

> 長的句子一定要停頓，才背得下來，你先背 You gave me
> many，要大聲，再背 happy childhood memories，這個
> 片語音節很多，你要唸很多遍，熟了之後，再背整句。

4

10. You always put me first.

You made me feel so special.

I couldn't have asked for more.

> 這三句話很感人，你要常說，你會成為一個 sweet talker，
> 會受到別人的喜愛，做起事情來會很順利。
>
> I couldn't have asked for more. 字面意思是「我不可能再
> 要求更多了。」即表示「我已經非常滿足了。」
>
> > 「could have + 過去分詞」，表示對過去能做而未做的事感
> > 到惋惜、遺憾（屬於假設法，只是 if 子句未說出而已）。
> > （詳見「文法寶典」p.315）

11. *You made me* feel so special. （你們讓我感到如此特別。）

這句話是一個句型，美國人很喜歡用 *You made me......*，
比如說：

⑴ 中文：**你害我**吃得太多。

英文：*You made me* eat too much.

⑵ 中文：**你害我**跌倒。

英文：*You made me* fall.

⑶ 中文：**你害我**生病。

英文：*You made me* sick.

那麼，「都是你害的」，英文就翻成 It's all your fault. （都是
你害的；都是你的錯。）

12. I respect the values you taught. (我尊重你們所教的價值觀。)

    value 的主要意思是「價值」，而複數形當作「價值觀」解釋，
    相當於 standards, principles 之意。

    如： My *values* are different from yours.
    　　　（我的價值觀和你的不同。）

13. I thank you for your sacrifice. (我感謝你們的犧牲。)

    不可說成 *I thank your sacrifice.* (誤)。因為 thank 只能接
    人做受詞，thank 的用法是：*thank sb. for sth.*。

4

14. You *raised* me well. (你們把我教養得很好。)

    raise 的基本意思是「提高」，在此是「養育」的意思，也可
    說成：You *brought* me *up* well.

15. *Let's drink to* honor my parents.

    > 表示「舉杯致敬」的用法及場合相當多，你可以說：
    >
    > *Let's drink to* the bride and groom.
    > （讓我們為新郎新娘乾杯。）
    > *Let's drink a toast to* Mr. Smith.
    > （讓我們為史密斯先生乾杯。）
    > *Let's drink to* our friendship.
    > （讓我們為友誼乾杯。）
    >
    > 你也可以直接說：
    >
    > *To* your health. （祝你健康。）
    > *To* our happiness. （祝我們大家快樂。）

4

16. You mean *the world* to me. (你們是我的一切。)

    = You mean *everything* to me.

    也可加強語氣說：

    > You mean *all the world* to me.
    > = You mean *the whole world* to me.

    表示「你們對我而言，是最重要的人；你們是我的一切。」

    > = You are very important to me.

17. A toast. (乾杯。) / Cheers. / Bottoms up.

    乾杯的說法很多，古代的人會把烤麵包 (toast) 泡在酒裏一起喝，因此，喝酒時說 A toast! 就是「乾杯！」的意思。

    要記住 A toast. 不可說成 *Toasts*. (誤) Cheers. 不可說成 *A cheer*. (誤) Bottoms up. 也一定要用複數形，這些都是固定用法，不可改變。

18. May + 主詞 + 原形動詞…… 爲「**祈願句**」句型。(詳見「文法寶典」p.368)

    如： May you succeed! (祝你成功！)
    　　May God bless you! (願上帝賜福給你！)

19. May the road rise to meet you.
    May the wind be always at your back.

    > 這二句話字面意思是：「願道路出現在你面前。願風永遠在你的背後。」一出門路就在你面前，風在你背後吹拂，不就是永遠順風嗎，故引申爲「願你心想事成。祝你一切順利。」

20. May God hold you in the palm of His hand.

    > 在本句中，是指基督教唯一的神，所以寫成 God，以便和其他宗教的諸神有所區別，這裏的 His 用大寫，來尊稱上帝 God。此句字面意義是「願上帝把你放在手掌心上。」把你放在手掌心上，即表示時時呵護著你、保護你，故引申爲「願上帝時時庇佑你。」

【作文範例】

A Letter to My Parents

Dear Mom and Dad,

You are my loving parents. I feel so lucky to be your child. All that I am today is because of you. The following words are from my heart.

From the day I was born, you did everything for me. You fed me when I was hungry, washed me when I was dirty and nursed me when I was sick. *Above all*, you held me when I cried. You helped me when I needed it. You gave me many happy childhood memories that I will never forget. You always put me first and made me feel so special. I couldn't have asked for more. I respect the values you taught and I admire the hard work you did. I thank you for your sacrifice. You tried so hard to raise me well. I know you did the best you could do.

Today, I will make you a promise from the bottom of my heart. *First*, I promise to make you proud of me. *Also*, I promise to always respect and love you. *Finally*, I promise to take care of you as long as I live.

Dear Mom and Dad, you light up my life. You mean the world to me. May God hold you in the palm of His hand.

Your loving child,

Pat

【中文翻譯】

給父母的一封信

親愛的爸爸、媽媽：

　　你們是深愛我的父母親。能當你們的孩子，我覺得很幸運。我今日所有的成就，都是你們的功勞。以下的話都是發自我的內心。

　　從我出生那一天起，你們為我做了一切。當我肚子餓了，你們餵我吃東西；當我弄髒了，你們幫我洗乾淨；當我生病了，你們無微不至地照顧我。最重要的是，當我哭泣的時候，你們會抱著我；當我需要幫助的時候，你們會伸出援手。你們給了我許多快樂的童年回憶，我永遠難忘。你們總是把我放在第一位，讓我覺得好特別，我不可能再要求更多了。我尊重你們所教導的價值觀，我欽佩你們的努力，我感謝你們的犧牲。你們如此努力，把我教養得很好，我知道你們盡了最大的力量。

　　今日，我要給你們一個承諾，這是發自我的內心深處。首先，我保證讓你們以我為榮；再者，我保證會永遠尊敬你們、愛你們；最後，我保證在我有生之年，一定會好好照顧你們。

　　親愛的爸爸、媽媽，你們照亮了我的生命。你們是我的一切。願上帝時時庇佑你們。

愛你們的孩子，

派特

5. A Speech to Honor Our Teachers
向老師致敬的演講

5

Ladies and gentlemen:	各位先生，各位女士：
I'd like to say a few words to honor our teachers.	我想要說幾句話，來向我們的老師致敬。
We owe everything to them.	我們的一切，都要歸功於老師。
Teachers, you did a great job.	老師，您教得真好。
We all admire and like you so much.	我們非常敬佩而且喜歡您。
Without you, our graduation would be much less meaningful.	沒有您，我們的畢業就沒有什麼意義了。
We want to honor and praise you.	我們要向您表示敬意，也要讚美您。
Your teaching was a gift.	您特別努力教導我們。
Thank you for the things you've done for us.	謝謝您為我們所做的一切。

**

honor ('ɑnɚ) v. 向～致敬　　owe (o) v. 歸功於
owe sth. to sb. 將某事歸功於某人　　admire (əd'maɪr) v. 欽佩
graduation (ˌgrædʒʊ'eʃən) n. 畢業
meaningful ('minɪŋfḷ) adj. 有意義的

Our days as your students are over.	我們當學生的日子已經結束。
We are sad to leave you.	我們真捨不得離開您。
But we were lucky to have you.	但是我們很幸運,曾經擁有您。
You did more than just teach.	您不只是教導我們。
You were friends and role models.	您是我們的朋友,也是我們的榜樣。
We will remember you forever.	我們將永遠記住您。
Your dedication was easy to see.	您對我們的奉獻,我們都很清楚。
You were patient and kind every day.	您每天都很有耐心,很親切。
You put us first, drove us hard, and sacrificed a lot.	您將我們擺在第一位,嚴格督促我們,您犧牲不少。

5

** ————————

role model 榜樣;模範

dedication (͵dɛdə'keʃən) *n.* 奉獻;投入

patient ('peʃənt) *adj.* 有耐心的

drive (draɪv) *v.* 督促　　sacrifice ('sækrə͵faɪs) *v.* 犧牲

We promise you three things.	我們答應您三件事情。
We'll remember what you've taught.	我們將記住您的教導。
We'll continue to excel.	我們要保持第一。
We'll make you proud in the future.	您將來會以我們爲榮幸。

Teachers:	老師：
We are not saying good-bye.	我們現在不說再見。
This is just the beginning.	這只是開始。
We take your teaching and	我們將永遠銘記您的教誨
knowledge with us into the future.	和您所傳授的知識。

5

Now, let's raise our glasses	現在，我們一起來將杯子
and toast.	舉起，乾杯！
To the best teachers since	向有史以來最好的老師致
Confucius!	敬！
Teachers, don't forget us because	老師，不要忘了我們，因
we sure won't forget you.	爲我們一定不會忘記您。

**

promise〔'prɑmɪs〕*v.* 承諾；答應
excel〔ɪk'sɛl〕*v.* 勝過別人　　raise〔rez〕*v.* 舉起
toast〔tost〕*v.* 乾杯　　Confucius〔kən'fjuʃəs〕*n.* 孔子

【背景説明】

　　　　這篇演講非常感人，是無價之寶，感謝別人是成功之道，我們應該將這篇演講稿熟背。

1. 一般在美國教室裏，學生稱呼老師，都是用 Mr.，Mrs. 或 Miss 加上姓（family name），像 Mr. Brown（布朗先生），Mrs. Robinson（魯賓遜太太）、Miss Smith（史密斯小姐）等，美國人不像中國人説 *Teacher Liu* 之類的話，應該説 Mr. Liu。

　　在演講的時候，對校長就説 Principal，對所有老師，你就可以説 Teachers，特別指定老師，就要用 Mr. Brown 之類的稱呼。

2. We want to honor and praise you.

　　在中國的文化中，所謂「稱讚」都是對晚輩，稱讚晚輩，美國人可用 praise 這個字，來稱讚任何人，包括長輩，如：

　　Let's praise our teachers.（讓我們來讚美我們的老師。）
　　= Let's say something nice about them.

　　講這些話有點肉麻，但是美國人常説。

3. *drive us hard* 嚴格督促我們（= *push us hard*）

　　We made it because you *drove us hard*.
　　（我們能夠成功，是因爲你嚴格督促我們。）

4. Your teaching was *a gift*.

　　當某樣東西比預期好的時候，你就可以説它是一項禮物 a gift，像是額外得到的東西。

　　美國人喜歡常説 gift。別人只要額外幫助你，或請你吃飯，你就可以説：It's *a gift*.

再例如： You have done so much for me already.

This is really *a gift*.

（你已經為我做了很多。這是你額外給我的禮物。）

Your teaching was *a gift*. 英文解釋是：You taught us beyond the call of duty. 字面的意思是：「您的教導超過您所須負的責任」，引申為「您特別努力教導我們。」

如果你看到一個大人物突然來了，你就可以說：

Your presence is *a gift*. 字面的意思是，你的來到是一項禮物，引申為「非常感謝你來。」

下雨下了很多天，天氣突然變好，你就可以說：

The sunshine is *a gift*. （想不到陽光出現了。）

gift 的英文解釋是 something unexpected and beyond what was required（超過預期、超過所需的某事）。

gift 的翻譯有無限多的翻法，要看前後句意而定，反正你要常說就對了，說多了，你就自然可以體會它的意思。

5

5. We'll continue to excel. （我們要保持第一。）

excel 當不及物動詞，字面的意思是「勝過他人」，它的形容詞是 excellent。

We'll continue to excel. 這句話的字面意思是「我們要繼續勝過他人。」引申為「我們要保持第一。」這句話的英文解釋是：

We'll continue to be the best.

= We'll maintain the highest standard.

（我們將保持第一；我們將保持最高水準。）

6. We take your teaching and knowledge with us *into the future*.

這句話字面的意思是：「我們將把您的教誨和傳授的知識帶到未來」，引申為：「我們將永遠記住您的教誨和傳授的知識。」

【作文範例】

A Letter to Our Teachers

Dear teachers,

We are so happy to have graduated and we owe it all to you. You did a great job. We all admire and like you so much. Without you, our graduation would be much less meaningful. *Therefore*, we honor and praise you. Your teaching was a gift, and we want to thank you for the things you've done for us.

Our days as your students are over and we are sad to leave you. We were lucky to have you because you did more than just teach. You were friends and role models. We will remember you forever.

Your dedication was easy to see. You were patient and kind every day. You put us first, drove us hard, and sacrificed a lot. *In return*, we promise you three things. *First*, we will remember what you've taught. *Second*, we will continue to excel. *And third*, we will make you proud in the future.

Teachers, we are not saying good-bye. This is just the beginning. We take your teaching and knowledge with us into the future. Teachers, don't forget us because we sure won't forget you.

Sincerely,
The Class of 2011

6. *Making an Introduction*
介紹他人

Ladies and gentlemen:	各位先生、各位女士：
This is Michael Wang.	這位是王麥可。
You've all heard about him.	你們都聽說過他。
He's an ace.	他是一流人才。
He's a gem.	他是有價值的人。
He's the best of the best.	他是最頂尖的人物。
He's tops.	他是最好的。
He's the best.	他最好。
He's A number one.	他是第一流的。
He is wonderful.	他真棒。
He is one in a million.	他是百萬中選一。
He is a needle in a haystack.	像他這種人，很難找到。

6

**————————————

ace〔es〕n. 一流的人才；紙牌的 A
gem〔dʒɛm〕n. 寶石；有價值的人　　tops〔tɑps〕adj. 最好的
A number one 第一流的（A 唸成〔e〕）
one in a million 無與倫比的；出色的
needle〔'nidl̩〕n. 針　　haystack〔'he,stæk〕n. 稻草堆
a needle in a haystack 比喻「難得的人」

Ladies and gentlemen:　　　　　各位先生、各位女士：
He is an expert.　　　　　　　　他是個專家。
He is a man of action.　　　　　他是個會做事的人。
He can get the job done.　　　　他能把工作做好。

He's as solid as a rock.　　　　他非常實在。
He's as stable as can be.　　　　他非常穩定。
He's a man we can't do without.　他是個我們不能沒有的人。

My dear friends:　　　　　　親愛的朋友們：
Mr. Michael Wang is a good　　王麥可先生是我的好朋友。
　friend of mine.
You'll have a chance to chat　　待會你們會有機會和他談話。
　with him later.
Let's make him feel at home.　　我們要讓他感到很自在。

Ladies and gentlemen:　　　　各位先生、各位女士：
Here he is.　　　　　　　　　　他就在這裏。
Michael Wang.　　　　　　　　王麥可。
Let's give him a big hand.　　　我們給他熱烈的掌聲。

** ——————————————————

expert (ˈɛkspɝt) *n.* 專家　　　solid (ˈsɑlɪd) *adj.* 堅實的；可靠的
stable (ˈstebḷ) *adj.* 穩定的　　***as ~ as can be*** 非常～
can't do without 不能沒有
give sb. a big hand 給某人熱烈鼓掌

【背景說明】

1. 這一課太有用了。裏面的句子平常會話的時候，都可以用
   得到。例如，你看到一個功課好的同學，你就可以說：
   You're an ace.　You're a gem.　You're the best of the best.
   You're tops.　You're the best.　You're A number one.

   美國人稱讚多於責備，所以他們有很多稱讚的句子。他們
   不僅當面稱讚，背後也稱讚。介紹別人的時候，尤其要說
   很多句稱讚的話，愈多愈好。

2. You're an ace.

   這句話美國人說得太多了，在班上，老師發考卷的時候，
   如果你的分數最高，老師就會說：You're an ace.（你最棒。）
   ace 這個字，主要意思是，在撲克牌中的 A，在玩撲克牌的
   時候，A 是最大的，故引申爲「最好的；一流的人才」。
   看到一個人，把事情做得很好，你就可以說：You're an
   ace.

3. You're a gem.

   gem 是「寶石」，是指珍貴的東西，這句話字面的意思是
   「你是一個寶石」，引申爲「你很有價值，無可取代。」

4. You're the best of the best.

   這句話是 You're the best one of the best. 的省略。

5. You're tops.

   tops 是形容詞，tops〔tɑps〕adj. 最好的，這句話千萬
   不要說成 You're the tops.（誤）tops 源自 top「頂端」，
   這句話的意思是「你是最頂尖的。」

6

6. You're A number one.

你看到你所欽佩的人、你的偶像,你可以說:You're number one. (你第一。) 你也可以加強語氣說:You're A number one. 句中 A 的發音要注意,要唸成〔e〕,不可唸成〔ə〕。整句的重音在 A。

7. You're wonderful.

你見到誰,都可以講這句話。例如,東西掉了,別人幫你撿起來,你就可以說:You're wonderful. (你真好。)

8. You're one in a million.

這句話字面的意思是「你是百萬中之一」,引申為「你是難得的人才。」你可以開玩笑說:You're one in a billion.

9. You're a needle in a haystack.

這句話字面的意思是「你是稻草堆中的一根針」,引申為「你是難找到的人才。」needle「針」,這個字如果背不下來,先背 need,用已會的單字,來背不會的單字,是一種好方法。haystack 背不下來,先背 hay「稻草」,再加上 stack「堆」,這樣子就容易背了。

10. He is an expert.
He is a man of action.
He can get the job done.

你看到誰都可以用這三句話來稱讚他。有不少人什麼事剛開始都很熱衷,結果什麼事都做一半,能夠把事情做完的人,你就說:He can get the job done.

有些人光說不練,有很多計劃都沒有付諸行動,只要說了,立刻採取行動的人,我們就說他:He is a man of action. (他是會做事的人。) 當你看到一個人,對他自己所做的事情,很專注、很熟練,你就可稱讚他說:You're an expert. (你很專業。)

11. He's as solid as rock.

   字面意思是「他像岩石一樣堅固」，引申為「他非常實在。」

12. He's as stable as can be.

   這句話是由 He's as stable as (stable) can be. 演變而來，字
   面的意思是「他能夠多穩定就有多穩定。」表示「他非常穩定。」
   你也可以說：He's as stable as a table.（他非常穩定。）

13. He's a man *we can't do without.*

   can't do without 是成語，表「不能沒有」。這句話的意思就
   是「他是我們不能沒有的人。」這句話也可以說成：

   He's a man *who we can't do without.* 現在美國口語中，都
   用 who 來代替 whom。但 whom 這個字，在美語中，除了偶
   爾在文章中出現以外，已經很少出現了，除非是文謅謅的人。

14. Please feel at home.

   在家裏面，是讓人最自在的地方，你衣服脫光，也沒有人管
   你。這句話字面的意思是「請覺得是在自己家一樣」，引申為
   「請不要拘束。」家裏也是自己最熟悉的地方，家裏的一切，
   自己最清楚，所以 be at home in 表示「精通於」，例如：
   He is at home in driving.（他很會開車。）

15. Let's give him a big hand.（讓我們給他熱烈的掌聲。）

   > 演講完了以後，叫別人鼓掌，你就可以說這句話，也可以說：
   >   Let's give him a hand.（讓我們給他鼓掌。）
   >   Let's applaud him.（讓我們給他鼓掌。）
   >   Let's put our hands together.（讓我們給他鼓掌。）
   > give *sb.* a hand 除了當「給某人鼓掌」以外，還可以當
   > 做「幫助某人」解（= *help sb.*）。例如：Give me a hand,
   > please.（請助我一臂之力。）

6

【作文範例】

An Introduction

I would like to introduce my good friend, Michael Wang. I am sure that you've already heard a lot about him. That is because his accomplishments are well known. There is no doubt that he's one of the best in his field. *In fact*, I'd go so far as to say that he's one in a million. *Therefore*, Michael deserves his good reputation and we are so lucky to have him with us today.

You will all have a chance to chat with Michael later. Feel free to ask him any question. Remember, he is an expert. *Moreover*, he is a man of action who can get the job done. I think we will soon find that we can't get along without him. But for now, let's all give Michael a warm welcome and make him feel at home. Let's give him a big hand.

【中文翻譯】

介紹他人

我想介紹我的好朋友，王麥可。相信你們都聽說過他，因為他的成就眾所皆知。無疑的，他是他的專業領域中的佼佼者。事實上，我敢說，他是百萬中選一。因此，麥可實至名歸，而今天我們很幸運，能請到他來。

待會你們會有機會和麥可談話。你們可以問他任何問題。記住，他是個專家。而且，他是個會做事的人，他能把工作做好。我認為我們很快就會覺得，我們不能沒有他。但是，現在，讓我們大家給他熱情的歡迎，讓他感到很自在。我們給他熱烈的掌聲。

7. *How to Stay Healthy*
如何保健

Ladies and gentlemen:
各位女士，各位先生：

It's great to see all your smiling faces.
能看到各位微笑的臉，眞是太棒了。

I'm here to talk about our health.
我來這裏，是要跟大家談一談我們的健康。

Everybody wants to be healthy.
大家都想要健康。

We all desire a long and healthy life.
我們都希望能長壽而且健康。

But what's the best way to make it happen?
但要實現這個願望，最好的方法是什麼呢？

To begin with, we are what we eat.
首先，吃什麼，就長成什麼樣子。

Eat well, and you'll look good.
如果你吃得好，就長得好看。

Eat junk, and you'll look bad.
如果你亂吃東西，就長得不好看。

7

**

desire〔dɪ'zaɪr〕*v.* 渴望
make it happen 實現；做到 (= *do it*)
to begin with 首先
We are what we eat. 【諺】吃什麼，就長成什麼樣子。
junk〔dʒʌŋk〕*n.* 垃圾；破爛

Some age gracefully.	有些人愈老，氣質愈好。
Some age terribly.	有些人愈老愈可怕。
The way we age depends on us.	我們變老的樣子，完全取決於我們自己。
Don't overeat.	不要吃太多。
Don't starve yourselves.	不要挨餓。
Always *eat* in moderation.	吃東西一定要適量。
Eat smart.	要吃得高明。
Eat right.	要吃得正確。
Always find something nutritious to eat.	一定要找有營養的東西吃。
Eat more fruit.	多吃水果。
Eat more vegetables.	多吃蔬菜。
Don't eat too much *red meat*.	不要吃太多紅肉。

7

**

age〔edʒ〕*v.* 變老　　gracefully〔'gresfəlɪ〕*adv.* 優雅地
depend on 取決於
overeat〔'ovɚ'it〕*v.* 吃過量　　starve〔stɑrv〕*v.* 使挨餓
moderation〔͵mɑdə'reʃən〕*n.* 節制
in moderation 適度地；有節制地　　smart〔smɑrt〕*adv.* 高明地
right〔raɪt〕*adv.* 正確地　　nutritious〔nju'trɪʃəs〕*adj.* 營養的
red meat 紅肉（如牛肉、羊肉等）【***white meat*** 白肉（如雞肉、
　魚肉等）】　　fruit 是物質名詞，不可加 s。

Beef and pork are full of cholesterol.	牛肉和豬肉含有很多膽固醇。
Cholesterol will clog arteries.	膽固醇會阻塞血管。
Fish and chicken are much healthier.	魚肉和雞肉比較有益健康。
Drink water.	喝水。
Drink juice.	喝果汁。
Stay away from soda pop.	不要喝汽水之類的飲料。
I have a remedy for a cough.	我有一個治療咳嗽的方法。
Drink two big glasses of pineapple juice with lime.	喝兩大杯鳳梨原汁加檸檬。
Soon the cough will go away.	咳嗽很快就會好。
Don't smoke.	不要抽煙。
Don't drink.	不要喝酒。
Don't do drugs.	不要吸毒。

7

**

beef〔bif〕*n.* 牛肉　　pork〔pork〕*n.* 豬肉
cholesterol〔kə'lɛstəˌrol〕*n.* 膽固醇　　clog〔klɑg〕*v.* 阻塞
artery〔'ɑrtərɪ〕*n.* 動脈；大血管　　juice〔dʒus〕*n.* 果汁
stay away from 遠離　　***soda pop*** 汽水之類的飲料（ = *soda* = *pop*）
remedy〔'rɛmədɪ〕*n.* 治療法（ = *cure*）
cough〔kɔf〕*n.* 咳嗽　　pineapple〔'paɪnˌæpl̩〕*n.* 鳳梨
lime〔laɪm〕*n.*（皮薄的）檸檬；萊姆（一般的檸檬叫 lemon）
do drugs 吸毒（ = *take drugs* = *go on drugs*）

Smoking causes cancer.	抽煙會致癌。
Drinking leads to liver diseases.	喝酒會得肝病。
Drugs invite an early death.	吸毒容易早死。

Second of all, exercise daily.	第二，要每天運動。
Work out every day.	每天運動。
Keep yourselves in shape.	要使自己保持健康。

Exercising gives us energy.	運動使我們有活力。
It keeps our bodies young.	運動讓我們的身體保持年輕。
It keeps **our minds** sharp.	運動使我們的思路敏捷。

Our minds need knowledge.	我們的頭腦需要知識。
Our souls need love.	我們的心靈需要愛。
Our bodies need exercise.	我們的身體需要運動。

7

** ————————

cause〔kɔz〕v. 導致；引起（= *lead to* = *invite*）
liver〔'lɪvɚ〕n. 肝
second of all 第二（= *second* = *secondly*）
work out 運動（= *exercise*）
keep sb. **in shape** 使某人保持健康
sharp〔ʃɑrp〕adj. 敏捷的　　soul〔sol〕n. 心靈；靈魂

Do you agree?	你同意嗎？
Is this true?	這是真的嗎？
How do you feel after exercising?	你運動後有什麼感覺？
President Chiang Kai-shek had his own method to keep fit.	先總統蔣公自己有一套保持健康的方法。
He walked one thousand steps before every meal.	他每餐飯前會走一千步。
He walked another thousand steps after the meal.	每餐飯後再走一千步。
An airline pilot once told me a simple cure for insomnia and jet lag.	有位航空公司的飛行員，曾告訴我一個治療失眠及時差的簡單方法。
Take a lot of exercise right after you get up in the morning.	每天一早起來，就做大量的運動。
This will help you sleep better.	這樣會幫助你睡得更好。

7

** ───────────────

fit〔fɪt〕*adj.* 健康的　　step〔stɛp〕*n.* 一步

meal〔mil〕*n.* 一餐　　airline〔'ɛr͵laɪn〕*n.* 航空公司

pilot〔'paɪlət〕*n.* 飛行員　　cure〔kjʊr〕*n.* 治療法

insomnia〔ɪn'sɑmnɪə〕*n.* 失眠

jet lag 時差（不可寫成*jetlag*）

Exercise can be fun.	運動也可以很有趣。
I jog on my treadmill while watching TV.	我會邊看電視邊在我的跑步機上慢跑。
It's so enjoyable I forget I'm working out.	這樣做很愉快,所以我會忘了自己是在做運動。
Good health is not free.	良好的健康是無法憑白得到的。
Nothing worthwhile is easy.	沒有任何有價值的東西是容易得到的。
You have to work and sweat.	你必須拼命努力。
Sweat is good.	拼命努力是好的。
Pain is gain.	痛苦就是收成。
No pain, no gain.	不勞則無獲。

7

** ─────────────────

jog〔dʒɑg〕v. 慢跑　　treadmill〔'trɛd,mɪl〕n. 跑步機
enjoyable〔ɪn'dʒɔɪəbl̩〕adj. 愉快的;有趣的
free〔fri〕adj. 免費的
worthwhile〔'wɝθ'hwaɪl〕adj. 值得的;有價值的
sweat〔swɛt〕v. 流汗;拼命工作
pain〔pen〕n. 痛苦;辛苦　　gain〔gen〕n. 收益;獲得
No pain, no gain. 不勞則無獲。(這是美國人的說法,英國人
　則說成:No pains, no gains.)

Thirdly, ***listen to your bodies***.	第三，聽從你的身體。
When you feel tired, take a rest.	當你覺得累了，就休息。
When you feel sleepy, go to bed.	當你覺得想睡，就去睡。
Move your bowels once a day.	每天上一次大號。
Pee whenever you need to.	需要上一號時，就去上。
Never hold it in.	絕對不要忍住。
When I was a kid, my father taught me one important thing.	在我小時候，我父親教我一件很重要的事。
Always take care of your feet.	一定要好好照顧你的腳。
Your feet are the most important part of your body.	腳是身體最重要的部位。
Wash your feet every day.	要每天洗腳。
Change your socks every day.	要每天換襪子。
Keep your feet clean and dry.	要使你的腳保持清潔與乾爽。

7

**

take a rest 休息　　sleepy〔'slipɪ〕*adj.* 想睡的

move〔muv〕*v.* 使移動　　bowels〔'bauəlz〕*n. pl.* 腸

move *one's* ***bowels*** 上大號（= *take a number two*）

pee〔pi〕*v.* 上小號（= *take a number one*）

hold it in 忍住　　***take care of*** 照顧

socks〔saks〕*n. pl.* 短襪（stockings〔'stakɪŋz〕*n. pl.* 長襪）

A doctor told me a story about how to take care of our skin.	有一位醫生告訴我，一個關於如何保養皮膚的故事。
An old lady lived in a castle and never went out into the sun.	有個老太太住在一座城堡裏，從來沒出去曬過太陽。
Her skin was as fair as a baby's.	她的皮膚就像嬰兒一樣白。
His advice is this:	他的建議是：
Never go outside without an umbrella, rain or shine.	不論晴雨，出門一定要撑傘。
Be sure to use an umbrella with UV protection.	一定要使用抗紫外線的傘。

7

Fourthly, thin is in.	第四，現在流行瘦。
Fat's not where it's at.	不要胖。
North, south, east, or west, thin is best.	不管你到東南西北，瘦都是最好的。

** ─────────────

castle〔ˈkæsl̩〕*n.* 城堡　　***go out into the sun*** 出去曬太陽
fair〔fɛr〕*adj.*（皮膚）白皙的【不可用 *white*】
rain or shine 不論晴雨　　***UV***（= *ultraviolet*）*adj.* 紫外線的
UV protection 抗紫外線　　in〔ɪn〕*adj.* 流行的
where it's at 我們的目標；人們所需要的（= *what we are aiming for*；*what is needed*）

Stay slim.	要保持苗條。
Avoid getting fat.	避免發胖。
You must burn more calories	你所燃燒掉的卡路里，必須
than you eat.	比吃進來的卡路里多。

I have three methods for losing	我有三個減肥的方法。
weight.	
Number one: Eat two oranges	第一：在餐前吃兩顆柳橙。
before each meal.	
A friend of mine lost twelve	我有一個朋友，一個月就瘦
pounds in a month.	了十二磅。

7

Number two: Rise early.	第二：要早起。
Exercise on an empty stomach.	要空腹時運動。
Don't eat anything for an hour	運動後一個小時內不要吃東
after exercising.	西。

** ————————

slim〔slɪm〕*adj.* 苗條的；瘦的 (= *thin* = *slender*)
burn〔bɜn〕*v.* 燃燒　　calorie〔'kælərɪ〕*n.*【熱量單位】卡路里
lose weight 減輕體重
orange〔'ɔrɪndʒ〕*n.* 柳橙；橙子 (不容易剝)【tangerine〔͵tændʒə'rin〕
　　n. 椪柑 (容易剝)；mandarin〔'mændərɪn〕*n.* 大椪柑；大橘子 (容
　　易剝)，台灣的柳丁為台灣特產，美國人稱為 Taiwanese orange。】
rise〔raɪz〕*v.* 起床 (= *get up* = *wake up*)
stomach〔'stʌmək〕*n.* 胃

Number three: Eat just a little bit as your lunch, like a slice of bread and a glass of orange juice.

第三：午餐只吃一點點，像是一片麵包和一杯柳橙汁。

You will certainly become hungry in the afternoon.

你下午一定會很餓。

Naturally you will eat an early dinner.

當然你就會很早吃晚餐。

Whenever you feel like eating, change into your sportswear and go get some exercise.

每當你想吃東西，就換上運動服，去做點運動。

By doing so, you can lose one kilogram a week.

這樣做，一週可減一公斤。

More exercise, less eating, is the rule.

少吃多動爲原則。

In conclusion, remember, image is everything.

總之，要記住，形象是一切。

Stay fit and look healthy.

保持健康，並看起來健康。

People judge you by your appearance.

人們會以你的外表來判斷你。

7

**

slice〔slaɪs〕*n.* 一片　　naturally〔'nætʃərəlɪ〕*adv.* 當然；自然地
change into 換上　　sportswear〔'sports,wɛr〕*n.* 運動服
kilogram〔'kɪlə,græm〕*n.* 公斤
in conclusion 總之（= all in all = in summary）
image〔'ɪmɪdʒ〕*n.* 形象　　judge〔dʒʌdʒ〕*v.* 判斷
appearance〔ə'pɪrəns〕*n.* 外表

Good health is precious.	良好的健康很珍貴。
Good health is priceless.	良好的健康是無價的。
It's a lifetime of joy.	良好的健康會讓你一輩子都快樂。
Exercise is the way.	運動是方法。
Good nutrition is the key.	好的營養是關鍵。
A healthy life is waiting for you.	健康的人生正等著你。
Start today.	就從今天開始。
Change your life.	改變你的一生。
Let's all get healthy.	讓我們都變得很健康。

7

Thank you for joining us.	謝謝大家來參加。
Thank you for your attention.	謝謝大家專心聽講。
May you live long and stay healthy forever.	祝大家長壽，並且永遠健康。
Good-bye and good luck.	再見，祝各位好運。

**

precious〔'prɛʃəs〕*adj.* 珍貴的
priceless〔'praɪslɪs〕*adj.* 無價的；珍貴的（= *invaluable* = *precious*）
lifetime〔'laɪf͵taɪm〕*n.* 一生   nutrition〔nju'trɪʃən〕*n.* 營養
key〔ki〕*n.* 關鍵   join〔dʒɔɪn〕*v.* 參加；加入
attention〔ə'tɛnʃən〕*n.* 注意；專心（聽講）

【背景說明】

　　這篇演講稿雖然長，卻很好背。背完之後，就可以
用演講中的內容，來勸導別人。

1. It's great to see all your *smiling* faces.

　　如果你看到聽眾都沒笑的話，你就可以說：
　　　　It's great to see all your friendly faces.
　　或說：It's great to see you all.

2. to begin with (首先)，可用 first of all、first、firstly
　來代替。

3. Eat junk. (亂吃東西。)
　= Eat junk food.

> junk food 是指非自然的食物，如洋芋片 (potato chips)、
> 可樂 (cola)、餅乾 (cookies)、漢堡 (hamburgers)，相
> 反的是自然的食物 (natural food)，如：水果 (fruit)、蔬
> 菜 (vegetable)、穀類 (grains)、牛奶 (milk)、起司
> (cheese) 等。

　　在中國，媽媽叫小孩不要亂吃東西，通常是不要亂吃地攤
的東西；在美國，媽媽叫小孩不要亂吃東西，是不要亂吃
junk food，像 potato chips 之類的東西，所以 Don't
eat junk. 翻成中文，就是「不要亂吃東西。」junk 的主要
意思是「垃圾」，所以有人把 junk food 翻成「垃圾食物」。

4. Some age gracefully.

　　age 是「變老」，gracefully 是「優雅地」，age gracefully
字面的意思是「優雅地變老」，引申為「愈老愈有氣質」。
age terribly 字面是「變老變得很可怕」，引申為「老得很
難看」。

有些老人看起來很難看，像巫婆啊！有些老人非常有精神、
有氣質，這完全看你如何保養，所以美國人常說：

> You are what you eat. （你吃什麼，就長成什麼樣子。）
> You are what you do. （做什麼職業，就長成什麼樣子。）

像屠夫就長得滿臉橫肉，像老師就長得一臉書卷氣。

5. Don't overeat. （不要吃太多。）
= Don't eat too much.

6. Eat *smart*. （要吃得高明。）

> smart 有副詞形式，是 smartly，像 Do it smartly. （做事
> 聰明一點。）smart 本身當副詞時，要當成慣用句來背，
> 如：Play it *smart*. （做得正確。）
>
> smart 多當形容詞，如：
>
> > He looks smart. （他看起來聰明。）
> > Your decision was a smart move. （你的決定做得很對。）

7. Don't starve yourselves. （不要挨餓。）
= Don't be starved.
= Don't be hungry.

> 不可說成 *Don't starve.* 因為 starve 是反身動詞，後面一
> 定要接受詞。

8. soda pop （汽水之類的飲料）等於 soda = pop。

> soda pop 是任何有氣飲料的總稱，像 Coke （可口可樂）、
> Pepsi （百事可樂）、Sprite （雪碧）、Seven-up （七喜）。
> Coke 和 Cola 不同，Coke 是「可口可樂公司」的專有品
> 牌，Cola 則泛指任何品牌的可樂，像 Pepsi Cola （百事
> 可樂）、Coca Cola （可口可樂）、RC Cola （榮冠可樂）。

9. Drugs *invite* an early death. （吸毒容易早死。）

> invite 的主要用法是「邀請」，在此作「引起；招致」解。

10. 「運動」的說法很多，美國人最喜歡用 exercise 或 work out，美國人不說 take exercise，但說 take some exercise 或 take a lot of exercise。

11. It's so enjoyable I forget I'm working out.
    = It's so enjoyable *that* I forget I'm working out.
    = It's so enjoyable, I forget I'm working out.

    當 so 後面的字群較短時，可將 that 省略，或改為逗點。

12. *Thin is in.*（現在流行瘦。）

    in 是美國人的口頭禪，現在年輕人常說「很 in」，就是「很流行」。如：Eating mango slush is in.（現在流行吃芒果冰。）

    Thin is in. 是 *Being* thin is in. 的省略。

13. Fat's not where it's at. 是 *Being* fat is not where it's at. 的省略。

    > 在 Fat's not where it's at. 中的 Fat's，不可說成 *Fat is*，這是口語的習慣用法，就是這麼奇怪。
    >
    > where it's at 美國人常說，作「我們的目標」解。如：
    >
    > > Winning the game is *where it's at*.
    > > （贏得這場比賽是我們的目標。）
    > > Going to the best school is *where it's at*.
    > > （考上最好的學校是我們的目標。）
    > > Buying a house is *where it's at* for me.
    > > （買房子是我的目標。）
    >
    > 當講 where it's at 的時候，語氣上具有急迫性，表示你很想去做這件事情，想達到這個目標。

14. 我們中國人說「東西南北」，美國人說的是「北南東西」，就是 north, south, east, or west，這是幽默好玩的話，比如說，你可以跟朋友說：

> North, south, east, or west, where would
> 　you like to go? (你想去哪裏呢？)
>
> North, south, east, or west, you're the best.
> 　(全世界你最好。)
>
> 上面兩句中，North, south 也可以不説。下面是一句常用
> 的諺語：East or west, home is best. (無論到哪裏，家
> 是最好的。)

15. kilogram (公斤) 也可以説成 kilo，但是 kilometer (公里)，
　　就不能只説 kilo 了，不然的話，就搞不清楚是公斤或公里了。

16. It's a lifetime *of joy*. (一生快樂。)
　　　　　　(一生) (快樂的)

　　the joy *of a lifetime* 則是指「一生當中最快樂的事」。
　　(快樂的事) (一生當中的)

17. Start today. = Begin today.

　　美國人喜歡説今天開始如何如何，像：

　　　　Start today. (就從今天開始。)
　　　　Change your life. (改變你的一生。)
　　　　Quit smoking. (戒煙吧。)

18. Let's all get healthy. 中，get 等於 become。

　　如：　Let's all get rich. (我們全部變成有錢人吧。)
　　　　　= Let's all become rich.

19. 「May ＋ 主詞 ＋ 原形動詞」表示「祝福」，句尾可用驚嘆號
　　或句點。如：

　　　　May you be happy. (祝你快樂。)
　　　　May you live long! (祝你長壽！)
　　　　May you be beautiful forever! (祝你永遠美麗！)

【作文範例】

1. Weight Loss

Thin is in. Fat's not where it's at. North, south, east, or west, thin is best. Stay slim. Avoid getting fat. We must burn more calories than we eat. *I have three methods for losing weight*.

Number one: Eat two oranges before each meal. A friend of mine lost twelve pounds in a month that way. *Number two:* Rise early. Exercise on an empty stomach. Don't eat anything for an hour after exercising. *Number three:* Eat just a little bit as your lunch, like a piece of bread and a glass of orange juice. You will certainly become hungry in the afternoon. Naturally you will eat an early dinner. Whenever you feel like eating, change into your sportswear and go get some exercise. By doing so you can lose one kilogram a week. More exercise, less eating, is the rule.

2. Eat Healthy

We are what we eat. If we eat well, we will look good. If we eat junk, we will look bad. Some age gracefully. Some age terribly. The way we age depends on us. Don't overeat. Don't starve yourselves. Always eat in moderation. Eat smart. Eat right. Always find something nutritious to eat.

Eat more fruit. Eat more vegetables. Don't eat too much red meat. Beef and pork are full of cholesterol. Cholesterol will clog arteries. Fish and chicken are much healthier.

Eat more foods with calcium. Eat more dairy products. They will strengthen bones. Drink water. Drink juice. Stay away from soda pop. I have a remedy for a cough. Drink two big glasses of pineapple juice with lime. Soon the cough will go away. Don't make fast food a habit. It's greasy, artificial and full of calories. Eat it once in a blue moon. Don't smoke. Don't drink. Don't do drugs. Smoking causes cancer. Drinking leads to liver diseases. Drugs invite an early death.

7

3. How to Stay Healthy

Everybody wants to be healthy. We all desire a long and healthy life. But what's the best way to make it happen? *To begin with*, we are what we eat. Eat well, and you will look good. Eat junk, and you will look bad.

Firstly, don't overeat. Don't starve yourselves. Always eat in moderation. Eat smart. Eat right. Always find nutritious things to eat. Eat more fruit. Eat more vegetables. Don't eat too much red meat. Beef and pork are full of cholesterol. Cholesterol will clog arteries. Fish and chicken are much healthier. Eat more foods with calcium. Eat more dairy products. They will strengthen bones. Drink water.

Drink juice. Stay away from soda pop. I have a remedy for a cough. Drink two big glasses of pineapple juice with lime. Soon the cough will go away. Don't make fast food a habit. It's greasy, artificial and full of calories. Eat it once in a blue moon. Don't smoke. Don't drink. Don't do drugs. Smoking causes cancer. Drinking leads to liver diseases. Drugs invite an early death.

Secondly, we must exercise daily and keep ourselves in shape. Exercising gives us energy. It keeps our bodies young. It keeps our minds sharp. Our minds need knowledge. Our souls need love. Our bodies need exercise. President Chiang Kai-shek had his own method to keep fit. He walked one thousand steps before every meal. He walked another thousand steps after the meal. An airline pilot once told me a simple cure for insomnia and jet lag. Take a lot of exercise right after you get up in the morning. This will help you sleep better. Good health is not free. Nothing worthwhile is easy. You have to work and sweat. Sweat is good. Pain is gain. No pain, no gain.

Thirdly, listen to your bodies. When you feel tired, take a rest. When you feel sleepy, go to bed. Move your bowels once a day. Pee whenever you need to. Never hold it in. Wash your hands before each meal. Brush after each meal. Shower at least once a day. When I was a kid, my father taught me one important thing. Always take care of your feet. Your feet are the most important part of your body.

Wash your feet every day. Change your socks every day. Keep your feet clean and dry. A doctor told me a story about how to take care of our skin. An old lady lived in a castle and never went out into the sun. Her skin was as fair as a baby's. His advice is this: Never go outside without an umbrella, rain or shine. Be sure to use an umbrella with UV protection.

Fourthly, thin is in. Fat's not where it's at. North, south, east, or west, thin is best. Stay slim. Avoid getting fat. We must burn more calories than we eat. *In conclusion*, image is everything. Stay fit and look healthy. People judge us by our appearance. Our health is precious. Good health can't be bought. Health is more important than wealth.

Some say good health is beauty. Others say it's vitality. All agree it's a lifetime of joy. So, let's exercise. Let's burn a few calories. Let's give our bodies a work out. Start today. Change your life. Let's all get healthy.

4. Advantages of Exercising

If we want to be healthy, we must exercise daily and keep ourselves in shape. Exercise gives us energy. It keeps our bodies young. It keeps our minds sharp.

President Chiang Kai-shek had his own method to keep fit. He walked one thousand steps before every meal. He walked another thousand steps after the meal. An airline pilot once told me a simple cure for insomnia. Take a lot of exercise right after you get up in the morning. This will help you sleep better. Good health is not free. You have to work and sweat. Nothing worthwhile is easy. Sweat is good. Pain is gain. No pain, no gain.

5. Maintaining Our Bodies

In order to maintain our bodies, we must listen to our bodies. When you feel tired, take a rest. When you feel sleepy, go to bed. Move your bowels once a day. Pee whenever you need to. Never hold it in.

Wash your hands before each meal. Brush after each meal. Shower at least once a day. When I was a kid, my father taught me one important thing. He said, "Always take care of your feet. Your feet are the most important part of your body. Wash your feet every day. Change your socks every day. Keep your feet clean and dry."

A doctor told me a story about how to take care of our skin. An old lady lived in a castle and never went out into the sun. Her skin was as fair as a baby's. His advice is this: Never go outside without an umbrella, rain or shine. Be sure to use an umbrella with UV protection.

7

8. *How to Achieve Success*
成功之道

Ladies and gentlemen:
I'm so happy to be here today.
The subject I'm going to
talk about is how to
achieve success.

各位先生，各位女士：
我很高興今天能來到這裡。
我所要談論的題目，就是要
如何才能成功。

Everybody wants to be
successful.

人人都想成功。

We all want to make it big.
But how do we get there?

我們大家都想飛黃騰達。
但是要如何才能做到呢？

8

First of all, you must have
a goal.
It must be clear-cut.
It must be your passion.

首先，你必須要有目標。

你的目標必須非常明確。
你的目標必須是你所愛好的。

**

achieve〔əˋtʃiv〕*v.* 達成；（經努力）獲得
make it big 成功；出人頭地　　***get there*** 達到目的；獲得成功
goal〔gol〕*n.* 目標　　clear-cut〔ˋklɪrˋkʌt〕*adj.* 明確的
passion〔ˋpæʃən〕*n.* 強烈的愛好

You can also have many minor
   goals in life.
Achieve them one at a time.
But always stay on the track
   of your main goal.

你的人生中也能夠有許多次
要的目標。
要一次一個慢慢達成。
但要一直朝著你的主要目標
前進。

Second, *believe* in yourselves.
Your potential is unlimited.
The world is yours to conquer.

第二，相信你自己的能力。
你的潛力無限。
這個世界由你來征服。

Dream big dreams.
Reach for the stars.
The sky is your limit.

要有遠大的夢想。
要達成不容易做到的事。
你的潛力無限大。

Look ahead.
Don't look back.
Don't dwell on the past.

向前看。
不要回頭看。
不要懷念過去。

8

**————————

minor (ˈmaɪnɚ) *adj.* 次要的　　*at a time* 一次
stay (ste) *v.* 保持　　*be on the track of* 朝著～前進
believe in 信任　　potential (pəˈtɛnʃəl) *n.* 潛力
conquer (ˈkɑŋkɚ) *v.* 征服　　big (bɪg) *adj.* 偉大的
reach for 伸手去拿　　*dwell on* 懷念；老是想著

Go for it.	大膽試一試。
Just do it.	趕快做。
Make it happen.	去做吧。
***Third*, *commit* yourselves.**	第三，要專心。
Dedicate yourselves.	要投入。
Totally focus on your goal.	把注意力完全集中在你的目標上。
Try your best.	盡力。
Do your best.	盡全力。
Give it your best shot.	盡你最大的努力。
Give it your best effort.	盡你最大的力量。
Don't hold anything back.	不要做任何保留。
Don't be afraid to let yourselves go.	不要害怕去發揮自己的潛力。

8

** ———————

***Go for it*.** 大膽試一試；冒一下險；趕快做。

commit *oneself* 專心；全力以赴

dedicate *oneself* 獻身；投入　　totally 〔'totḷɪ〕 *adv.* 全部地

focus 〔'fokəs〕 *v.* 集中　　***try*** *one's **best*** 盡力

do *one's **best*** 盡力　　***give it*** *one's **best shot*** 盡最大的努力

shot 〔ʃɑt〕 *n.* 射擊；嘗試　　***hold back*** 保留

let *oneself **go*** 盡量發揮自己的潛力

To succeed, you must work like hell.	爲了成功，你必須拼命工作。
You must work like a dog.	你必須拼命工作。
You must work your fingers to the bone.	你必須拼命努力工作。

Fourth, **follow** the best.	第四，跟著最好的走，拜好的師傅。
Select good role models.	選擇好榜樣。
Study and learn from them.	向他們學習。

Take their advice.	聽從他們的勸告。
Follow their suggestions.	接受他們的建議。
Hitch your wagons to their stars.	以他們的成就爲你們的目標。

Pick their brains.	擷取他們的智慧。
Offer your services.	提供你的服務。（替你的榜樣工作。）
They are your blueprints of success.	他們是你未來成功的藍圖。

8

** ————————————

like hell 拼命地　　*work like a dog* 拼命工作
work one's fingers to the bone 努力工作　　*role model* 榜樣
hitch one's wagon to a star 胸懷大志；有遠大抱負
pick one's brains 擷取某人的智慧
blueprint〔'blu,prɪnt〕*n.* 藍圖

Fifth, *fear* none, respect all.	第五，不怕任何人，尊敬所有人。
Fear nobody.	不必懼怕任何人。
Respect everybody.	要尊敬每一個人。
Don't feel inferior.	不要自卑。
Don't feel superior.	不要驕傲。
Always know your place.	務必要懂得分寸。
Don't denigrate others.	不要抹黑他人。
Don't put others down.	不要貶低他人。
Criticizing will diminish you.	批評他人只會降低你自己的格調。
Sixth, *seek* challenges.	第六，尋求挑戰。
Don't back down.	不要退縮。
Tough tasks make you stronger.	困難的工作會使你更堅強。
Be willing to sweat.	要願意付出心血。
Treat challenge as an opportunity.	將挑戰視為機會。
Don't let anything stop you.	別讓任何事阻擋你。

8

** ————————————

inferior〔ɪnˈfɪrɪɚ〕*adj.* 較差的　　superior〔səˈpɪrɪɚ〕*adj.* 較優的
know one's *place* 懂分寸；舉止謙虛
denigrate〔ˈdɛnəˌgret〕*v.* 抹黑；毀謗　　*put down* 貶低
criticize〔ˈkrɪtəˌsaɪz〕*v.* 批評　　diminish〔dəˈmɪnɪʃ〕*v.* 減弱
seek〔sik〕*v.* 尋找　　*back down* 退縮
tough〔tʌf〕*adj.* 困難的　　willing〔ˈwɪlɪŋ〕*adj.* 願意的
sweat〔swɛt〕*v.* 流汗；付出心血

Seventh, *seek* feedback.	第七,尋求別人的意見。
Get helpful advice.	獲得有益的忠告。
Never be afraid to ask.	不要怕去請敎別人。
Swallow your pride.	不要驕傲。
Eat humble pie.	要謙虛。
You need criticism to improve.	你需要批評才能進步。
Attack bad habits.	戒掉壞習慣。
Have courage to change.	要有勇氣改變。
This is the key to success.	這是成功的關鍵。
Eighth, *be* a sponge for knowledge.	第八,像海綿一樣吸收知識。
Soak up as much as you can.	盡量吸收。
You can never get enough.	知識永遠都不夠。
Be a student for life.	要終生學習。
Collect and study the best.	收集最好的,並加以研究。
You must always be eager for more.	你必須永遠渴望得到更多知識。

8

**——

feedback〔ˈfidˌbæk〕*n.* 回饋;反應　　swallow〔ˈswɑlo〕*v.* 吞下
pride〔praɪd〕*n.* 驕傲　　humble〔ˈhʌmbḷ〕*adj.* 謙虛的
criticism〔ˈkrɪtəˌsɪzəm〕*n.* 批評　　attack〔əˈtæk〕*v.* 攻擊
key〔ki〕*n.* 關鍵　　sponge〔spʌndʒ〕*n.* 海綿　　*soak up* 吸收
for life 終生　　eager〔ˈigɚ〕*adj.* 渴望的　　*be eager for* 渴望

Ninth, *be* patient.	第九，要有耐心。
Stick to your guns.	堅持你的立場。
Sometimes you have to wait.	有時你必須等待。
Never give up.	永遠不要放棄。
Never give in.	永遠不要屈服。
Never say never.	永遠不要說不能做。
Keep on trying.	繼續努力。
Stay in the ring.	不要放棄。
Don't throw in the towel.	不要認輸。
Only those who persist will win.	只有堅持到底的人才會成功。
Only those who persevere will succeed.	只有能堅持到底的人才會成功。
Only those who stick it out can achieve success.	只有堅持到底的人才能成功。

8

** ————————————

stick to one's guns 堅持立場

give up 放棄　　*give in* 屈服　　*keep on* 繼續

stay in the ring 不要放棄　　*throw in the towel* 認輸

persist〔pəˋsɪst〕 v. 堅持

persevere〔͵pɝsəˋvɪr〕 v. 堅持到底　　*stick it out* 堅持到底

***Tenth*, *you must be ready*.**　　第十，你必須做好準備。
Opportunity strikes fast.　　機會來得很快，稍縱即逝。
Don't miss the chance by being　　不要因為沒有準備而失去
　unprepared.　　機會。

Set plans.　　要做計劃。
Make a "to do" list.　　把要做的事列一張表。
Follow through on everything.　　然後逐項完成。

Keep the good.　　好的事物保留。
Discard the bad.　　不好的事物拋棄。
Know the difference between　　要知道這兩者的差別。
　the two.

You must be in the right place.　　你選擇的地方要對。
You must be there at the right　　你選擇的時機也要對。
　time.
But, most importantly, you　　但最重要的是，你必須有所
　must be prepared.　　準備。

8

** ————————————

　　strike fast 來得快（ = *come fast* ）
　　set〔 sɛt 〕*v.* 制定　　***set plans*** 做計劃（ = *make plans* ）
　　follow through 進行到底；貫徹始終
　　discard〔 dɪs'kɑrd 〕*v.* 丟棄

Ladies and gentlemen, we all want to be the best.	各位先生、各位女士，我們都想要成為最好的。
Wanting is not enough.	光是想要是不夠的。
You must get on your feet and take action.	你必須站起來、採取行動。
Push yourselves to excel.	鞭策自己勝過別人。
Force yourselves to break through.	強迫自己去突破。
Don't waste your one chance in life.	別浪費你們一生難得的機會。
Thank you for being here today.	感謝大家今天來到這裡。
I hope your dreams will come true.	希望你們的夢想都將實現。
You will come out with flying colors.	你們將會非常成功。
Thanks ever so much.	非常感謝。

8

** ——————————

get on one's *feet* 站起來　　*take action* 採取行動
push〔pʊʃ〕v. 鞭策
excel〔ɪk'sɛl〕v. 勝過（比較：excellent *adj.* 優秀的）
force〔fors〕v. 強迫　　*break through* 突破
one chance in life 一生難得的機會　　*come true* 實現
come out with flying colors 非常成功

【背景説明】

　　這篇演講稿很長，有 109 個句子，因爲經過特別編排，背起來很容易，不要怕，***You can do it***. 你看，背完演講後，你等於背了 109 個句子。融會貫通後，變成 109 個句型。你的英文馬上就會有很大的進步。

　　要特別注意斜黑字體，***First of all…a goal***; ***Second, believe***…; ***Third, commit***… ，Second 是第二，所以用 b 字開頭；Third 用 c 字開頭。

　　Fourth, follow…; ***Fifth, fear***…; ***Sixth, seek***…; ***Seventh, seek***…;爲了記憶，Fourth 後面接 f 開頭的 follow，Fifth 後面接 f 開頭的 fear；Sixth 和 Seventh 後接 s 開頭的 seek，眞是絞盡腦汁，精心設計，爲了讓你容易背下來！

　　Eighth, ***Ninth***，都用 *be* 開頭，***Tenth*** 用 You must be ready. 起頭，都是爲了記憶方便。因爲演講稿很長，先三句一組背，再一段一段背，例如，先背 ***First of all*** 這段，每段爲一個小單位，這樣你才不會前面熟，後面不熟。

　　這篇文章的內容太重要了，可以用在日常生活中，只要你想説英文，你天天就可以用得到，可以對朋友説、同學説、學生説，任何對象都可以。

　　「演講式英語」的最大受益者，是英文老師，教多了，就會變成很好的演説家，事實上，人人都可成爲英文老師，你可以教你周圍的人，把這個方法傳出去。幫助別人，也幫助自己。

　　這篇演講稿花了一年多的時間設計、研究，經過實驗，不管你記憶力多差，你都背得下來。

8

1. The subject *I'm going to talk about* is how to achieve success.

   這是一個典型的開場白，*I'm going to talk about* 是形容詞子句，修飾 subject，核心主詞是 subject，動詞是 is。

2. We all want to *make it big*.

   make it big 是習慣用法，就等於 succeed。也可説成：
   We all want to *make it big time*.（我們都想要飛黃騰達。）

   big time 字面的意思是「大的時間」，引申爲「第一流；最好的」，make it big time 意思就是「要成爲最好的」，引申爲「要飛黃騰達；要成功」。

3. How do we get there? 本來的意思是「我們如何到那裏？」

   例如： We want to go to the post office.
   How do we get there?

   在本篇演講稿中，引申爲「我們如何才能做到呢？」

   如： We want to win.（我們想要贏。）
   How do we get there?（我們要如何才能做到呢？）

4. 美國人一開口就喜歡説 *first of all*，語氣比 first 或 firstly 要強烈。

5. 美國人很注重 goal（目標），他們常對別人説，You must have a goal.（你必須要有目標。）

   > 美國人常常東想西想，不太穩定，所以父母經常教導子女説，The goal must be *clear-cut*.（目標必須明確。）你甚至可加強語氣地説，The goal must be *clear-cut, plain and simple, black and white*. 句中的 plain and simple，就是「清清楚楚的」，black and white 就是「明明白白的」。很多人就是因爲目標不明確，才會失敗，所以，才會有這麼多英文的慣用語，來強調目標明確的重要性。

8

6. It must be your passion.

在幾乎所有的字典上，passion 都當作「激情；熱情；強烈的情感」解，但是最重要的意思是「愛好」，字典上卻沒有說明白。

例： Sports are my passion.（運動是我的愛好。）

中國人喜歡說「運動是我的興趣」，Sports are my interest.
passion 比 interest 要強烈，它的形容詞 passionate 是「熱情的」，例如：

> She is a very passionate girl.
> = She is passionate.（她非常熱情。）

所以，passion 有兩個重要的意思，第一是「愛好」，
第二是「熱情」。

我們常常跟別人說，「你要成功，就要有熱情」，英文就是：

> You must be passionate to succeed.

7. Always stay on the track of your main goal.

8

美國人很喜歡用 track 這個字造成的成語，如：

> You must *stay on track*.

這句話字面的意思是：「你必須待在軌道上」，引申為「你不要偏離方向；你不要誤入歧途。」

這句話也可以說成 You must stay on the right track.

相反的是 out of track（偏離軌道；誤入歧途）。

如： Don't go out of track.（不要誤入歧途。）

Always stay on the track of your main goal. 也可說成：

Always stay on the right track of your main goal.

由於在句中，track 後面有修飾語，所以加定冠詞 the，這句話字面的意思是：「永遠在主要目標的軌道上」，引申為「永遠朝著主要的目標前進，不要偏離。」

8. Believe in yourselves.

> 很多書上沒有說明清楚 believe 和 believe in 的差別。
> believe 是「相信～的話」，believe in 是「信任」、「信仰」、
> 「相信～的力量」等，有無限多意思，要看前後句意來判斷。
> 比較：I believe you.（我相信你的話。）
> 　　　I *believe in* you.（我信任你。）
> 任何及物動詞加上介詞就形成另外一個意思。例如，hear
> （聽到）、hear of（聽說）、hear from（接到～的訊息）等。

9. Dream big dreams.

> 美國人常喜歡説 "Dream big dreams."，就是教人要有遠大
> 的夢想。Reach for the stars. 字面意思是「伸手去抓星星」，
> 引申為「達成不容易做到的事。」The sky is your limit.
> 字面意思是「天空是你的界限」，引申為「你的潛力無限大。」
> 你唸唸這三句話，

> > *Dream big dreams.*
> > *Reach for the stars.*
> > *The sky is your limit.*

8

> 你看，唸起來有多順，想忘都忘不掉。和學生講話用得
> 到，寫畢業紀念冊也可以用。老師有個學生，王慶銘老師，
> 我送了他一本字典，他叫我題幾個字，我就把第二段整段寫
> 上去，他嚇了一跳，他説：「老師你怎麼那麼厲害？拿了筆，
> 隨便寫就寫了那麼多好的句子。」我告訴他説，這就是背
> 了「**演講式英語**」的好處。

10. 美國人常説：Look ahead. Don't look back. Don't dwell
on the past.

> 目標設定好後，就向前看，不要回頭看，不要懷念從前，
> 不要管從前如何如何。老是想著從前，就無法向前進。

11. Nike〔′naɪkɪ〕是有名的運動品牌，他們以（ ✔ ）和標語 Just do it. 做為行銷的廣告。所以 Just do it. 是美國人的口頭禪。

　　　例如老師叫學生上台來，學生不敢上去，老師就說：

　　　　　　Go for it.（勇敢去試一試。）
　　　　　　Just do it.（趕快做。）
　　　　　　Make it happen.（去做吧！）

　　Make it happen. 字面意思是「使這件事發生」，也就是 Do it. 這三句話都是「趕快去做」的意思，像中文的「坐而言，不如起而行」。

12. 成功的第三個秘訣，就是要專心、要投入（Commit yourself. Dedicate yourself.）也可以說成：Be committed. Be dedicated. 字典上，commit 和 dedicate 的解釋很多，這兩句話要當成慣用句來背，這是美國人掛在嘴巴上的口頭禪。你可以跟你的子女、學生、同學說這些話，叫他要專心（Commit yourself.）、要投入（Dedicate yourself.）。

13. Try your best. 就是「盡量努力。」等於 Do your best. try 字面意思是「嘗試」，在此作「努力」解。

> Give it your best shot. 來自於投籃或射擊，投進一球或射中目標，引申為「盡最大的力量」，等於 Give it your best effort.（盡最大的力量。）
>
> 你叫你的同學加油，你就可以說 "Try your best. Do your best. Give it your best shot." 這三句話。
>
> **說英文要練習一次說三句以上，說多了，就變成演講了，演講不一定要在講台上，隨時隨地都可以對任何人演講。**

8

14. Don't be afraid to let yourself go.

> 這句話的意思是:「不要害怕去發揮自己的潛力。」比如說,
> 有些事情是你可以做得到的,是在你的能力範圍內,可是因
> 爲某種因素,使你造成恐懼感,而不敢去嘗試,美國人很喜
> 歡叫人突破自我,他們常説:

> > You can do it. (你可以辦得到。)
> > Seek a breakthrough. (尋求突破。)
> > Let yourself go. (發揮你自己的潛力。)

15. Don't hold anything back. (不要做任何保留。)
   = *Don't hold back anything.*
   = *Don't hold back.*

> 例如,某個人很拘束,不敢開口説英文,你就可以和他
> 説, "Don't hold anything back." 也就是 "Don't be
> afraid to let yourself go.",句中的 let yourself go,
> 就是「發揮自己的潛力」。

8

16. You must *work like hell*. 句中的 work like hell,就等於
   work like a dog,等於 *work your fingers to the bone*,
   美國人也常説 work like the devil,工作像在地獄中啊!
   像狗一樣拼命工作啊!像 devil (魔鬼) 一樣工作啊!都表
   示「拼命工作」,工作到手指磨破,看到骨頭,當然也是
   「拼命工作」。這些都表示什麼?表示**美國人是一個幽默的
   民族**,一般教科書中,未能充分反映出美國的文化,學了
   當然沒有什麼用處,因爲與現實脱節。沒有學到美國人平
   常所説的話,英文怎麼學得好?

17. 成功的第四個祕訣是 *Follow the best.*（跟著最好的走。）
拜師父就要拜最好的，老師有個員工，他弟弟想當廚師，結
果找路邊攤師傅學，將來，充其量不過在路邊攤稱王，我介
紹他去全國最有名的大廚那裡學習，才學了一半，就可以開
業當大廚了。

出生於西班牙的畢卡索，直到 23 歲去了法國，拜了師父，
才開始發揮他的天才。拜了師父，選擇好的榜樣，都是成
功之道，Select good role models. 而且還要 Study and
learn from them. 還要 Take their advice. Follow their
suggestions.（聽他們的勸告。接受他們的建議。）才會成功。

18. *Hitch your wagons to their stars*. 字面意思是「把你的馬車
栓在他們的星星上」，引申為「以他們的成就為你的目標。」
來自諺語：Hitch your wagon to a star.（要理想崇高；
要胸懷大志。）

8

19. Pick their brains.（吸取他們的智慧。）（pick 的主要意思是
「採；摘；撿」）要做個成功的人，就要擷取成功者的智慧，
成功者通常年齡較大、體力較差，你要主動向你的 role
model 說，你可以 offer some services 給他，幫他做些事，
這些成功者都是你未來成功的藍圖，They are your blueprints
of success. 也可以說成：They are your blueprints *for*
success.

20. *Fear none, respect all*. 是很多人的座右銘，意思就是：
Fear nobody.（不怕任何人。）Respect everybody.（尊敬
每一個人。）也就是說，看到壞人絕不害怕，對周圍所有人
都尊敬。這是慣用句，也可說成：Fear none *and* respect all.
有 *and* 語氣較弱。

21. 成功的第六個祕訣就是：

> Seek challenges.（尋求挑戰。）
> Don't back down.（不要退縮。）

很多人看到新的挑戰就退縮，成功者看到挑戰，反而視爲是一次機會。

22. Tough tasks *make you* stronger.

這是一個美國人常説的句型，下面都是美國人常説的話：
Chicken soup *makes you* stronger.（雞湯使你更強壯。）
Spinach *makes you* stronger.（菠菜使你更強壯。）
Fish *makes you* smarter.（吃魚會讓你更聰明。）
Football *makes you* tougher.（橄欖球會讓你更堅強。）
Exercise *makes you* healthier.（運動使你更健康。）

23. 成功者總是 *Seek feedback*.（尋求意見。）

美國人做完某件事情後，通常會徵詢別人的意見，説：
Give me some feedback.（給我一些意見。）

feedback 這個字，即使是最大的英漢大辭典，也沒有完全解釋正確，不能把 feedback 老是當「回饋」解釋，只要你做了什麼事，別人給你的「意見、反應」，都叫 feedback。

8

24. *Swallow your pride*.
Eat humble pie.

> 這二句話唸起來很順，不可説成 *Eat a humble pie*.（誤）
> 這二句話字面的意思是「把驕傲吞下去。吃謙虛的餅。」，
> 也就是説，「不要驕傲。要謙虛。」

25. ***Attack bad habits***.

> attack 字面的意思是「攻擊」，Attack bad habits. 就像
> 我們中文說的「要消滅壞習慣。」
>> ***Attack*** bad habits. (消除壞習慣。)
>> = ***Get rid of*** bad habits.
>> = ***Kick*** bad habits.
>
> 「要養成好習慣」就是：Form good habits.

26. Be *a sponge* for knowledge.

美國人太喜歡說 sponge 這個字了，這是他們的習慣，我
們也要常說才對。美國人認爲頭腦就像 sponge (海綿)
一樣。

> 如： You are so smart. (你很聰明。)
> You soak up English like *a sponge*.
> (你學英文像海綿；你學英文一敎就會。)

27. Be a student *for life*.

for life 的意思是「終生；一輩子」，

> 如： He went to prison *for life*. (他被終生監禁。)
> I'll live here *for life*. (我將一輩子住在這裏。)

Be a student *for life*. 的意思是「做一個終生學習者」，

Be a student *of life*. 字面的意思是「做一個生活的學生」，
引申爲「要由生活中汲取經驗。」

28. Collect and study the best.

> 中國人只說「我要學最好的」，美國人為什麼要說 collect 呢？
> 因為美國老師教你方法，叫你去收集，叫你去挑選資料，選
> 擇最好的去研讀，不像中國老師什麼都幫你準備好了。所以，
> 美國人喜歡用 collect 這個字，像：collect wisdom from the
> wise（向聰明的人收集智慧），collect experience from mistakes
> （從錯誤中得到經驗）。

29. 成功的第九個祕訣，就是要有耐心（Be patient.）美國人常
    說：Stick to your guns.

> stick to 是「堅持；貼在上面」，Stick to your guns. 字面的意
> 思是「手貼著你的槍」，表示「你堅持不舉手投降、準備抗爭」，
> 引申為「堅持你的立場。」

30. *Never give up*.
    Never give in.
    Never say never.

> give up 為「放棄」，give in 是「屈服」，二者意義相近，這三句
> 都是美國人的口頭禪，鼓勵人們不要放棄，不要屈服，永遠不要
> 說做不到。

8

31. 美國老師在課堂上，常教導同學：

> Keep on trying.（繼續努力。）
> Stay in the ring.（不要放棄。）
> Don't throw in the towel.（不要認輸。）

> Stay in the ring. 來自拳擊比賽，ring 在此指「拳擊台」，待在拳擊
> 台上，表示「不要放棄；不要停止；堅持到底。」拳擊賽時，如果拳
> 擊手身體狀況很糟的時候，拳擊手的經理，就會把毛巾丟入拳擊台中
> （throw in the towel），表示「認輸；放棄」。例如，有些同學打電
> 話來說，考得太差，一直沒進步，覺得很洩氣，我就會跟他說：
> "Keep on trying. Stay in the ring. Don't throw in the towel."

32. You must be ready.

> 美國人做什麼事，都很早就準備好，他們常常預測任何突發的狀況，他們做什麼都有 Plan A、Plan B，甚至 Plan C 之類的計劃，像機會來了，他們該怎麼辦。
>
> 美國父母常教導子女說：
>
> **You must be ready** in case something happens.
>
> 美國人的旅行，大多在一年前就準備好了，深怕突發狀況，因為美國人相信莫非定律（Murphy's Law），就是不管準備得多周全，都一定會有突發狀況，所以他們覺得，再怎麼準備都不為過（You can't be too ready. You can't be ready enough.）

33. *Opportunity strikes fast.*（機會來得很快，稍縱即逝。）
    = *Opportunity comes fast and goes fast.*

8

> strike 的主要意思是「敲打」，
>
> 如：**Strike** while the iron is hot.（打鐵趁熱。）找遍所有的字典，也沒有 strike 當「來」的意思，我們應該把這句話，當成慣用句來背。
>
> 這句話美國人常說，你也要常說。例如：
>
> A: Here comes the girl you like.
>
> （你喜歡的那個女孩來了。）
>
> B: I'm afraid to talk to her.（我不敢去跟她說話。）
>
> A: Go for it! *Opportunity strikes fast.*
>
> （勇敢去追！機會稍縱即逝。）
>
> Opportunity strikes fast. 字面的意思是「機會出現得很快」，引申為「機會來得快，但是去得也快；機會稍縱即逝。」

34. 美國人做事喜歡及早準備，
文具行就有賣 "to do" list，
就是一張備忘卡片，上面
有□1. ⋯⋯ □2. ⋯⋯
□3. ⋯⋯ ，follow through
「完成」的事就打個 "√" 。

```
THINGS TO DO TODAY
Day_____ Date_____
1. □ _____
2. □ _____
3. □ _____
4. □ _____
5. □ _____
6. □ _____
7. □ _____
8. □ _____
9. □ _____
10. □ _____
11. □ _____
12. □ _____
□ SPECIAL ATTENTION:
_____
_____
_____
Record Expenses and Special Memos
on Reverse Side
TOPS ⊛ FORM 2140 ⊛          LITHO IN U.S.A.
```

35. Follow through on everything.

follow through 這個成語很重要，例如：

He had a good plan but he did not follow it through.
（他有一個好計劃，但並未貫徹。）

這個成語是 follow *sth.* through「把某事貫徹」，
sth. 必須是短的字，如：

Follow a plan through.
= Follow through on a plan.

你不可能說 Follow [⋯⋯] through.

through 那麼遠，沒辦法修飾 follow，所以才用 Follow
through on [⋯⋯] .

36. Discard the bad.

discard 這個字來自打撲克牌，discard 「不要的牌」，
意思是「丟棄」。
不要的｜牌

37. You must be *in the right place*.
    You must be there *at the right time*.

> 中國人說「天時、地利、人和」，美國人也喜歡說：
> You must do things *in the right place, at the right time,*
> *with the right people.* (你做事情要講究天時、地利、人和。)
> 類似的說法很多，如：
>> A: I'm so unlucky today. (我今天真倒楣。)
>> B: That's OK. You're just *in the wrong place,*
>> *at the wrong time, with the wrong people.*
>> (沒關係。你只是選錯地方、選錯時間、選錯人。)

38. Only those *who persist* will win.

    Only those *who persevere* will succeed.

    Only those *who stick it out* can achieve success.

> persist 堅持
> = persevere 堅持到底
> = stick it out 堅持到底

這三句話同樣句型，一句比一句強，三句話一起，說起來很
有力量。persist＜persevere＜stick it out，這三個都有「堅
持」的意思，stick it out 的語氣最強。

39. 鞭策自己叫 "*Push yourself.*"

> 鞭策自己，勝過他人，就是 "*Push yourself* to excel." 要鞭策
> 自己到極限，就是 "*Push yourself* to the limit." Push yourself
> to excel. 和 Force yourself to break through. (要強迫自己突
> 破。) 意思相同。

40. Don't waste your one chance in life.

= *Don't waste your only chance in life.*

這表示人一生當中，說不定只有一次機會做大事，因為美
國人的想法是，Tomorrow may never come. 所以要把
握每一次的機會。

41. You will come out with flying colors.

color 基本意思是「顏色」，colors 是表示「旗幟」，字面意思
是「你將帶著飛揚的旗幟出現」，引申為「你將會非常成功」。

42. Thanks *ever so* much.

ever so 是「非常」的意思，等於 very。美國口語中，用
thanks 的講法很多，你可以輪流地說：

> *Thanks*. (謝謝。)
> *Thanks* so much. (多謝。)
> *Thanks* ever so much. (非常感謝。)
>
> *Thanks* a lot. (多謝。)
> *Thanks* a million. (多謝。)
> *Thanks* a bunch. (多謝。)

8

這篇演講稿太棒了，演講稿中的內容，都可以用在作文當中。

【劉毅老師的話】
這篇演講稿太精彩了。背熟了之後，
可以鼓勵別人，也可激勵自己，一生都用
得到這篇演講。

【作文範例】

How to Achieve Success

Everybody wants to be successful, but not everyone can do it. In order to achieve success, we must take some steps to improve ourselves. *First of all*, we must set a clear-cut goal and always stay on track toward that goal. *Second*, we should believe in ourselves and not be afraid to dream big dreams. *Third*, we must commit ourselves and always make our best effort. *Fourth*, we need to be patient. Sometimes we have to wait for success, but it will come as long as we never give up.

In addition to improving ourselves, we can look outside ourselves for ways to increase our chances of success. We should select good role models and then study and learn from them. *Besides*, we should respect others, but not feel inferior to them, for we must also respect ourselves. We should take their criticism graciously and never be afraid to ask for advice. *Also*, we must seek out challenges because tough tasks make us stronger. *Finally*, we must be ready to take advantage of opportunities. We must not miss a chance just because we are unprepared. *In conclusion*, we must take action if we want to be successful, and I believe that the steps above can help us achieve our goals.

9. *Just Do It*
坐而言，不如起而行

Ladies and gentlemen:	各位先生，各位女士：
Please listen carefully.	請仔細聽。
I've got a message for you.	我要對你們傳達一個訊息。
Just do it.	坐而言，不如起而行。
Don't wait to be asked.	別等別人要求才行動。
Do what needs to be done.	做該做的事。
You've seen it everywhere.	這句話到處都看得見。
You've heard it one hundred times.	你已經聽過一百遍了。
Of course, it's the Nike slogan.	當然，它是耐吉的廣告詞。
This is a great motto.	這是很棒的座右銘。
It's a super philosophy.	它是絕妙的人生哲理。
Make it your way of life.	遵循這個原則。

9

** ———————————————

message〔'mɛsɪdʒ〕*n.* 訊息　　slogan〔'slogən〕*n.* 廣告詞
motto〔'mato〕*n.* 座右銘
philosophy〔fə'lasəfɪ〕*n.* 人生哲理

Learn this mindset today.	今天就學會這種想法。
Put it into practice.	付諸實行。
Live by it forever.	永遠遵守它。
Begin now.	現在就開始。
Look around this room.	環顧這個房間。
What would you change if you could?	如果可以的話,你會做什麼改變?
Always think this way.	要總是這樣想。
Look around and say:	要環顧四周,並自問:
What can I do to improve?	我能做什麼改善?
Every task is a test.	每項任務都是考驗。
Every job is a chance.	每件工作都是機會。
Improve, improve, improve.	改進、改進、再改進。
Go the extra mile.	特別努力。
Go the extra distance.	格外努力。
Be a "just do it" person.	做一個起而行的人。

9

** ——————————————

mindset ('maɪnd,sɛt) *n.* 心態;想法
put ~ into practice 實行~   ***live by*** 遵守
task (tæsk) *n.* 任務

Outwork everybody.
Be an overachiever.
Do more than is expected.

工作要比別人更認真。
做個表現突出的人。
比預期的達成更多。

Achieve more.
Learn more.
Create more opportunities.

達成更多任務。
學習更多事物。
創造更多的機會。

Take charge.
Take control.
You have what it takes.

你負責。
你掌控。
你有這種能力。

Work like the devil.
It won't kill you.
It will make you stronger.

拼命工作。
不會累死的。
只會更茁壯。

Be a go-getter.
Seize the initiative.
Be a mover and shaker.

做個有幹勁的人。
把握主動權。
做個重要的人。

9

**

outwork〔aʊt'wɝk〕*v.* 比～認真工作
overachiever〔'ovərə'tʃivɚ〕*n.* 表現比預期要好的人
take charge 負責　　*take control* 掌控
like the devil 拼命地　　go-getter〔'go'gɛtɚ〕*n.* 有幹勁的人
seize the initiative 採取主動　　*mover and shaker* 重要的人

Start with small things. 從小事開始。

Help people in need. 幫助有需要的人。

Jump in and lend a hand. 加入其中，伸出援手。

On seeing some litter, pick it up. 一看到垃圾，就撿起來。

On seeing a crowd at a door, 一看到門邊有人，就幫忙開
　　hold it open. 著門。

On a crowded bus, give up your 在擁擠的公車上，讓出你的
　　seat. 座位。

Say to yourself: 自己跟自己說：

It needs to be done. 這件事需要完成。

I can do it. 我做得到。

I am the one to do it. 就是要我來完成。

9

There you have it. 你們大家都知道了。

Get started now. 現在馬上開始。

Good day. Good luck. Just 祝你愉快。祝你幸運。趕快
　　do it. 做吧。

**　**

---

　in need 有需要的；窮困的

　jump in 投入；著手　　*lend a hand* 幫忙

　on + V-ing 一～的時候　　litter〔ˈlɪtɚ〕*n.* 垃圾

　pick up 撿起來　　crowded〔ˈkraʊdɪd〕*adj.* 擁擠的

　give up 讓出；放棄　　seat〔sit〕*n.* 座位

【背景説明】

這篇演講稿中的句子，都是美國人常説的，背完之後，記得要常常運用到會話中，要多使用，才不會忘記，有事沒事也要常常口裏唸唸有辭地複習。

1. *I've got* a message for you.（我要對你們傳達一個訊息。）
   = *I have* a message for you.
   = *I got* a message for you.
   【美國口語中，常將 have 省略。（詳見「文法寶典」p.330）】

   I've got 不可以説成 *I have got*。【have got 是英式英語】

2. Just do it. 是美國人的口頭禪，因爲美國人大都喜歡光説不練。

   所以他們常教導子女：

   Don't talk about it.（不要光說。）
   Don't think about it.（不要光想。）
   Just do it.（趕快去做。）

3. 如果美國人問你：What are you doing? 你就可以回答：
   I'm doing what needs to be done.

   美國人通常不主動，主管常跟部屬説：Don't wait to be asked.
   （不要等到別人要求，才行動。）來強調主動出擊的重要。

   下面這三句話，你可以跟弟弟、妹妹或你的下屬説：

   Just do it.（趕快做。）
   Don't wait to be asked.
   　　（不要等到別人要求。）
   Do what needs to be done.（做該做的事。）

9

4. ✔ 是 Nike 的 logo〔'logo〕*n.* 品牌標誌。

> Just do it. 是他們的 slogan（廣告詞；標語；口號）。
>
> 類似的例子還很多，如香奈兒著名的雙 C 符號 ⅭⅭ，與 Louis Vuitton 的縮寫 LV，都是著名的 logo，而非 slogan。
>
> 美國陸軍的口號（slogan）是：
>
> Be all you can be.（發揮你全部的力量。）

5. Make it your way of life. 根據上面一句話 it 指的是 philosophy。

> 字面的意思是：「使這個哲理成為你的生活方式」，可引申為「把這個哲理當做你的人生觀」，意思就是「遵循這個原則」。
>
> 其他例子如：
>
> *Make* being on time *your way of life.*（你要準時。）
>
> = *Make it your way of life* to be on time.

Make eating healthy *your way of life.*

> 這句話字面的意思是：「你要把吃得健康當成你的生活方式」，引申為「你要吃得健康」。
>
> *Make* exercising regularly *your way of life.*
> （你要定時運動。）
> *Make* dressing properly *your way of life.*
> （你要穿著整齊。）
> *Make* cleanliness *your way of life.*（你要保持乾淨。）
> *Make* being frugal *your way of life.*（你要節省。）
> *Make* modesty *your way of life.*（你要謙虛。）

你要常說 *Make...your way of life.* 不要怕，說錯沒關係，別人聽不聽得懂沒關係，你要常說就對了。

6. Eating well is *my way of life*.

> 這也是美國人常說的句型，這句話字面的意思是：「吃好的
> 東西是我生活方式」，表示「我習慣於吃好東西。」
>
> Wearing expensive clothes is Jennifer's *way of life*.
> （珍妮佛習慣於穿昂貴的衣服。）
> Wearing sexy outfits is Elsa's *way of life*.
> （艾爾莎喜歡穿性感的衣服。）

7. mindset 是「心態；想法」，等於 mentality。

> The American mindset is different from ours.
> （美國人的想法，和我們不一樣。）
>
> I understand your mindset. （我了解你的想法。）
> = I understand your mentality.
> = I understand what you're thinking.

8. Live by it forever. （永遠遵循它。）

> live by 的字面意思是「靠～生活」，引申為「遵循」，等於
> abide by。也可以說成：Abide by it forever.

9. Begin now. 也可以說成 Start now. 這是美國人常喜歡說的話。

9

10. 美國人很喜歡用 improve 這個字，improve 是成功之道，所
以他們非常強調。Improve, improve, improve. 公司不好需
要 improve，公司第一名，也需要 improve，否則就無法保
持領先。

11. 美國人常用 Every task is a test. Every job is a chance.
    來鼓勵人們把握每一次的機會。

12. *You have what it takes*.（你很有能力。）

> 是 You have *what it takes* to accomplish something. 的
> 省略。當某人沒信心時，你就可以說：
>
> You have what it takes.
>
> 懷疑他人能力時，你可以問：
>
> Do you have what it takes?（你有這種能力嗎？）
>
> You have what it takes. 很重要，你看到任何人都可以
> 跟他說這句話。
>
> 你可以說：
>
> You can do it.（你可以做到。）
> I'm sure of it.（我確信。）
> *You have what it takes*.（你有能力。）

9

no matter what it takes（無論如何），也很常用，來表示
堅決的意願。

如：*No matter what it takes*, I will do it.
　　（無論如何，我都要做。）
　　No matter what it takes, I will finish it.
　　（無論如何，我都會完成。）

你要常說 "*no matter what it takes*"，這是道地的美語。

13. ***Outwork everybody.***

> out 加上動詞，形成很多字，字典上也許沒有，但美國人常說。
>
> ***outwork***（比～工作更認眞）= *work more than*
>
> > I ***outwork*** you.（我比你工作更認眞。）
> >
> > = I *work more than you.*
>
> ***outstudy***（比～更用功）= *study more than*
>
> > ***Outstudy*** everybody.（比每個人都用功。）
> >
> > = *Study more than everybody.*

14. 美國人常用這三句話：

> > Take charge.（你負責。）
> >
> > Take control.（你掌控。）
> >
> > You have what it takes.（你有能力。）
>
> 來鼓勵領導人物。
>
> 想叫別人負責，就說：
>
> > Take charge at work.（在工作時，當個領導人物。）
>
> Take charge. 和 Take control. 兩句意義相同。

9

15. Work like the devil.

> 美國人印象當中，devil（魔鬼）都是速度很快的，而且永遠不
> 休息的。所以 Work like the devil. 表示像 devil 一樣地工作，
> 引申爲「拼命工作」，等於
>
> > Work like hell.（拼命工作。）
> >
> > = Work your fingers to the bone.（拼命工作。）
> >
> > = Work until you drop.（拼命工作。）

16. It won't kill you. 這句話很常用。

> 如： Don't be afraid to do this. (不要害怕做這件事情。)
> *It won't kill you.* (你不會累死。)

> 意思不是真的會殺死你，意思是叫你放輕鬆，這是美國人幽
> 默的説法。又如女生追男生常喜歡説：

>> Don't be afraid of me. *I won't bite.* (不可説成 *I won't bite you.*)
>> (不要害怕。我不會吃掉你。)

> 這些都是幽默的話。

17. Be a go-getter.

> go-getter 是表示「有幹勁的人」，来自 go (*and*) get。有幹勁
> 的人常説：I will go get it. (我會去拿；我會去做。) 在公司
> 裏面，懶人都不願意去做事，勤快的人常説：I'll go get it.
> 例如，老板要任何東西的時候，你都可以説：I'll go get it. 電
> 話鈴響了，門鈴響了，你都可以説：I'll go get it. 你看到老板
> 要去拿東西的時候，你就可以説：I'll go get it for you. (我
> 去幫你拿。) 所以 Be a go-getter. 就是「要有幹勁」的意思。

9

18. Seize the initiative. 字面意思是「抓住主動權」，引申爲「採取
主動」和 Take the initiative. 意義相同。

19. a mover and shaker 源自 a person who can move the world
and shake the world，字面的意思是「可以移動世界、搖動世
界的人」，引申爲「舉足輕重的人；重要人物」。大人物則是 big
shot, big wheel 和 big toe。

> 你在公司裏面，老板會跟你説：
> *Be a mover and shaker.* (做個重要的人。)
> 這和 big shot (大人物) 有時候有區別。

20. jump in 的意思是「不要等別人叫你去，你自己要參與」，等
　　 於 get involved。當一群人在討論事情的時候，有人不參與，
　　 你就可以説：

　　　　 You can jump in anytime.（你可以隨時參與。）

21. Speak to yourself. 也可説成：Say to yourself. 美國各地區
　　 不同，西岸的美國人大都講 Speak to yourself. 東岸的美國人
　　 則常説 Say to yourself. 一般美國人兩種説法都説。

22. There you have it. 是慣用句。

> 字面的意思是：「現在你有了」，引申爲「現在你知道了。」
> 演講結束時，就可以説 There you have it.
>
> 　把東西遞給別人時，也可以説：
> 　　 There you have it.（好了，拿去。）
> 　= There you go.
> 　= Here you are.
> 　= Here it is.

23. 我們背幾個「現在開始」的説法：

　　　　 Start now.
　　 = Get started now.
　　 = Begin now.【不可説 *Get begun now.*（誤）】
　　 = Commence now.

9

24. Good day. Good luck. Just do it.

Good day. 是由 Have a good day 簡化而來。

白天見面或道別時都可以使用。

白天見面説 Good day. 翻成中文，就是「你好。」

白天道別的時候，也可以説 Good day. 翻成中文，就是「再見。」

【問候語一覧表】

白天見面 Good day.	早晨見面	Good morning. 或 Morning.
	正午見面	【中午 12:00 只有一秒鐘時間，所以 不説 *Good noon.*（誤）】
	下午見面	Good afternoon. 或 Afternoon.
	傍晚見面	Good evening. 或 Evening.

白天再見 Good day.	早晨再見	Have a good morning. （不説 *Good morning.*）
	正午再見	【中午 12:00 只有一秒，沒有表達方法】
	下午再見	Have a good afternoon. （不説 *Good afternoon.*）
	晚上再見	Have a good evening. （也可説 Good evening.） Have a good night. Good night. （常説 Good night.）

一般人認爲，晚上見面説 Good evening.，晚上再見説
Good night.。事實上，也有美國人再見時説 Good evening.

例如：I've got to go now. Good evening.

（我現在要走了。再見。）

9

【作文範例】

Just Do It

We have all heard the phrase, "Just do it," a super philosophy, which is the slogan of the Nike Corporation. It means that when there is something that needs to be done, we should do it as soon as we can. We should not think too much. *Above all*, we should not procrastinate or put it off.

Putting things off is common with people. Most people wait until the last moment. They think that as long as they meet the deadline, they are okay. The problem with this attitude is that, unless all goes well, they cannot deal with anything that is unpredictable. *Furthermore*, because they procrastinate, they spend all their time worrying, suffering from unnecessary pressure. *On the other hand*, if they do things as soon as they can, jobs won't pile up and they can be relieved of that unnecessary pressure. They can even enjoy some leisure.

9

To sum up, we should follow the motto, "Just do it," because it will do us much good.

【中文翻譯】

坐而言，不如起而行

我們大家都聽過 "Just do it" 這個片語，它是種超級哲學，也是耐吉公司的標語。它的意思是，如果有某件事必須完成，我們就應該儘快去做。我們不該想太多。最重要的是，我們不該拖延。

拖延事情是一般人的通病。大多數人都會等到最後一刻。他們認為，只要趕上期限，就可以了。這種態度的問題在於，除非一切都很順利，否則他們就無法應付任何意料之外的事。此外，因為拖延，所以他們花費所有的時間在擔心，承受不必要的壓力。另一方面，如果他們能儘快做所有的事情，那麼工作就不會累積，也可以免除不必要的壓力。他們甚至可以享受一些閒暇時光。

總之，我們應該遵循 "Just do it" 這個座右銘，因為它將對我們很有益處。

9

10. Happy Birthday Speech
生日快樂演講

Congratulations!	恭禧！恭禧！
It's your birthday.	今天是你的生日。
Happy birthday to you.	祝你生日快樂。
You were born today.	今天是你出生的日子。
Today is your special day.	今天是你特別的日子。
This is your day.	今天你是主角。
How do you feel?	你覺得怎麼樣？
Do you feel special?	你有沒有覺得很特別？
What's your birthday wish?	你生日的願望是什麼？
You look great ——	你看起來真棒，
even better than last year.	甚至比去年還好。
You are aging gracefully.	你愈來愈有氣質。
You're not getting old.	你沒有變老。
You're getting wiser.	你變得愈來愈有智慧。
You're getting better.	你變得愈來愈好。

10

**──────────

congratulations〔kənˌgrætʃəˈleʃənz〕*n. pl.* 恭禧
wish〔wɪʃ〕*n.* 願望　　age〔edʒ〕*v.* 變老
gracefully〔ˈgresfəlɪ〕*adv.* 優雅地　　wise〔waɪz〕*adj.* 有智慧的

Light the candles.	點蠟燭。
Turn off the light.	關掉電燈。
Let's sing "Happy Birthday."	我們一起唱「生日快樂歌」。
"Happy birthday to you...."	「祝你生日快樂……。」

Make a wish!	許個願！
Take a deep breath!	深呼吸！
Blow out the candles!	把蠟燭吹熄！

Good job!	做得好！（你吹得不錯！）
You did it!	你做到了！（你吹熄了！）
Your wish will come true.	你的願望將會實現。

What was your wish?	你許了什麼願？
What did you wish for?	你有什麼願望？
I hope it was a good one.	我希望它是個很好的願望。

Don't tell me.	不要告訴我。
I know it's a secret.	我知道那是個祕密。
If you tell, it won't come true.	如果你洩露，它就不會實現。

10

**

light〔laɪt〕*v.* 點燃　*n.* 電燈　　candle〔'kændl〕*n.* 蠟燭
turn off 關掉　　***make a wish*** 許願　　breath〔brɛθ〕*n.* 呼吸
take a deep breath 深呼吸　　***blow out*** 吹熄
come true 實現　　***wish for*** 希望；想要
secret〔'sikrɪt〕*n.* 祕密　　tell〔tɛl〕*v.* 洩密

Please say something. 請說幾句話。

Speech, speech. 演講，演講。

Give us a few words. 對我們說幾句話。

The birthday boy or girl can say: 壽星可以說：

Words fail me. 我不知道該說什麼。

I'm speechless. 我說不出話。

I don't know what to say. 我不知道說什麼才好。

What a wonderful birthday! 這個生日真棒！

I won't ever forget it. 我永遠不會忘記。

I'm the luckiest person in the 我是全世界最幸運的人。
  world.

You guys are so great. 你們大家真好。

You are all the best. 你們都是最棒的。

Thanks for being here. 謝謝你們來這裏。

10

** ————————————

fail〔fel〕*v.* 拋棄；使失望（fail 的主要意思是「失敗」）

speechless〔'spitʃlɪs〕*adj.*（一時）說不出話來的

not ever 絕不；永遠不會（= *never*）

guy〔gaɪ〕*n.* 人；傢伙

I'd like to thank my parents.	我要感謝我的父母。
I'd like to thank my friends.	我要感謝我的朋友。
I don't deserve this.	我真不敢當。
The gifts are nice.	這些禮物真好。
The cards are great.	這些卡片真棒。
But it's you that make it special.	但是,都是由於你們,讓這一切變得如此特別。
I made two wishes.	我許了兩個願。
One is a secret.	一個是祕密。
The other is for you.	另一個要獻給大家。
I wished for your good health.	我希望大家健康。
I wished for your happiness.	我希望大家快樂。
Let's have good luck in the year ahead.	讓我們在今後的一年內,充滿好運。

10

Finally, I'd like to say:	最後,我想說的是:
With friends and family like you,	有像你們這樣的家人和朋
every day feels like my birthday.	友,我每天都覺得像是在過生日。

** ————————————————

deserve (dɪˋzɝv) *v.* 應得 (賞罰)
ahead (əˋhɛd) *adj.* 未來;今後   feel (fil) *v.* 感覺像;似乎

【背景說明】

1. Congratulations!（恭禧！恭禧！）

> congratulations 這個字，一定要用複數，什麼時候都可
> 以說，如朋友結婚、過生日、升官、發財都可以說。
>
> 中國人說「恭禧！恭禧！」，通常說兩句「恭禧」，但是
> 要記住，美國人只說一句 Congratulations! 就行了，美國
> 人不習慣說兩句。Congratulations. 或 Congratulations!
> 都可以，這個字後面，可用句點或感嘆號。

2. Happy birthday to you.（生日快樂。）

> 這句是慣用句，也可以只說：Happy birthday. 為什麼是慣
> 用句呢？因為它沒有動詞。

3. You were born today.

> 這個句子用過去式動詞 were，表示你是在過去的今天出生，
> 也就是「今天是你出生的日子。」

4. This is your day.

> 字面的意思是：「今天是你的日子。」意思就是「今天你是
> 主角。」當你的朋友畢業、結婚的時候，你都可以跟他說這
> 句話。

10

5. You are aging gracefully.

> aging 是「變老」，gracefully 是「優雅地」，字面的意思
> 是「你優雅地變老」，引申為「你愈來愈有氣質」。
>
> 【比較】You age gracefully.（一般語氣）
> 　　　　You are aging gracefully.（加強語氣）

「現在進行式」的語氣，比「現在式」要強烈，表示「稱讚」。
「現在進行式」不一定表示現在正在進行的動作，有八種功用。

（詳見「文法寶典」p.342）

6. You're not *getting* old.
   You're *getting* wiser.
   You're *getting* better.

   get 的「現在進行式」，表示「愈來愈～」。（詳見「文法寶典」p.343）

7. I know it's a secret.
   If you *tell*, it won't come true.

   tell 通常當「授與動詞」，有兩個受詞，但在這裏 tell 是「完全不及物動詞」，作「洩密」解。If you *tell*, it won't come true. (如果你洩密，它就不會實現。) come true 作「實現」解。

8. Speech, speech.

   美國人在舉行 party 的時候，如果想叫別人講話，通常會拿小湯匙來敲杯子，喊 "Speech, speech." 意思就是「發表演講，發表演講」，這裏的 speech 是 make a speech 的省略。

   【注意】Speech, speech. 只講兩個字，是在 party 中，大家起鬨的時候說的。

10

9. *You guys* are so great.

   美國人對一群男女會說 *you guys* (你們)，對一群男生，或者甚至一群女生，都可以說 *you guys*，但是，只有看到單獨一個女孩，不能說 *you guy*，你可以說：Excuse me, miss. 或 Excuse me, ma'am. 而 *you guys* 是美國人的口頭禪，你只要說 you guys，美國人就會認為你的英文很棒了。

10. I don't deserve this.

    deserve 這個字，作「應得 (賞罰)」解，所以，*I don't deserve this*. 有正反兩個意思：

① 我真不敢當。

【意思是「我覺得我不該得到這種獎勵或讚賞等」。】

② 我不該受到這種對待。

【意思是「我不該受到這種處罰或譴責等」。】

這句話也可説成：I don't deserve it. 當別人送你禮物，或是給你加薪，你都可以説：I don't deserve it. 或 I don't deserve this.

11. I wished for your good health.

I *wished for* your good health. (我希望你身體健康。)

= I *wished* <u>you</u> <u>good health</u>. (我希望你身體健康。)
              間接受詞   直接受詞

wish for 的主要意思是「希望」，有時候也可作「想要」解。

如：   She *wishes for* what she can't have.

    = She *wants* what she can't have.

    （ 她想要她沒辦法得到的東西。 ）

12. The birthday boy or girl can say:

美國人過生日的時候，不管年齡多大，無論老少，男的都叫 birthday boy，女的叫 birthday girl，就像中國人叫「壽星」一樣。

10

13. Words fail me.

fail 當及物動詞，有兩個意思：①拋棄（某人）②使失望。這句話字面的意思是，「話拋棄我」，引申為「我無話可説。」，或「我不知道該説什麼。」

    His courage *failed* him. (他失去勇氣。)

    = He *lost* his courage.

    You *failed* me. (我對你很失望。)

    = You *disappointed* me.

別人送你禮物、稱讚你、給你錢，你都可以說這三句話：

> *Words fail me.*
> *I'm speechless.*
> *I don't know what to say.*

這三句話可說是萬用句，要把英文學好，不要忘記，一次
要說三句以上，有事、沒事，就要用英文對別人講話，講
很多，像是發表演講一樣。

14. Let's have good luck in the year ahead.

in the year ahead 是指「在未來的一年內（從現在算起）」，
也可翻成「在今後的一年內」。而 *in the year next*「明年
（是從明年 1 月 1 日算起）」等於 next year。

15. Every day *feels* like my birthday.

feel 的這種用法，很少人會用，feel 在這裏作「感覺是；
似乎（= *seem*）」解。如：*It feels* cold in this room.（這
個房間感覺很冷。）

到了游泳池，接觸到水，你就可以說：The water *feels*
fine.（這個水摸起來感覺很好。）

feel 這個字的主要意思是「感覺」，一切意思都由「感覺」
演變而來。一般人不懂的原因是，feel 這個字，也可用「非
人」當主詞。

你只要記住，在「非人」當主詞時，feel 等於 seem，一切
就迎刃而解。

Every day *feels* like my birthday. 意思是「我每天都覺得
像是在過生日」，就是「我每天都快樂。」

10

【作文範例】

My Birthday Wish

Today is a special day for me because it is my birthday. I'm not worried about getting older. Instead of getting old, I'm getting wiser. I'm getting better every day. *Therefore*, I am happy to celebrate this day with you. Before I blew out the candles on my cake, I made a wish. It's a good wish so I hope it will come true.

I can't tell you what I wished for, but I can say that I am the luckiest person in the world. I'm lucky because I have great friends and family like you. The gifts are nice and the cards are great, but it's you that make my birthday special. Actually, I made two wishes. Only one is a secret. The other is for you. I wished for your good health and happiness. With friends and family like you, every day feels like my birthday.

10

【中文翻譯】

我的生日願望

　　今天是我特別的日子，因為今天是我的生日。我不擔心會變老。我沒有變老，而是變得愈來愈有智慧。我每一天都變得愈好。因此，我很高興能和你們一起慶祝這一天。在我吹熄蛋糕上的蠟燭之前，我許了一個願望。這是個很好的願望，所以我希望它能實現。

　　我不能告訴你們，我的願望是什麼，但是我敢說，我是全世界最幸運的人。我很幸運，因為我有像你們這些很棒的朋友及家人。這些禮物真好，還有這些卡片也很棒，但是，都是由於你們，讓我的生日變得如此特別。事實上，我許了兩個願。有一個是祕密。另一個要獻給大家。我希望大家健康快樂。有像你們這樣的家人和朋友，我每天都覺得像是在過生日。

10

11. *Why We Should Study English*
為什麼我們應該學英文

11

Ladies and gentlemen:	各位先生，各位女士：
I'm glad you could make it.	很高興你們能來到這裏。
Please pay attention to what I say.	請注意我所說的話。
Learning English is an investment.	學英文是一種投資。
Our profit will be great.	我們會獲益良多。
It's the best thing *we* can do.	這是我們所能做的最好的事情。
We must learn English.	我們必須學英文。
We have no choice.	我們沒有選擇的餘地。
It's the way of the world.	這是世界的潮流。
English is here to stay.	英文會一直存在。
It's spoken everywhere.	到處都在說英文。
It's a worldwide movement.	這是全世界的趨勢。

** ────────────────

make it 成功；辦到；能來　　*pay attention to* 注意
investment〔ɪn'vɛstmənt〕*n.* 投資　　profit〔'prɑfɪt〕*n.* 利益
worldwide〔'wɜld'waɪd〕*adj.* 全世界的
movement〔'muvmənt〕*n.* 趨勢

11

English is essential.	英文是非常重要的。
It's a ticket to success.	它是成功的關鍵。
It's such a useful skill.	它是一種非常有用的技能。
We need *English* to succeed.	我們需要英文才能成功。
We can't do without it.	我們沒有它就不行。
Here are the reasons why *we should study English*.	以下就是為什麼我們應該學英文的原因。
First, speaking English well *is a sign of success*.	第一，英文說得好，是成功的表徵。
It makes us more fascinating.	英文說得好，會讓我們更有魅力。
It makes everybody envy us.	會讓每個人都羨慕我們。
It gives us power.	英文給我們力量。
Knowing English earns respect.	懂英文能贏得尊敬。
Our status and confidence will increase.	我們的地位和信心將會提升。
Second, English is fun.	第二，英文很有趣。
It's a blast.	爆好玩的。
We will really enjoy this language.	我們會真正喜歡這種語言。

** ————————————————

essential〔ə'sɛnʃəl〕*adj.* 必要的；非常重要的（= *very important*）
skill〔skɪl〕*n.* 技能   sign〔saɪn〕*n.* 表徵；標誌
fascinating〔'fæsn̩‚etɪŋ〕*adj.* 有魅力的；迷人的（= *charming*）
envy〔'ɛnvɪ〕*v.* 羨慕
status〔'stetəs‚'stætəs〕*n.* 地位（這個字有二種發音，一般字典只有〔'stetəs〕）
blast〔blæst〕*n.* 爆好玩的事

11

English *will make* us happier.	英文能使我們更快樂。
We will make more friends.	我們將會結交更多朋友。
We will become better people.	我們將會變得更好。

Third, *English will open our eyes.*	第三，英文能使我們大開眼界。
We can learn many new things.	我們能學到許多新的事物。
English films, songs, and literature are informative.	英文電影、英文歌曲，以及英國文學，都能增進我們的知識。

Fourth, *English is global.*	第四，英文全球通用。
We should become a global people.	我們應該成為有世界觀的人。
The world is getting smaller.	世界變得愈來愈小。

English is great for traveling.	旅行時英文很有用。
It's like a secret weapon.	它就像是個祕密武器。
It will help us anywhere.	在任何地方它都能幫助我們。

** ————————————

make friends 交朋友
open one's eyes 使某人大開眼界；大吃一驚
film〔fɪlm〕*n.* 電影　literature〔'lɪtərətʃə〕*n.* 文學；文學作品
informative〔ɪn'fɔrmətɪv〕*adj.* 能增進知識的
global〔'globḷ〕*adj.* 全球的
weapon〔'wɛpən〕*n.* 武器　*secret weapon* 祕密武器

11

Ladies and gentlemen:	各位先生，各位女士：
English is a great language.	英文是很棒的語言。
We will never be bored.	我們絕不會厭倦。
We can do many things with it.	我們能用英文做很多事情。
Let's enjoy the English- speaking world.	讓我們來享受說英文的世界。
Let's not get left behind.	我們不要落伍。
Let's not get left all alone.	我們不要孤孤獨獨一個人， 和別人不一樣。
It's never too late.	永遠不嫌遲。
Trust me, I know.	相信我，我懂。
We can learn at any age!	不論我們年紀多大，都可以學！
Let's not be dinosaurs.	我們不要成爲恐龍。
They all died out.	牠們都消失了。
They became extinct.	牠們已經絕種了。
I appreciate your time.	我很感激大家所花費的時間。
Let's not wait another minute.	我們一分鐘都不要再等。
Let's start learning English right now.	讓我們現在就開始學英文吧。

** ————————————————

leave behind 遺留　　dinosaur〔ˈdaɪnəˌsɔr〕*n.* 恐龍
die out 死光；消失；絕種（= *become extinct*）
extinct〔ɪkˈstɪŋkt〕*adj.* 絕種的；滅絕的
appreciate〔əˈpriʃɪˌet〕*v.* 感激

11

【背景説明】

　　"Why We Should Study English"（爲什麼我們應該學英文），這是流行的話題。老師可以告訴學生，家長可以告訴小孩，爲什麼要學英文。背了這篇文章，你就會用英文告訴他們了。

　　這篇文章有經過特殊設計，要注意到斜體字，當你背不下來的時候，你就要研究，這一句和上一句的關連，這一組和上一組的關連。斜黑字是表示連接的關鍵字，自己也可以舉一反三，研究出背的方法，怎麼樣自己才能記得下來。

1. I'm glad you could make it.（我很高興你們能來。）

> 　　*You can make it*. 這類的句子很常用，例如，過馬路，碰到綠燈，你就可以説：I think *we can make it*.（我想我們來得及。）到了目的地，你就可以説：*We made it*.（我們到了。）
>
> 　　凡是某人某件事做成功了，如考試及格、考上理想的學校，你就可以説：*You made it*.（你成功了；你及格了；你考上了。）所以，*You can make it*. 這類的句子有無限多的意思，要看前後句子的意思而定。
>
> 　　I'm glad you *could make* it. 用過去式的原因，是由於説話的時候，你們已經辦到了，也就是已經來了，所以用過去式 *could make*。

2. It's the best thing we can do.

　　這句話非常有用，要掛在嘴巴上講，你不管講完什麼話，提出什麼建議，都可以説這句話。例如，你説過了 Learning English is an investment. 你就可以説：It's the best thing *we* can do. 在句中，we 用斜黑的原因，是要連接下面的 *We* must learn English.

11

3. We must learn English.
   We have no choice.
   It's the way of the world.

> 這三句話是一個説話的公式，你可以舉一反三。
>
> 例： You *must* go home. (你必須回家。)
>
> *You have no choice.* (你沒有選擇的餘地。)
>
> *It's the way* to go. (這是該做的事。)
>
> 你只要記住，must.... 後面就可以用 ··· have no choice。
>
> 例： I *must* go to work. (我必須去工作。)
>
> *I have no choice.* (我沒有選擇的餘地。)
>
> *It's the way* to go. (這是該做的事。)
>
> 這種例子太多了，你最好天天都要練習説這個會話公式。
>
> We *must* obey traffic rules.
>
> (我們必須遵守交通規則。)
>
> *We have no choice.* (我們沒有選擇的餘地。)
>
> *It's the way* not to get a ticket.
>
> (這樣就不會接到罰單了。)
>
> 美國人習慣説 I have no choice. 之類的話。像：
>
> I really want to help you, but *I have no choice.*
>
> (我眞的很想幫你，但是我無能爲力。)

4. It's *the way of the world.* (這是世界的潮流。)

> way 是指「做法」。
>
> Learning English is *the way of the world.*
>
> (學英文是世界的潮流。)
>
> Healthy eating is *the way of the world.*
>
> (現在流行健康飲食。)

11

5. English is here to stay.

這句話字面的意思是：「英文待在這裡不走。」即「英文會永遠存在。」等於 *English will always be used.*

6. English is a *worldwide* movement.

worldwide 〔ˋwɝldˊwaɪd 〕*adj.* 全世界的

這個字是由兩個字所組成，world＋wide（寬），世界這麼寬，就是指「全世界的」。其他類似的有：nationwide（全國的）、citywide（全市的）。

movement 〔ˋmuvmənt 〕*n.* 移動；運動

這句話字面的意思是「英文是全世界的移動」，也就是「英文是全世界的運動」，引申為「英文是全世界的趨勢。」

7. English is a *ticket* to success.
 ＝ English is a *key* to success.

你開門需要鑰匙（key），你坐車需要車票（ticket），故引申為：「英文是成功的關鍵。」

8. We can't *do without* it. (我們沒有英文就不行。)

do without「沒有～也行」，can't do without「沒有～不行」，很多情形都可以用。如：We can't *do without* water. (我們沒有水就不行。)

do 是完全不及物動詞，如：That will do. (行、行、行。) *do without* 這個成語很特別，在一句話中，without 後的受詞明確時，可以省略，也可以保留。如：There wasn't any coffee left, so we had to *do without* (*it*). (咖啡一點也沒剩，所以我們必須將就不喝了。)

11

9. It's *a blast*. (爆好玩的。) = *It's a lot of fun.*

blast 的主要意思是「爆炸」，在此引申爲「爆好玩的」，你如果説 blast 這個字，美國人會笑。

如美國人問你説：Are you having fun? (你玩得高興嗎？) 你可以回答：Yeah, I'm having *a blast.* (痛快死了。) *have a blast* = *have a great time* (玩得很愉快)

10. We will become better people.

better people 是 good people 的比較級。美國人喜歡用 good 來形容人。我們中國人喜歡説「他很好」，美國人就説：He is a good person. 中國人説：「他很會開車。」美國人會説：He is a *good* driver.

We will become *better* people. 的意思就是「我們將變得更好。」

11. English is global. (英文全球通用。)

而 global people 則是指「有世界觀的人」。

The world is getting smaller. (世界變得愈來愈小。)

get、become 的現在進行式，表示「愈來愈～」。(詳見「文法寶典」p.343)

12. We should become a global people.

(我們應該成爲有世界觀的人。)

people 是集合名詞，可表「集合體」，有單複數形式，也可以表「個體」，本身就是複數形。(詳見「文法寶典」p.51)

這裏的 a global people 表示「一個整體」，就像 people 表示集合體「民族」一樣。在這裏的 a global people 是指「一群有世界觀的人」。

11

13. English will *open our eyes*.
（英文能使我們大開眼界。）

open our eyes 就等於 broaden our horizons（拓
展我們的眼界）。horizon〔hə'raɪzn〕*n.* 地平線；眼界

例：Seeing the Grand Canyon really *opened my eyes*.
（看到了大峽谷，眞使我大開眼界。）

open *one's* eyes 也有「大吃一驚」的意思，
如：When I told him so, he *opened his eyes*.
（當我告訴他實情時，他大吃一驚。）

14. Let's not *get left behind*.（我們不要落伍。）

表示「我們不要讓自己落伍，被人遺忘；我們不要被留
在後面。」去旅行的時候，你可以跟朋友說：

Don't *get left behind*.（不要落到後面去了。）
Let's not *get left all alone*.（我們不要孤單一個人。）

你也可以跟朋友說：

Don't *leave* me *all alone*.
（不要把我單獨一個人丟下不管。）
I don't want to *be left all alone*.
（我不想要自己一個人單獨被留下。）

15. *Trust me, I know*. 是慣用句，很常用。

爲什麼是慣用句呢？因爲二個子句，沒有連接詞。
I know 表示 *I know* how to do it 或 *I know* what it's all
about，或 *I know* it all。

美國人也常說：Believe me, *I know*. 或 Listen to
me, *I know*. 凡是想叫別人聽你的話時，都可加上 *I
know*，加強語氣。

11

16. Let's not be dinosaurs. (我們不要成爲恐龍。)

　　這句話的字面意思是「我們不要成爲恐龍。」恐龍在世界上已經絕跡，故本句可引申爲「我們不要落伍。」
dinosaur〔'daɪnə,sɔr 〕*n.* 恐龍；落伍的人；老古板

17. I appreciate your time.

　　appreciate 這個字，後面只能接事情，它的眞正意思是「重視；賞識」。(詳見 p.341)

18. Let's not wait another minute.

　　在句中的 another minute 是名詞當副詞用，wait 後面的 for 省略。這句話也可説成 Let's not wait for another minute. (詳見「文法寶典」p.101)

19.
{ Let's *start learning* English right now.
= Let's *start to learn* English right now.

{ Let's *begin learning* English right now.
= Let's *begin to learn* English right now.
= Let's learn English right now.

　　start 和 begin 後面都可以接動名詞或不定詞，意義相同。(詳見「文法寶典」p.434)

【作文範例】

11

Why We Should Study English

There are several reasons why we should study English. *First*, speaking English well is a sign of success. It makes us more fascinating and makes everybody envious. It also earns us respect. *As a result*, our status and confidence will increase. *In addition*, English is fun. We can really enjoy this language because we can learn many things through it. *Furthermore*, English will make us happier because by being able to speak English we will make more friends.

English will also open our eyes. We can learn a lot from English films, songs and literature. They are all so informative. *Finally*, English is global. The world is getting smaller because of English. English is therefore great for traveling around the world. It's like a secret weapon that can help us anywhere.

In conclusion, English is a great language. If we study English, we will never be bored because we can do so much with it.

11

【中文翻譯】

爲什麼我們應該學英文

　　我們爲什麼應該學英文，理由有很多。首先，英文說得好，就是一種成功的象徵。它不但使我們更迷人，而且會讓大家羨慕我們，也會替我們贏得尊敬。因此，我們的地位就會提高，自信也會增加。此外，英文是很有趣的。我們會因爲能利用英文學習到很多東西，而非常喜歡這個語言。而且，因爲能說英文，我們會交到更多朋友，變得更快樂。

　　英文也能拓展我們的眼界。我們可以從英文影片、歌曲和文學作品中，學到許多。它們都能提供我們很多知識。最後一點，英文全球通用。世界因爲英文而變得愈來愈小。環遊世界時，英文非常好用，它就像隨處都能幫助我們的祕密武器一樣。

　　總之，英文是一種很棒的語言。如果我們學英文，絕對不會覺得厭倦，因爲我們可以利用英文做很多的事情。

12. *How to Be Romantic*
如何製造浪漫的氣氛

12

Hello, lovely people. | 哈囉，可愛的人們。
I feel passionate today. | 我今天心情很好。
Let's talk about love and romance. | 讓我們來談談愛與浪漫。

Are you **romantic?** | 你浪漫嗎？
Do you do sweet things? | 你會做一些很貼心的事情嗎？
Do you speak the language | 你懂得如何浪漫嗎？
  of love?

Life is **romantic!** | 生命是很浪漫的！
There is beauty everywhere! | 到處皆有美！
Don't waste a chance for | 不要浪費任何表現愛的機會！
  romance!

People are **romantic.** | 每個人都很浪漫。
Lovely nature is **romantic.** | 美好的大自然是浪漫的。
Open your eyes and see the beauty. | 用開放的心，看美好的東西。

＊＊─────────────

lovely〔ˈlʌvlɪ〕 *adj.* 可愛的　　passionate〔ˈpæʃənɪt〕 *adj.* 熱情的
romance〔roˈmæns〕 *n.* 浪漫
romantic〔roˈmæntɪk〕 *adj.* 浪漫的
sweet〔swit〕 *adj.* 令人高興的　　nature〔ˈnetʃɚ〕 *n.* 大自然

12

It's all around us!	美就在我們的周圍！
You can't deny it!	你無法否認！
Now is your chance to wake up and feel it!	你現在要把握機會，去感受美好的事物！
Romance is exciting.	愛情是令人興奮的。
It's a hot, wild adventure.	它是個激情的、狂熱的冒險。
Just follow your feelings of passion.	只要跟著你喜愛的感覺走。
Romance your spouse.	對你的另一半表達愛意。
Romance your boyfriend or girlfriend.	對你的男女朋友談情說愛。
Try to *romance* someone you like.	試著對你喜歡的人浪漫一點。
You've seen many movies.	你已經看過許多電影。
Now it's time to act.	現在行動的時候到了。
Here are some tips for romance!	以下是一些表現浪漫的秘訣！

** ———————————

deny〔dɪ'naɪ〕*v.* 否認　　wild〔waɪld〕*adj.* 狂熱的
wake up 醒來；覺醒　　adventure〔əd'vɛntʃɚ〕*n.* 冒險
follow〔'fɑlo〕*v.* 跟著　　passion〔'pæʃən〕*n.* 愛好
romance〔ro'mæns〕*v.* 和…談情說愛；向…表達愛意
spouse〔spaʊz〕*n.* 配偶　　act〔ækt〕*v.* 行動　　tip〔tɪp〕*n.* 秘訣

12

First, send flowers.	第一步，送花。
Present a beautiful bouquet.	送一束美麗的花。
Flowers say it best.	花最能表達愛意。
Give a single red rose.	也可以送單獨一朵紅玫瑰。
It has the scent of love.	它具有愛的芳香。
Melt someone's heart.	能融化對方的心。
***Second**, **speak** the language of love.*	第二，你要會說愛的語言。
Really flatter your date.	好好地稱讚你的約會對象。
Honest compliments can work miracles.	誠實的讚美可以產生奇蹟。
Say:	你可以說：
You look fantastic.	你看起來美極了。
I really love your style.	我非常喜歡你的樣子。
I can't take my eyes off you!	我的目光無法離開你！

** ————————————————————

send〔sɛnd〕*v.* 送　present〔prɪˈzɛnt〕*v.* 贈送
bouquet〔buˈke〕*n.* 花束　single〔ˈsɪŋgl̩〕*adj.* 單一的
rose〔roz〕*n.* 玫瑰　scent〔sɛnt〕*n.* 味道
melt〔mɛlt〕*v.* 融化　heart〔hɑrt〕*n.* 心
flatter〔ˈflætɚ〕*v.* 諂媚　date〔det〕*n.* 約會對象
honest〔ˈɑnɪst〕*adj.* 誠實的　compliment〔ˈkɑmpləmənt〕*n.* 讚美
miracle〔ˈmɪrəkl̩〕*n.* 奇蹟　***work miracles*** 產生奇蹟
fantastic〔fænˈtæstɪk〕*adj.* 極好的　style〔staɪl〕*n.* 風格

12

__Third__, give __chocolates__ anytime.	第三，隨時皆可送巧克力。
It's a passionate candy.	這是一種表現熱情的糖果。
They say it's an aphrodisiac.	人們說，這是一種催情劑。
Other candy will do.	其他糖果也可以。
Just remember to say:	只要記得說：
"Sweets for a sweet person!"	「甜甜的糖果給甜甜的你！」
__Fourth__, have a "__dark__" dinner date.	第四，來個「昏暗的」晚餐約會。
Candlelight is the best.	燭光是最好的。
Dancing flames increase desire!	跳動的火焰可以增加熱情！
Make sure there is soft music.	要確定有輕音樂的陪伴。
Add a slow dance if you can.	如果可以的話，再加個慢舞。
Your date will be at your mercy.	你的約會對象將任你擺佈。

** ————————————

chocolate〔'tʃɔklɪt〕*n.* 巧克力　　candy〔'kændɪ〕*n.* 糖果
aphrodisiac〔ˌæfrə'dɪzɪˌæk〕*n.* 催情劑　　do〔du〕*v.* 可以
sweets〔swits〕*n. pl.* 糖果　　sweet〔swit〕*adj.* 甜美的
candlelight〔'kændl̩ˌlaɪt〕*n.* 燭光
dancing〔'dænsɪŋ〕*adj.* 跳動的　　flames〔flemz〕*n. pl.* 火焰
increase〔ɪn'kris〕*v.* 增加　　desire〔dɪ'zaɪr〕*n.* 慾望
soft music 輕音樂　　add〔æd〕*v.* 增加
at one's mercy 任由某人擺佈

Finally, *take a quiet stroll.*	最後，悠閒地去散個步。
Of course, nighttime is the best.	當然，夜晚是最佳時刻。
Hold hands if you possibly can.	如果可能的話，要手牽著手。
Only a peaceful place will do.	要找個安靜的地方才可以。
Walk slowly, talk sweetly, breathe deeply.	慢慢地走，甜蜜地談話，深深地呼吸。
Gaze at the stars, gaze at the moon, tell your date how you feel.	望著星辰、望著月亮，告訴對方你的感受。
Now everybody, be brave!	現在，各位，勇敢一點！
Romantics take risks.	浪漫的人是會冒險的。
They put their feelings on the line.	他們會坦白說出心中的感覺。

**————————————————

quiet〔'kwaɪət〕*adj.* 安靜的；悠閒的
stroll〔strol〕*n.* 散步　　***take a stroll*** 散步（= *take a walk*）
nighttime〔'naɪt,taɪm〕*n.* 夜晚　　hold〔hold〕*v.* 握著；抓住
peaceful〔'pisfəl〕*adj.* 寧靜的　　sweetly〔'switlɪ〕*adv.* 甜蜜地
breathe〔brið〕*v.* 呼吸　　deeply〔'diplɪ〕*adv.* 深深地
gaze〔gez〕*v.* 凝視　　brave〔brev〕*adj.* 勇敢的
romantic〔ro'mæntɪk〕*n.* 浪漫的人　　***take risks*** 冒險
put ~ on the line 坦白地說出

12

Cut to the chase.	不要再拐彎抹角。
Don't play cat and mouse.	不要玩貓捉老鼠。
Don't play hard to get.	不要故意擺出讓別人追不到的樣子。
Remember, failure is OK.	記住，失敗沒有關係。
It's the effort that counts.	努力最重要。
Sooner or later you'll succeed!	你遲早會成功的！
*Now, **go be romantic!***	現在就去浪漫一下吧！
You'll never regret it.	你絕對不會後悔的。
Your fantasies will come true!	你的幻想將會實現！

**

cut〔kʌt〕v. 停止
chase〔tʃes〕n. 追逐
Cut to the chase. 不要拐彎抹角。
mouse〔maʊs〕n. 老鼠
failure〔'feljɚ〕n. 失敗　　effort〔'ɛfɚt〕n. 努力
count〔kaʊnt〕v. 重要　　***sooner or later*** 遲早
regret〔rɪ'grɛt〕v. 後悔　　fantasy〔'fæntəsɪ〕n. 幻想

【背景説明】

　　這篇演講稿非常精采，内容豐富，做一個懂得浪漫的人，你看到的一切，都很美好。整篇演講稿，經過特殊設計後，很好背，如 *S*econd, *s*peak…，S 和 s；***Third***, give ***chocolates***…，第三配合第三個字母 C，"chocolates"；***Fourth***, have a "***dark***" dinner…，第四配合第四個字母 D，"dark"。背好這篇演講稿，可用裡面的内容，給你身旁的人建議，他們會佩服你很有學問，不只是英文方面，還有更多的内涵。

12

1. Hello, *lovely people*.

美國人喜歡幽默，懂得浪漫的人，演講的開場白就可以説：
Hello, *lovely people*.（哈囉，可愛的人們。）
老師對學生可以説：Hello, *lovely students*.
若同學站在台上，就可説：Hello, *my lovely classmates*.
（哈囉，我可愛的同學們。）
這句話等於 Hello, my dear classmates.

　　"Hello, *lovely people*." 不可説成 "*Hello, my lovely people*."（誤），因爲這些人並不是你的同學或學生。老師對學生可以加 my，如：Hello, *my lovely students*.

2. *I feel passionate today*.

　　passionate 表示「熱情的」，這句話字面意思是「我今天感到很熱情」，也就是「我今天心中充滿愛。」心中充滿愛的意思是，看到一切都覺得美好，例如，吃到很難吃的東西，都不會覺得難吃，看到任何人都高興，所以這句話可引申爲「我今天心情很好。」這句話也可説成：I feel full of love today.
心中有愛的人，看了什麼都好，*I feel passionate*.的相反是
I feel indifferent.（我對什麼都漠不關心；我對什麼都冷漠。）

12

　　早上起來，可以自言自語說：*I feel passionate today.* Today is the day to make a difference.（我今天心情很好。今天我要有不同的表現。）*I feel passionate today.* 比 I feel great today. 還要強烈，因為你除了心情好以外，還含有想把愛傳播出去的意思。

3. Do you do *sweet things*?

　　sweet things 字面意思是「甜的事情」，這句話字面意思是「你有沒有做甜的事情？」引申為「你有沒有做一些貼心的事情？」例如，幫別人開車門、拿東西、讚美別人，說些好聽的話，都是 *sweet things*。

sweet 這個字也可單獨使用，例：

　　A: Let me carry it for you.（讓我幫你拿。）
　　B: Oh, that's so *sweet*.（噢，真體貼。）
　　A: Here's a present for you.（這是給你的禮物。）
　　B: Oh, that's such a *sweet thing* to do!（噢，真貼心！）

　　sweet 這個字，充滿著愛，你要常用，例如你的朋友說：I'll treat you to the movies tonight.（我今晚要請你看電影。）你就回答：*Sweet!*（好極了！）

　　兩個美國男人在一起時，看見前面來了一位美女，他們常會說：*What a sweet thing!*（多麼可愛的馬子！）今天天氣很好，你除了可以說：What a lovely day! 之外，你還可以說：*What a sweet day!*

4. Do you speak the language of love?

　　這句話字面是「你會說愛的語言嗎？」引申為「你懂不懂浪漫？」英文解釋是：Do you know how to be a good lover? 或 Do you know how to be romantic?

5. Don't waste a chance for romance!

　　字面意思是「不要浪費任何浪漫的機會！」引申為「不要浪費任何表現愛的機會！」或「不要浪費任何可以談戀愛的機會！」美國人認為談戀愛，不一定要有結果，儘量去做比不做好。

12

在美國喬治亞州（Georgia），有一個地方叫 Savannah
（塞拿），在河邊有一條街，叫做 River Walk（河畔步道），那
裡的氣氛非常浪漫，在週末時，很多熱情的美國年輕人，看到
女人，不管老的小的、已婚未婚、漂亮不漂亮，他們都會熱情
地跑去，和她打招呼，甚至跪下來向她求婚，很多人在那裡當
天就結婚了，因此，那個地方已成為美國有名的擇偶聚集地。

6. People are romantic.

　　romantic 這個字來自羅馬人（Roman），即使到現在，
義大利人，尤其是羅馬人，還保存著浪漫的個性。你看到「教
父」這部電影，外面在槍戰，廝殺得天昏地暗，屋子裡面他
們還在唱歌跳舞，充滿浪漫的氣氛。在浪漫的人眼中，一切
都美好。這句話意思就是「人人都很浪漫。」每個人內心都
充滿了愛，只是有些人放在心中，不表示出來而已。

7. Lovely nature is romantic.

　　這句話的意思是「美好的大自然是浪漫的。」比如說，躺
在沙灘上看夕陽，氣氛非常浪漫，對浪漫者來說，大自然的
一切都是美好的，只要張開眼睛，一切都是美。

8. Open your eyes and see the beauty.

　　這句話字面意思是「張開眼睛，去看美好的事物。」
人的眼睛本來就是張開的，所以，這句話的真正含意是
「用開放的心，看美好的事物。」如果你的心不開放、
不浪漫，你看一切東西都是醜陋的。

9. Now is your chance to *wake up* and feel the beauty!

本句話原本是 "Your **chance** to wake up and feel the beauty
　　　　　　（核心主詞）　完　全　主　詞

is now!" 由於完全主詞太長，整個句子頭重腳輕，所以用倒
裝句（詳見文法寶典 p.636），這句話用倒裝句，說起來才順口。

12

這句話字面意思是「現在就是你醒來，感受到美的機
會！」引申為「現在你要把握機會，去感受美好的事物！」

美國人很喜歡用 *wake up*，叫別人注意，例如：

A: I didn't hear what you said.
（我沒有聽到你在說什麼。）

B: You need to *wake up*.（你需要注意。）

當你的同學考試考不好，快要被退學了，還渾然不知
警惕時，你就可以和他說：*Wake up and smell the coffee.*
（要注意周遭的事情。）這句話源自「早餐咖啡都已經煮好
了，你還不起床？」，也可說成：*Wake up and smell
the bacon.*（源自「早餐培根都煎好了，你還不起床？」）

10. Just follow your feelings of passion.

字面的意思是「只要跟著你喜愛的感覺走。」passion 一
字，一般字典翻成「熱情」，在這裏作「愛好」解，例如，當
你喜歡一個人，就應該勇往直前，不要退縮，passion 這個
字本身就是一種感覺，所以這句話也可說成："Just follow
your passion." 加上 your feelings of，是加強語氣的用法。

11. Romance your spouse.

romance〔roˋmæns〕*v.* 向…表達愛意
spouse〔spaʊz〕*n.* 配偶（= husband *or* wife）

你的另一半，可說成 your spouse 或 your better half。

這句話意思就是「對你的另外一半表達愛意。」美國
人的文化是，雖然結了婚，仍然應該對另一半浪漫一點。

12. Now it's time *to act*.（現在就是要行動的時候了。）

= Now it's time *to take action*.

= *Take action* now.

= *Act* now.

12

13. Here are some *tips* for romance!
(這裡是一些表現浪漫的祕訣！)

> tip 這個字有很多意思，通常當「小費」解，在此作「祕訣」解。這個字源自於賽馬時，給管理馬廄的人小費，就會得到一些內幕消息，知道哪一匹馬能夠獲勝，所以 tip 還有「祕密消息；暗示；勸告」的意思。
>
> 這句話等於 Some *tips* for romance are here. 由於主詞太長，句子頭重腳輕而倒裝。

14. Present a beautiful bouquet. (送一束美麗的花。)

pre¦sent〔prɪ'zɛnt〕v. 贈送 (從字根上分析可知，present 有「送
before¦send　　　　　　　　　　　　　　　 到面前」的意思。)

bouquet〔bu'ke〕n. 花束 (注意這個字的發音，很奇怪，因爲來自法語)
bouquet 這個字不是指幾枝花在一起而已 (a bunch of flowers)，而是指一大束排得很漂亮的花。

　　a bunch of flowers　　　　　　a bouquet

15. Give a single red rose. (送單獨一枝紅玫瑰。)

> 用 single 來加強 a 的語氣，送一枝紅玫瑰表示「你是唯一」，送二枝表示「成雙成對、心心相印」，送三枝表示 "I love you."

16. Chocolate is an aphrodisiac.

> 美國人認爲，送巧克力是一種示愛的
> 表現，aphrodisiac〔͵æfrə'dɪzɪ͵æk〕n. 催
> 情劑，此字來自 Aphrodite〔͵æfrə'daɪtɪ〕，
> 是希臘神話中愛神的名字，相當於羅馬神
> 話中的維納斯 Venus〔'vinəs〕。

12

17. Other candy will do. (其他糖果也可以。)

　　　do 在此為完全不及物動詞，作「可以」解，等於
be good enough。

18. Sweets for a sweet person! (甜甜的糖果給甜甜的你！)

　　　送糖果給別人時，別忘了說這句話。第一個 sweets，
等於 candy「糖果」，第二個 sweet 當形容詞用，作「甜
的」解。sweets 當「糖果」解時，永遠是複數形，要有
s，但 candy 是不可數名詞，須用單數。

19. Your date will be *at your mercy.*
　　mercy〔'mɜsɪ〕*n.* 慈悲

> mercy 的用法很重要，看看下面的例子：
>
> 　　Have *mercy* on me. (可憐可憐我吧！)
> 　　【字面意思是「給我一點慈悲。」】
> 　　I'm at your *mercy.* (我任由你處置。)
> 　　【字面意思是「我在你的慈悲之下」，你要給我什麼，就給我什麼。】
>
> *at one's mercy* 當成成語來看，意思是「任由某人擺佈」。
>
> 　　date 這個字主要意思是「日期；約會」，go on a date
> 就是「去約會」，在這句話中，date 作「異性的約會對象」
> 解。Your date will be at your mercy. 意思就是「你的約
> 會對象將任你擺佈。」

20. *Take a* quiet *stroll.*
　　stroll〔strol〕*n.* 散步；閒逛
　　take a stroll 散步（= *take a walk*）
　　quiet〔'kwaɪət〕*adj.* 安靜的；悠閒的；不受干擾的
　　take a quiet stroll 悠閒地去散個步

　　　美國人很喜歡用 stroll 這個字，當你邀請別人去散步
時，你就可以說：Let's *take a stroll.* (我們去散步吧。)
清晨或傍晚，美國人都喜歡散步，吃完飯後，你要去散步，
你就可以說：I need to *take a stroll.* (我需要散步。)

12

21. **Walk slowly, talk sweetly, breathe deeply.**

　　當你腦筋不清楚，或緊張時，你要 breathe deeply
（＝ *take a deep breath*）做深呼吸。這三個動作沒有連
接詞，強調緊湊、一氣呵成。(詳見「文法寶典」p.465)

22. **Romantics *put* their feelings *on the line*.**

romantic〔ro'mæntɪk〕*n.* 浪漫的人
put ~ on the line　坦白地說出（＝ *lay ~ on the line*）

　　on the line 源自於 on the frontline「在前線」比喻「冒
險」，所以，*put ~ on the line* 還有「用～承擔風險」的意思。
下面三句話，美國人常說：

　　I *put* my reputation *on the line* for you.
　　(我用我的名譽為你承擔風險。)
　　I *put* myself *on the line* for you. (我為你冒險。)
　　I *put* my future *on the line* for you.
　　(我用我的前途為你冒險。)

23. ***Cut to the chase.***

　　chase〔tʃes〕*n.* 追逐；追求，cut 在這裡作「停止」解，
這句話字面意思是「停止追求」，引申為「**不要再拐彎抹角
了。**」等於 Stop beating about the bush.

　　Cut to the chase. 查遍所有中外字典都找不到，但美國人
常用，我們一定要學會使用這句話，如：Let's *cut to the
chase* and get to the point. (我們不要拐彎抹角，直接講重點。)

24. **Don't play cat and mouse.**

mouse〔maʊs〕*n.* 老鼠

　　這句話字面意思是「不要玩貓捉老鼠的遊戲。」引申為
「**不要玩感情遊戲**，一個跑，一個追。」play cat and mouse
和 play hide and seek (捉迷藏) 完全不同。

12

25. Don't play <u>hard to get</u>.
名詞片語

　　有些人喜歡弄別人的感情，讓別人覺得他很難得到，被人追了幾年，連手都沒牽過，這句話源自 Don't play the "hard to get" game. 意思就是「不要故意擺出讓別人追不到的樣子。」

26. *It's* the effort *that counts*.

effort〔ˈɛfət〕*n.* 努力
count〔kaʊnt〕*v.* 計算；重要；有價值；有用

　　count 主要意思是「計算」，這裡作「重要」解，這句話的意思是「努力最重要。」美國人一般送的禮物都不是很值錢，但包裝很精美，根據美國人的習俗，不管你收到什麼禮物，你都要表現出很高興的樣子，他們從小所受的教育是，禮物不重要，心意最重要，他們常說：*It's* the thought *that counts*. （心意最重要。）我們可以把 *It's* ~ *that counts*. 看成一個句型，如：*It's* the result *that counts*. （結果最重要。）

27. Go be romantic!（去浪漫一下！）

　　這句話是由 Go and be romantic! 演變而來。美國人在命令句的 come 或 go 後，常接原形不定詞。（詳見「文法寶典」p.419）

28. Your fantasies will come true!（你的幻想將會實現！）

fantasy〔ˈfæntəsɪ〕*n.* 幻想

　　這句話源自 Your dreams will come true. （你的夢想會實現。）come 在此作「變成」解。

come true 實現（ = *become a fact* = *be realized* = *be fulfilled* ）

――【劉毅老師的話】――
　　背完演講後，就可以利用演講的內容，和朋友說，說多了，就成為你自己的語言。

【作文範例】

How to Be Romantic

Everybody is romantic in his or her heart, but not

everyone expresses it. *In fact*, life is romantic and lovely

nature is romantic. There is beauty everywhere. You

should open your eyes and hearts to feel the beauty and,

most of all, love. You should never waste a chance for

romance. You have to follow your feelings of passion.

　　However, how can you be romantic? Here are some

tips for romance. *First of all*, you can send flowers.

Either a beautiful bouquet or just a single red rose is fine.

Flowers say love best. *However*, chocolates or other

candy will do, with the sentence "Sweets for a sweet

person!" *Second*, always romance your spouse or

boyfriend or girlfriend, complimenting him or her at any

time. *For example*, you might say, "You look fantastic.

I really love the way you are." *Third*, you can often take

him or her for a quiet stroll. It is best to walk hand in

hand and slowly. *Last but not least*, always remember

to do sweet things, such as carrying bags for her,

reminding him to wear a jacket, calling to talk about

anything, etc.

People are romantic. Be brave and put your feelings on the line. You'll never regret it. You will definitely find your true love.

12

【中文翻譯】

如何製造浪漫的氣氛

人人心中都很浪漫，但並不是每個人都會表現出來。事實上，生命是浪漫的，美好的大自然也是浪漫的。到處皆有美，你應該張開你的眼睛、敞開你的心胸，去感受美，更重要的是，去感受愛。你不該浪費任何可以表現愛意的機會。你必須跟隨自己的感覺走。

然而，你要如何製造浪漫的氣氛呢？以下是一些表現浪漫的秘訣。首先，你可以送花。無論是一束美麗的花，或是單獨一枝紅玫瑰都很棒，花朵最能訴說愛意。然而，巧克力或其他糖果也可以，再加上一句話：「甜甜的糖果給甜甜的你！」第二，總是要對你的另一半，或男女朋友，表達愛意，隨時讚美他或她。例如，你可以說：「你看起來美極了。我真喜歡你的樣子。」第三，你可以常常帶他或她，悠閒地去散個步，手牽手、慢慢走是最好的。最後一項重點是，永遠記得要做一些貼心的事情，像是幫她拿袋子、提醒他穿外套、打電話聊一聊等等。

其實每個人都很浪漫。你要勇敢一點，坦白說出你自己的感覺。你不會後悔的，你一定會找到你的真愛。

13. Don't Be Afraid to Make Mistakes
不要害怕犯錯

13

Ladies and gentlemen:　　　各位先生，各位女士：
I've learned a great lesson.　我學到了很棒的一課。
I want to share it with you.　我要和你們分享。

Mistakes are okay.　　　　犯錯是可以接受的。
They are part of life.　　　犯錯是人生的一部份。
That's how you learn.　　　是學習的法則。

Be bold.　　　　　　　　要大膽。
Take risks.　　　　　　　要冒險。
Don't be afraid to fail.　　不要害怕會失敗。

No one is perfect.　　　　沒有人是完美的。
Everyone has faults.　　　每個人都有缺點。
You can't improve without　如果沒有缺點，你就無法進
　them.　　　　　　　　步。

** ———————————————————————

share〔ʃɛr〕v. 分享　　okay〔'o'ke〕adj. 可以的（= O.K. = OK）
bold〔bold〕adj. 大膽的　　*take risks* 冒險
fail〔fel〕v. 失敗　　perfect〔'pɝfɪkt〕adj. 完美的
fault〔fɔlt〕n. 缺點　　improve〔ɪm'pruv〕v. 改進；進步

13

Mistakes *make you stronger*. | 犯錯使你更堅強。
They make you better. | 犯錯使你變得更好。
Learn from them and improve. | 從錯誤中學習才會改進。

Mistakes aren't embarrassing. | 犯錯沒有什麼好難為情的。
They are valuable experience. | 犯錯是珍貴的經驗。
Successful people *know* this. | 成功的人都明白這一點。

No one likes to be wrong. | 沒有人喜歡犯錯。
It's *no* fun to look stupid. | 看起來像個笨蛋，並不好玩。
But everyone makes *mistakes*. | 但是每個人都會犯錯。

Learn from *mistakes*. | 從錯誤中學習。
All great people do. | 偉人皆如此。
This is the secret to improvement. | 這就是進步的秘訣。

You must *try*. | 你得嘗試。
Making an effort is the key. | 努力是關鍵。
Try or you won't learn. | 試吧，否則你就學不到東西。

** ───────────────

embarrassing〔ɪm'bærəsɪŋ〕*adj.* 令人尷尬的；令人難為情的；
令人丟臉的
valuable〔'væljuəbl̩〕*adj.* 珍貴的
stupid〔'stjupɪd〕*adj.* 笨的；愚蠢的
secret〔'sikrɪt〕*n.* 秘訣 < *to* >　　*make an effort* 努力
key〔ki〕*n.* 關鍵

13

Learning English isn't easy.	學英文並不容易。
You will make mistakes.	犯錯是難免的。
The more you make, the faster	錯得越多，進步得越快。
you will progress.	
Build upon each ***mistake***.	以錯誤爲基礎。
Success is a step-by-step process.	成功無法一步登天。
Great efforts bring great	下的功夫越深，得到的收穫
rewards.	越大。
Face your fear.	面對你的恐懼。
It's not life-and-death.	這不是生死攸關的事。
It's only language study.	只是學習語言。
Have a learning attitude.	要有學習的態度。
Laugh off simple mistakes.	小錯一笑置之。
Remember them and move on.	記在心上，繼續前進。

** ———————————————————

progress〔prə'grɛs〕*v.* 進步　***build upon*** 以～爲基礎

step-by-step 一步接一步的；按部就班的

process〔'prɑsɛs〕*n.* 程序；步驟

reward〔rɪ'wɔrd〕*n.* 報酬；成果　face〔fes〕*v.* 面對

life-and-death 生死攸關的　attitude〔'ætə,tjud〕*n.* 態度

laugh off 對～一笑置之　***move on*** 繼續前進

13

Don't ridicule mistakes.	不要譏笑失敗。
Life is about learning.	人生即是學習。
<u>*Without trial and error* we are nothing</u>.	如果沒有嘗試與錯誤，我們將一事無成。
<u>*If you don't make mistakes*</u>, you will never progress.	如果你不犯錯，你就不會進步。
Go out and make them now!	放手一搏，去犯錯吧！
Make mistakes.	去犯錯。
Make lots of mistakes.	犯一堆錯。
It's better to try and fail than to never try at all.	試過了卻失敗，總比永遠不試好。
Nothing ventured, nothing gained.	不入虎穴，焉得虎子。
Thank you everybody.	感謝大家。
I hope you liked my speech.	希望你們喜歡我的演講。
Remember to learn from your mistakes.	記得從錯誤中學習。

**

ridicule ('rɪdɪ‚kjul) v. 譏笑；取笑　　trial ('traɪəl) n. 嘗試
error ('ɛrə) n. 錯誤　　***at all*** 一點也（不）【用於否定句】
venture ('vɛntʃə) v. 冒險　　gain (gen) v. 獲得

13

【背景説明】

　　這篇演講稿背的時候，特別要注意斜黑字，記住句子和句子之間，每一組和每一組之間的相關字，如：***Don't*** be afraid to fail. 接著下一組的 ***No one*** is perfect. 兩個否定的句子就連在一起了。再例如，Successful people ***know*** this. 和下一組的 ***No*** one likes to be wrong. 由於 know 和 No 兩個字發音相同，就連接起來了。這篇文章經過實驗，即使是七、八十歲的老人，都可以背得起來，文章中很多句子，都可以用來鼓勵別人，你背完之後，就可以運用了，就可以有很多的材料和別人説英文了。

1. 美國人很喜歡用 share（分享）這個字。***share*** 與 ***with*** 連用，也可省略 ***with*** 不説。不管是開心，或不開心的事，美國人都喜歡用 ***share*** 來代替 tell。如：I want to ***share*** an idea ***with*** you.（我要和你分享我的想法。）
中國人不説「我要和你分享」，中國人説「我要告訴你」。
   I have great news to ***share with*** you.
   　（我要和你分享一個好消息。）

　　中國人的思想是「我要告訴你一個好消息」，美國人的思想是「我要和你分享一個好消息」。這句話如果説成：I have great news to tell you. 就很奇怪了。因爲是好消息，外國人就喜歡用 ***share*** 這個字。

　　如果不是什麼重要的事，要告訴別人，可以説：I have news to tell you. 也可説：I have news to ***share with*** you. 反正，你要常説 ***share*** 這個字，講起話來才像美國人，這是中美文化的差異，美國人強調「分享」，中國人説「告訴」。如果 I want to ***share*** an idea ***with*** you. 翻成「我要和你分享我的想法。」這句中文不是我們常講的，你聽了別人説這句話，一定覺得不順，但是講英文，你就要用 ***share*** 這個字，説英文時，就要接受美國人「分享」的思想。

2. Mistakes are *part of life*.

> Mistakes are *part of life*. 字面的意思是:「犯錯是人生的一部份。」引申為「犯錯是人生當中必須經歷的;犯錯是難免的。」
>
> 美國人很喜歡說:~*is part of life*. 如:Learning *is part of life*. Working *is part of life*.
>
> *part of life* 通常是指每個人都會做的事,美國人常常喜歡掛在嘴邊說。
>
> 【例】 A: My mom was not happy with my grades.
> (我媽媽不滿意我的成績。)
> B: Well, *it's just part of life*.
> (嗯,這是難免的。)
>
> ※ *part of life* 也可說成 *part of one's life*。
>
> 【例】 Mistakes are *part of your life*.
> (你犯錯是難免的。)
> Mistakes are *part of our life*.
> (我們犯錯是難免的。)

3. That's how you learn.

這句話源自:That's the way *how you learn*. (誤)
【這是古老用法,現在不用】

關係副詞 how,引導形容詞子句,修飾先行詞 way。

現在的英文已經必須將 the way 省略,成為

That's *how you learn*. 【how you learn 變成名詞子句】

這句話也可說成:

That's the way (*in which*) *you learn*. 【in which 可省略】

4. Be bold. Take risks. (要大膽。要冒險。)

> 看到別人不敢說英文，或不敢做這個或那個，你就可以說：
>
> > ***Be bold***. (要大膽。)
> >
> > ***Take risks***. (要冒險。)
> >
> > Don't be afraid. (不要害怕。)
>
> 或者說：Be fearless. You have nothing to fear. 之類的話。
>
> 如果看到別人太毛躁，膽子太大，你就說：
>
> > Don't be too bold. (不要太大膽。)
> >
> > Don't take risks. (不要冒險。)
> >
> > ***Don't be a hero***. (不要逞英雄。)【這句話美國人最喜歡說】

13

5. It's no fun to look stupid. (看起來像個笨蛋，並不好玩。)

> no 通常是形容詞，當副詞時，有加強語氣的作用。
> no 當副詞時，等於 not…at all。
>
> > It's ***no*** fun to look stupid.
> >
> > = It's ***not*** fun ***at all*** to look stupid.
>
> 當然，也可說成：It's not fun to look stupid. 用 not
> 修飾 fun 的語氣，沒有 no 修飾 fun 的語氣強烈。
>
> 美國人勸他人時，會說 ***It's no fun*** to…. 當小孩子很頑
> 皮、跌跌撞撞時，你會說 ***It's no fun*** to get hurt. (受傷可
> 不好玩。)警察看到人家開快車時，會說 ***It's no fun*** to
> crash. (撞車可不好玩。)看到兩個人在打架，你可以說
> ***It's no fun*** to get killed. (被打死並不好玩。)看到小孩
> 衣服穿太少，可以說 ***It's no fun*** to get sick. (生病可不好
> 玩。)看到同學不愛讀書，可以說 ***It's no fun*** to flunk.
> (考不及格可不是好玩的事。)反正要常說 ***It's no fun*** to….
> 就對了。

6. Making an effort is the key.

> effort 這個字作「努力」解時，可當可數或不可數名
> 詞，所以這句話也可以說成 *Making effort* is the key.
> 或說成 *Making efforts* is the key. 句中的 Making 為核
> 心主詞，動名詞當主詞，所以動詞用單數。

13

7. *Build upon* each mistake.

> 這句話的意思是「你必須以每次的錯誤為基礎。」
> build 是及物動詞，加介詞 upon 以後，就變成成語，很多及
> 物動詞，都是加了介詞後，變成成語，像 hear from（接到～
> 的信息），build upon（以～為基礎）。

8. Success is a *step-by-step* process.
   （成功是按部就班來的；成功不是一步登天的。）

> 美國人做事喜歡按部就班，他們喜歡 one thing at a
> time（一次一件事情），他們喜歡 *step by step*（按部就班），
> 因為這樣子就不容易做錯。
>
> 美國老師常教小孩子：You must do things *step by step*.
> （你必須按部就班地做事。）就像我們常說的：「我們要一步
> 一腳印。」（ We must do things one step at a time. ）
> 一般說來，美國人的智慧並沒有中國人高，他們把每個人，
> 都假設成是腦筋不太好的人，所以，他們常把複雜的東西變
> 簡單，像做漢堡、製造汽車、蓋房子，都有一個按部就班的
> 程序，也就是：*a step-by-step* process（按部就班的程序），
> *step-by-step* 是形容詞，修飾 process。
>
> Success is a *step-by-step* process. 字面的意思是「成
> 功是按部就班的步驟。」引申為「成功無法一步登天。」

13

9. reward 的基本意思是「報酬」，也可作「獎賞」解。
award 只作「獎賞」解。

當某人替你完成一件很好的工作，你要給他額外的紅包
時，你就可以說：

This is your $\left\{ \begin{array}{l} \textit{reward} \\ \textit{award} \end{array} \right\}$ for a job well done.

（這是給你表現好的額外紅包。）

如果你要發薪水給他，你就可以說：

This is your **reward** for your work. 【不可用 *award*】

（這是你的酬勞。）

特別注意，頒獎時只能用 award。

This is your **award**. （這是你的獎品。）【不可用 *reward*】

10. *It's not life-and-death.*

看到別人失戀了，看到別人女朋友跑了，你就可以跟你
的朋友說： Cheer up. *It's not life-and-death.* （開心一點。
又不是什麼大不了的事。）

看到別人很匆忙，很急的時候，你就可以說：

What's the hurry? *It's not life-and-death.*
（急什麼？又不是生死攸關的事。）

It's not life-and-death. 字面的意思是「這不是生死攸
關的事。」在中國武俠小說裏，常會見到這句中文，但是，
在日常生活中，中國人不常說，可是美國人卻常常說。如：

A: Oh, no! I failed the test.
（噢，糟了！我考試不及格。）

B: Don't worry. *It's not life-and-death.*
（別擔心。沒什麼大不了。）

It's not life-and-death. 所引申的意思就是:「沒什麼大不了。」等於 It's no big deal. 的加強語氣。我們要常說美國人講的話:*It's not life-and-death.* 才像美國人。

13

11. Life is *about* learning.

表示你不管做什麼事,都要學習,無論是走路、坐車,都要學習。不可說成 *Life is learning.* (誤)

美國人常說:What's life *about*? (人生的重點在哪裏?)

你可以回答:Life is *about* learning. (人生就是要學習。)

或:Life is *about* happiness. (人生就是要快樂。)

about 在這裏的意思是「在～周圍;環繞著～」,引申爲「著重於」。

12. <u>*Without trial and error*</u> we are nothing.

Without trial and error 是介詞片語當副詞用,表條件,它的意思是「如果我們沒有嘗試犯錯」。這句話英文解釋是:If we don't try and err, we are nothing.

<u>Without trial and error</u> 畫底線的意思是,和下面一句 <u>If you don't make mistakes</u> 句意接近,所以,背起來好背,要記住組與組之間的關連,背起來就容易了。

We are nothing. 這句話字面的意思是「我們什麼都不是。」引申爲「我們一事無成。」相關的說法有:

We are nobody. (我們是小人物。)

We are something. (我們很有成就。)

13. ***Go out*** and make them now!

美國人很喜歡説 ***Go out*** and do it. 之類的話，表示不要
坐著不動，要採取行動，如：

Go out and make things happen. (趕快去做。)

13

14. It's ***better*** to try and fail ***than*** *to never try at all.*

不定詞 to 後面原則上應該加原形動詞，加副詞再加原
形動詞，是加強語氣的用法。(詳見「文法寶典」p.422)
在這裏是對稱性的問題，to try…和 to never try…的比較，
這裏一定要用 to never try at all，這種特殊的用法，在托
福中常考，可見它的重要。

15. Nothing ventured, nothing gained.

在諺語書中，或諺語辭典上，都是寫成 *Nothing
venture, nothing have.* 但在美國人口中，喜歡説：
Nothing venture, nothing gain. 或 Nothing ventured,
nothing gained. 意思是「如果不冒險，就一無所得；不
入虎穴，焉得虎子。」(詳見「英文諺語辭典」p.285)

───【劉毅老師的話】───
　　「演講式英語」適合各種程度，人人都
可以背。英文老師教多了，就可以不用看課
本上課。背了演講稿後，和外國人説起話
來，頭頭是道。

13

【作文範例】

Don't Be Afraid to Make Mistakes

While every one of us desires success, we know that very few successes can be achieved without the benefit of mistakes. *Therefore*, perhaps the first thing we should bear in mind is that mistakes are actually steppingstones to our success. *In fact*, mistakes will make us learn and improve. *In this view*, we won't regard mistakes as something embarrassing; *instead*, we will see them as valuable learning experiences.

Sometimes mistakes can open up new horizons. British scientist Alexander Fleming mistakenly left his experiment room window open. This led to the contamination of the culture he was developing. The next day when he looked at the culture, he found that most of the germs were dead. This was how Fleming discovered penicillin, a powerful antibiotic that revolutionized modern medicine. *In sum*, we should not be afraid to make mistakes. *After all*, nothing ventured, nothing gained.

【中文翻譯】

不要害怕犯錯

雖然我們每個人都想要成功，可是我們也知道，沒有經過失敗的教訓，而獲得成功的例子很少。因此，或許我們應該謹記在心，錯誤其實是我們邁向成功的踏腳石。事實上，錯誤能讓我們學習和進步。這樣看來，錯誤就不是一件可恥的事情；相反地，我們要把錯誤看成是很珍貴的學習經驗。

有時候，錯誤可以拓展我們的眼界。英國科學家亞歷山大富朗明，就曾經不小心讓他實驗室的窗子開著，使得他培育中的細菌受到感染。等隔天他再觀察那些培養菌時，才發現大部份的細菌都已經死了。這就是富朗明發現盤尼西林這種引起現代醫藥革命的有效抗生素的經過。總之，我們不應該害怕犯錯，畢竟，不入虎穴，焉得虎子。

14. *How to Make a Fortune*
致富之道

14

Ladies and gentlemen:	各位女士，各位先生：
I'm delighted to be here.	我很高興能來到這裏。
I'd like to offer some great	我想提供一些很棒的建議
advice to you.	給大家。
Money talks.	金錢萬能。
Money rules.	金錢主宰一切。
Money is power.	金錢就是力量。
Do you want to make a fortune?	你想賺大錢嗎？
Do you want to go from rags	你想由窮人變有錢人嗎？
to riches?	
Let me show you the way.	讓我來告訴你該怎麼做。

** ————————————————

fortune〔'fɔrtʃən〕*n.* 財富；巨款　　*make a fortune* 發財；賺大錢
delighted〔dɪ'laɪtɪd〕*adj.* 高興的
offer sth. to sb. 提供某物給某人（= *offer sb. sth.*）
Money talks. 【諺】有錢能使鬼推磨；金錢萬能。
rule〔rul〕*v.* 統治　　power〔'pauɚ〕*n.* 力量
rags〔rægz〕*n. pl.* 破爛衣服　　riches〔'rɪtʃɪz〕*n. pl.* 財產
go from rags to riches 從窮人變富人
show〔ʃo〕*v.* 指示；指點

14

First, follow your passion.	首先，要跟著你的愛好去走。
Find your natural ambition.	找出你天生的志向。
Decide to be the best in that field.	要下定決心，成為那個領域的佼佼者。
Do what you love.	要做你所喜愛的工作。
Love what you do.	愛你所做的工作。
Big money will follow you.	你錢想不要都不行，大錢會自己來。
Don't love money too much.	不要太愛錢。
Don't just work for money.	不要只是為了錢而工作。
Money should come from your passion.	錢應該來自你的愛好。
Second, work, work, work.	第二，要不停地工作。
Work till you drop.	工作到你累倒為止。
Work harder than you've ever worked before.	要比以往更努力工作。

** ───────────────────

follow〔'falo〕*v.* 跟隨；從事　　passion〔'pæʃən〕*n.* 愛好
ambition〔æm'bɪʃən〕*n.* 抱負；志向
natural ambition 天生的志向
decide to V. 決定；決心　　field〔fild〕*n.* 領域
big money 大筆的錢　　drop〔drap〕*v.* 累倒

You must give it your all.	你必須全心投入。
You must give 110%.	你必須盡全力。
You must invest blood, sweat, and tears.	你必須投注血汗和淚水。
You must sacrifice.	你必須有所犧牲。
You must be totally committed.	你必須全心投入。
Money doesn't grow on trees.	錢不會從天上掉下來。
Third, save, save, save.	第三，要拼命存錢。
From saving comes having.	勤儉爲致富之本。
A penny saved is a penny earned.	省一文就是賺一文。
Buy only what you need.	只買你所需要的。
Don't buy what you want.	不要買你所想要的。
Be as frugal as can be.	要非常節省。

14

** ────────────

give it one's all 盡全力 (= *give 100%* = *give 110%*)
invest〔ɪn'vɛst〕v. 投資；投注　　blood〔blʌd〕n. 血
sweat〔swɛt〕n. 汗　　tears〔tɪrz〕n. pl. 眼淚
sacrifice〔'sækrə,faɪs〕v. 犧牲　　totally〔'totl̩ɪ〕adv. 完全
be committed 投入 (= *commit oneself*)
grow on trees （好像長在樹上似地）伸手即可得到；極易得到
From saving comes having. = *Having comes from saving.*
penny〔'pɛnɪ〕n. 一分錢　　frugal〔'frugl̩〕adj. 節省的
as ~ as can be 非常 ~

14

Don't squander your hard-earned money.	不要浪費你辛苦賺來的錢。
Put your money in the bank.	把錢存在銀行。
Make a habit of saving money.	養成存錢的習慣。
If you have money, you can easily make money.	如果你有錢，很容易就能賺到錢。
Money makes money.	錢賺錢。
Money begets money.	錢生錢。
Fourth, invest in people.	第四，把錢投資在人身上。
Help deserving people.	幫助值得幫助的人。
Surround yourselves with quality people.	要和高水準的人在一起。
No man is an island.	沒有人是一座孤島。
You always need good people.	你一定會需要好的人。
You can't build a fortune all on your own.	你不可能只靠自己的力量賺大錢。

**

squander〔ˈskwɑndɚ〕v. 浪費
hard-earned〔ˈhɑrdˈɝnd〕adj. 辛苦得到的
make a habit of 養成～習慣   beget〔bɪˈgɛt〕v. 產生
deserving〔dɪˈzɝvɪŋ〕adj. 值得幫助的
surround〔səˈraʊnd〕v. 包圍；環繞
quality〔ˈkwɑlətɪ〕adj. 高級的；優秀的
build a fortune 發財（= *make a fortune*）   **on** one's own 靠自己

Money comes.	錢來來去去。
Money goes.	
But friendship always remains.	但是友誼永遠存在。
Be good to others.	要對別人好。
Treat all with kindness.	要對大家很親切。
Friends are life's golden treasure.	朋友是人生中珍貴的寶藏。

14

Fifth, cash is everything.	第五，現金很重要。
Wait, wait, wait.	要耐心等待。
Wait for the opportunities to invest.	等待投資的機會。
When the market drops, don't buy.	當股市下跌，不要買股票。
Wait until the market bottoms out.	要等到股市跌到底。
Then, invest just a little bit.	然後，只要投資一點點。

** ———————————

remain (rɪˈmen) v. 留下；存在
with kindness 親切地 (= *kindly*)
golden (ˈgoldn̩) adj. 貴重的；重要的
treasure (ˈtrɛʒɚ) n. 寶藏
market (ˈmɑrkɪt) n. 股票市場 (= *stock market* = *stock*)
drop (drɑp) v. 下跌
bottom out （股市）跌到最低點後即將回升

Don't be greedy.	不要貪心。
Don't overdo it.	不要做得過火。
Always hold on to a lot of cash.	一定要保有大量的現金。
When the market is booming, don't follow the crowd.	當股市暴漲，不要跟著一窩蜂走。
Don't go with the flow.	不要盲目跟從。
Don't jump on the bandwagon.	不要跟著湊熱鬧。
Always diversify your holdings.	一定要分散持股。
Always diversify your stock shares.	要持有各種股票。
Only buy blue chips when opportunity invites.	當機會出現時，只買績優股。

14

** ——————————

greedy〔'gridɪ〕*adj.* 貪心的　　*overdo it* 做得過火
hold on to 抓住　　boom〔bum〕*v.* 暴漲
follow the crowd 跟著一窩蜂走（*= go with the flow = jump on the bandwagon*）
bandwagon〔'bænd,wægən〕*n.* 電子花車
jump on the bandwagon 趕時尚；湊熱鬧【原指「搭乘競選活動樂隊車」】
diversify〔daɪ'vɜsə,faɪ〕*v.* 使多樣化
holdings〔'holdɪŋz〕*n. pl.* 持有股份
stock share 股票；股份（*= stock = share*）　　*blue chip* 績優股
invite〔ɪn'vaɪt〕*v.* 發出邀請；吸引力；出現（*= appear*）

Once they are bought, don't sell them.　一旦買了股票，就不要賣。

Keep them like you don't have them.　持有這些股票，像是自己不曾擁有一樣。

Wait thirty years, and you'll make a fortune.　等個三十年，就發財了。

14

Sixth, real estate is also great.　第六，房地產也是很棒的投資。

Invest first in your house.　先投資自己要住的房子。

Buy it at the right time in a good location.　買的時機要對，要買地段好的房子。

Location, location, location.　地點最重要。

Location is the key.　地點是關鍵。

A house in a good location will always appreciate.　地點好的房子一定會增值。

**

real estate 房地產

location〔loˈkeʃən〕*n.* 地點

key〔ki〕*n.* 關鍵　　appreciate〔əˈpriʃɪˌet〕*v.* 增值

14

Buy a house when the prices are low.	在房價低的時候買房子。
When nobody's buying, it's time for you to buy.	當沒人想買房子時,就是你該買的時候。
But, remember, don't spend all your cash.	但要記得,不要把所有的現金都花掉。
Buying a house is a big deal.	買房子是件大事。
You must be very picky.	你必須非常挑剔。
Be patient even if it takes a few years.	就算需要花好幾年的時間,也要有耐心。
You have to check and check.	你必須再三檢查。
Check the house, check the price, and even check the neighbors.	檢查房子、檢查價格,甚至要檢查鄰居。
A good neighborhood is very important.	好的鄰居很重要。

**─────────────

big deal 大事　　picky〔'pɪkɪ〕adj. 挑剔的
patient〔'peʃənt〕adj. 有耐心的
take〔tek〕v. 花費（時間）　　neighbor〔'nebɚ〕n. 鄰居
neighborhood〔'nebɚ͵hʊd〕n. 鄰近地區；鄰居間的情誼
a good neighborhood 好的鄰居

You have to bargain and bargain.	你必須討價還價。
Offer a very low price, and wait.	出一個非常低的價錢，再耐心等待。
If there is no competitor, time is on your side.	如果沒有競爭者，時間對你有利。
All in all, time is of utmost importance.	總之，時間是最重要的。
Only young people have the time to invest and wait.	只有年輕人才有時間投資並且等待。
Health is much more important to older people.	對年紀較大的人而言，健康則更為重要。
Cash flow is also vital.	現金周轉也很重要。
You need to have cash to invest.	你需要有現金才能投資。
Without cash you will miss many opportunities.	沒有現金的話，你就會錯過很多機會。

14

** ————————————

bargain〔'bɑrgɪn〕*v.* 討價還價　　offer〔'ɔfɚ〕*v.* 出（價）
competitor〔kəm'pɛtətɚ〕*n.* 競爭者
on *one's* ***side*** 站在某人這一邊
all in all 總之　　utmost〔'ʌt,most〕*adj.* 最大的；極度的
of utmost importance 最重要的（*= most important*）
cash flow 現金周轉　　vital〔'vaɪt!〕*adj.* 極重要的
miss〔mɪs〕*v.* 錯過

Do you know why so many market players ended up bankrupt?　你知道為什麼有那麼多玩股票的人到最後會破產？

Do you know why so many investors went broke?　你知道為什麼有那麼多投資人會破產？

It's because they got too greedy.　那是因為他們太貪心了。

They invested too much.　他們投資太多。

They lacked cash flow.　他們缺乏現金周轉。

Grasp all, lose all.　貪多必失。

Ladies and gentlemen:　各位女士，各位先生：

Time flies.　光陰似箭。

Time passes by swiftly.　時間過得很快。

** ————————————————

market player 玩股票的人

$$end\ up + \begin{cases} with + N. \\ adj. \end{cases}$$ 最後～

如：end up with death = end up dead（最後死了）

investor〔ɪn'vɛstɚ〕*n.* 投資人　　*go broke* 破產

lack〔læk〕*v.* 缺乏　　grasp〔græsp〕*v.* 緊抓

fly〔flaɪ〕*v.*（時間）飛逝　　*pass by*（時間）過去

swiftly〔'swɪftlɪ〕*adv.* 快速地

But you will not feel sad, because as time goes by, you will have more and more good friends.	但是你不會覺得難過，因為隨著時間的過去，你會有愈來愈多好朋友。
Your house will become more valuable.	你的房子會增值。
Your stock holdings will eventually increase.	你持有的股票最後會增加。
You're still young.	你還年輕。
You're not pressed for time.	你不趕時間。
Sooner or later you will become a wealthy man.	你遲早會成爲有錢人。
I hope you think about what I've said today.	我希望大家能想想我今天所說的。
I wish you all a bright future.	我祝各位有個光明的未來。
Have a good day.	再見。
Thank you very much.	非常謝謝大家。

14

** ——————————

as time goes by 隨著時間的過去
valuable (ˈvæljʊəb!) *adj.* 有價值的
holdings (ˈholdɪŋz) *n. pl.* 持有股份
eventually (ɪˈvɛntʃʊəlɪ) *adv.* 最後　　*be pressed for time* 時間緊迫
sooner or later 遲早　　wealthy (ˈwɛlθɪ) *adj.* 有錢的
bright (braɪt) *adj.* 光明的；充滿希望的
Have a good day. 再見。(= *Have a nice day.* = *Have a good one.*)

【背景説明】

　　這篇演講稿很豐富，讀了這篇演講，就知道怎麼樣發財，演講中的內容，天天都有機會和別人説。

1. I'm *delighted* to be here.

　　delighted 已經由情感動詞變成純粹的形容詞，等於 happy = pleased。delight 這個字還可以當動詞，作「使高興」解，如：It delights me. (它使我高興。)
　　　= I am *delighted* by it.
　不能用 *It's delighting to me.* (誤)
　可用 It's delightful to me. (正)

2. advice (勸告) 是抽象名詞，不可説 *an advice*，要用 some advice，或 a piece of advice。

3. Money talks. Money rules. Money is power. 這三句話都是諺語，相反的説法是：Money isn't everything. (金錢非萬能。)

4. Follow your *passion*. 等於 Follow your interest.

　　passion 一般都當「熱情」解，很少字典翻爲「愛好」，但是 passion 這個字當作「愛好」，卻是最常用的。

　　有一位大學剛畢業的學生，他去問三個事業上最成功的人，問他未來應該做什麼？他們都問他説：Where does your interest lie? 或説：What are you interested in? (你的興趣在哪裏？) 而且跟他説："Follow your passion." (跟著你的愛好走。) 所以跟著愛好走，就是成功之道。

14

5. ambition 除了當作「野心」以外，也可以當「志願」解。

6. ***Decide to*** be the best in that field.
= ***Be determined to*** be the best in that field.

7. work, work, work 也可說成 work, work, and work 有
時為了表示緊湊，一氣呵成，可將連接詞 and 省略。
（詳見「文法寶典」p.465）

14

8. ***Put your money in the bank.*** (把錢存在銀行裏。)

> 中國人習慣說：「要把錢存起來。」如果你說：*Save your money.* 就不合乎美國人的習慣，美國人習慣說：***Put your money in the bank.*** 因為「銀行」傳入中國還不到一百年，中國人說話的習性尚未改變，所以說，叫別人把錢存起來，應該說：***Put your money in the bank.*** 而不是 *Save your money.*
>
> 　　Save your money. 意思是叫別人「把錢省下來」，而不是「把錢存起來」。

9. invest in people 是 invest *something* in people 的省略，
something 是指 care, love, money 等。

10. No man is an island. 是一句諺語，字面的意思是：「沒有
任何人可以是一座孤島」，引申為「人不能孤立。」你看到
一個人孤孤獨獨，不交朋友，你就可以用這句話來勸告他，
這個諺語很常用。

14

11. You can't build a fortune all *on your own*. 也可説成：
    You can't make a fortune all *on your own*.

    > 美國人很喜歡用 *on one's own* 這個成語，如：
    >
    > > I can do it *on my own*. (我可以自己做。)
    > > I can go home *on my own*. (我可以自己回家。)
    >
    > 你要常説，才像美國人説的話。

12. Money comes. Money goes. But friendship always remains. 這是幽默的説法。當你和朋友一起，把錢花光了，你就可以説這三句。

    > 也可以説：Money comes.
    > Money goes.
    > But memory is always there.
    > 　　(錢來來去去。但是記憶永遠存在。)

13. Treat all with kindness. 也可以説成：Treat everybody with kindness.

14. 中國人説：「股票下跌。」事實上，美國人説：「股票市場下跌。」所以「股票下跌」英文應説成 The market drops. 或 The stock drops. 或 The stock market drops. 也可以説 The stock index drops.

    > 任何東西跌到底，都是 bottom out，如：
    >
    > > The price of gold *bottoms out*.
    > > 　(黃金跌到最低點。)
    > > The price of oil *bottoms out*. (油價跌到底。)

15. boom 是「發出隆隆聲」，比喻「非常繁榮；非常發達」。
這個單字，美國人常用，例如：

> The market *is booming*.（股票上漲。）
> The business *is booming*.（現在景氣非常好。）
> The business of the restaurant *is booming*.
> （這家餐廳生意很好。）

14

16. 「股票」叫作 stock shares = stocks = shares = stock holdings。

17. 在賭場最大面額的籌碼，都是藍色的（blue chips），引申為「績優股」。

18. appreciate 這個字，一般當「感激」解，事實上，這個字原本的意思是「增值」。

$$\frac{ap \mid preci \mid ate}{up \mid price \mid v.}$$，根據字根分析是「價格向上升」，還引申為「重視」、「感激」。

19. picky 這個字，美國人很常說，如：

> He is very *picky*.（他很挑剔。）
> She is a very *picky* girl.（她是很挑剔的女孩子。）

20. if there is no *competitor* 可以說成 if there is no *competition*，一般人、一般字典，都不知道 *competition* 也常當「競爭者」解。

21. all in all「總之」，等於 in conclusion = to sum up。

22. of importance = important
    of utmost *importance* = very *important*
    (of + 抽象名詞 = 形容詞)

23.「*end up* + 形容詞」，表示「結果～」。

> 　　在字典上或課本上，常看到「end up with + 名詞」，
> 但是，現在美國人說話喜歡簡化，多用「end up + 形容
> 詞」，少用「end up with + 名詞」，除非沒有形容詞形式，
> 像：He ended up with nothing.（結果他一無所成。）
>
> 【比較1】 *He ended up dead.*【常用】
> 　　　　 = *He ended up with death.*【少用】
> 　　　　 （結果他死了。）
>
> 【比較2】 *He ended up absent.*【常用】
> 　　　　 = *He ended up with absence.*【少用】
> 　　　　 （最後他沒去。）
>
> 【比較3】 *He ended up bankrupt.*【常用】
> 　　　　 = *He ended up with bankruptcy.*【少用】
> 　　　　 （最後他破產了。）

24. Grasp all, lose all. 是諺語，來自 If you grasp all, you
    will lose all. 字面的意思是：「如果你什麼都要，什麼都會
    失去。」引申為「貪多必失。」諺語常常是條件句的省略，
    像 No money, no honey.（沒有錢，就沒有愛情。）又如：
    No pain, no gain.（不勞則無獲。）

25. wish 後面接子句，表示「不可能的希望」，但是 wish 也可以
    當授與動詞用，後接兩個受詞，如：

> I *wish* you success. (我祝你成功。)
> I *wish* you happiness. (我祝你幸福。)
> I *wish* you prosperity. (我祝你發達。)
> I *wish* you good luck. (我祝你好運。)

14

26. Have a good day. (再見。) 早、中、晚都可以用。

Good day. 是萬能的，見面時可以說，再見時也可以說。
Good morning. Good afternoon. 和 Good evening.
相當於中國人見面時說：「你好。」如果加上 have，就只
能用在「再見」時說。如：

> Have a good morning. (再見。)
> Have a good afternoon. (再見。)
> Have a good evening. (再見。)

　　很多名詞都可以加上 have，都可
以表示「再見」。看到要出遠門的朋友，
告別時，可以說：Have a good trip.
(祝你旅途愉快。) 別人要出去玩，你
就說：Have fun. (好好玩吧。) Have
a blast. (痛快地玩玩吧。)

　　看到別人要去參加 party，你就說：Have a good
party. 見到朋友要去吃飯，你可以說：Have a good meal.

【作文範例】

1. How to Make a Fortune

Most people hope to become rich someday. But few of them do. That is because they do not have a good method. They just dream of going from rags to riches overnight. They may buy lottery tickets and hope to get lucky. But that is not very likely. There is a much better way to make a fortune. Let me tell you how.

Making a fortune is a step-by-step process. *The first step is to* follow your passion. If you find your natural talent, you can easily be the best in that field. Then big money will come to you. *Second*, you must work harder than you ever have before. You must be totally committed and be willing to make sacrifices. *Third*, you must save as much money as you can. Remember, "a penny saved is a penny earned." If you have money, you can easily make more money.

It is my belief that the above steps are the best way to make a fortune. If you follow them you are bound to succeed. Follow your passion, work hard, and save. Then you really will go from rags to riches.

【中文翻譯】

致富之道

大部份的人，都希望將來有一天能變得很有錢，但是能做到的，卻只是少數。那是因為他們沒有好的方法。他們只是夢想能在一夕之間，由窮人變成有錢人。他們可能會買樂透，並且希望能幸運中獎。但這是不太可能的。想賺大錢，有一個更好的方法。讓我來告訴你該如何做。

致富是個按部就班的過程。第一步，就是要跟著你的愛好去走。如果你能發掘自己天生的才能，就能很容易成為在那個領域的佼佼者。那麼，大筆的錢就會自己來。第二，你必須比以往更努力工作。你必須完全投入，並且願意犧牲。第三，你必須儘量存錢。要牢記，「省一文就賺一文。」如果你有錢，很容易就能賺到更多的錢。

我認為以上的步驟是最好的致富之道。如果你能遵循這些步驟，那就一定會成功。跟著你的愛好走，努力工作，並且存錢。那麼，你就真的能從窮人變成有錢人。

2. Making a Good Investment

Making good investments is important. We want to protect what we have and leave something to our children. ***Therefore***, it is important to know what to invest in. The following are my suggestions on how you can make a good investment.

First, invest in people. You can't build a fortune all on your own. ***Hence***, you should surround yourself with good people. ***Second***, hold on to some cash. If you have cash, you can take advantage of opportunities. *Third*, invest in real estate. Buy it at the right time and in a good location. Remember, location is the key. A house with a good location will always appreciate. *Finally*, take your time. Don't be greedy and wait for the best time to invest.

In conclusion, it is important to think about your investments carefully. If you follow the advice above, I am sure that you will be successful. You will increase not only your wealth, but also your number of friends. Sooner or later you will become a wealthy man.

【中文翻譯】

做正確的投資

正確的投資是很重要的。我們都想保護自己所擁有的,並且想留些東西給孩子。因此,知道如何投資,是很重要的。以下就是我的建議,提供你正確投資的方法。

首先,要投資在人身上。你不可能完全靠自己來累積財富。因此,你就要和好人在一起。第二,要保有一些現金。如果你有現金,你就可以利用機會。第三,投資房地產,買的時機要對,而且要買地段好的房子。記得,地點是關鍵。地點好的房子一定會增值。最後,不要急,不要貪心,要等待最好的投資時機。

總之,謹慎地考慮自己的投資,是很重要的。如果你遵循以上的建議,我相信你一定會成功。你不僅財富會增加,而且朋友也會增加。你遲早會成為一個有錢人。

15. Paradise Is Waiting for You
天堂正等待著你

15

Ladies and gentlemen: | 各位先生，各位女士：
I'm so excited to be here. | 能來到這裏，我非常興奮。
I've got some hot news | 我有最新的消息要告訴你們！
  for you! |

I've discovered a place. | 我發現一個地方。
I'm dying to tell you about it. | 我很想要告訴你們這個地方。
It's a paradise here on earth. | 那是人間天堂。

It's a spectacular spot! | 它是一個景色很美的地方！
It has everything you need. | 那裡有你需要的每樣東西。
I wish I could live there | 但願我能永遠住在那裡。
  forever. |

** ─────────

hot〔hɑt〕*adj.*（新聞等）最新的；剛發生的
be dying to V. 渴望
paradise〔'pærə,daɪs〕*n.* 天堂；樂園；風景極美的地方
on earth 在地球上；在人世間
spectacular〔spɛk'tækjələ〕*adj.* 壯觀的
spot〔spɑt〕*n.* 地點（= *site*）

It's a magical sight.	它是一個神奇的景象。
It's like a fairy tale setting.	它彷彿是一個童話故事中的佈景。
There, all my dreams can come true.	在那裡，我所有的夢想都能成眞。
It's Shangri-La.	它是世外桃源。
It's Utopia.	它是理想國。
It's like heaven here and now!	它就像是現在的人間天堂！
I'm crazy about it!	我非常喜歡它！
I love it too much!	我非常愛它！
Here are some reasons why:	下面就是我的理由：

15

**

magical〔'mædʒɪkḷ〕*adj.* 神奇的；不可思議的

sight〔saɪt〕*n.* 景象

fairy tale 童話故事

setting〔'sɛtɪŋ〕*n.* (小說、戲劇等的) 背景

come true 實現；成眞

Shangri-La〔'ʃæŋgrɪˌlɑ〕*n.* 香格里拉；世外桃源 (出自 James Hilton 的小說 *Lost Horizon* 中，假想的喜馬拉雅山山谷名，代表理想世界)

Utopia〔ju'topɪə〕*n.* 烏托邦 (出自 Thomas More 的小說 *Utopia* 中，描述的理想國)

heaven〔'hɛvən〕*n.* 天堂；樂園

here and now 目前；此刻

First, *the people are so kind*.　　首先，這裡的人非常親切。
They're as warmhearted as can be!　他們非常熱心！
They treat you just like family!　　他們就把你當家人一樣！

They are all polite and helpful.　　他們全都很有禮貌，樂於助人。
They'll do anything you ask.　　你要求什麼，他們就會做什麼。
They really try to please you!　　他們真的在盡力地討好你！

There, I'm so at home.　　在那裡，我覺得舒服自在。
I feel like I belong.　　我覺得自己不是外人。
It's like I've lived there all my　　就好像我已經在那裡住了一輩
　　life.　　子。

Second, *the scenery is outstanding!*　第二點，那裡風景出奇地美麗！
The mountains are majestic!　　山峰雄偉壯觀！
It's a lush green oasis!　　它是一片鬱鬱蔥蔥的綠
　　洲！

15

**

as…as can be 非常
warmhearted〔'wɔrm'hɑrtɪd〕*adj.* 熱心的；親切的
treat〔trit〕*v.* 對待　　*at home* 像在家裡一樣舒服自在；無拘束
belong〔bə'lɔŋ〕*v.* 合得來；成為集體的一份子
scenery〔'sinərɪ〕*n.* 風景
outstanding〔aut'stændɪŋ〕*adj.* 突出的
majestic〔mə'dʒɛstɪk〕*adj.* 有威嚴的；雄偉的
lush〔lʌʃ〕*adj.* 草木茂盛的　　oasis〔o'esɪs〕*n.* 綠洲

The beaches are picture-perfect.	海灘風景如畫。
The sand is soft and white.	沙子既柔軟又潔白。
The whole setting is like a postcard.	整片景色就像一張明信片。

Third, there are tons of things to do. 　第三點，有很多事可以做。

There are activities for everyone.	有適合每個人的活動。
But relaxing is the first choice at this resort!	但在這休閒勝地最重要的事是放輕鬆！

15

You can swim, hike, or explore.	你可以游泳、爬山，或去沒去過的地方。
You can dance, sing, or get a massage.	你可以跳舞、唱歌，或做個按摩。
You can even have a swim in the nude.	你甚至可以裸泳。

**

perfect〔'pɝfɪkt〕*adj.* 完美的　　***picture-perfect*** *adj.* 風景如畫的
postcard〔'post,kɑrd〕*n.* 明信片
ton〔tʌn〕*n.* 噸　　***tons of*** 許多的
resort〔rɪ'zɔrt〕*n.* 休閒勝地　　hike〔haɪk〕*v.* 健行
explore〔ɪk'splor〕*v.* 探險　　massage〔mə'sɑʒ〕*n.* 按摩
nude〔njud〕*n.* 裸體　　***in the nude*** 裸體地

***Fourth**, the environment is so peaceful.*	第四點,周圍環境很平和。
There is no crime at all.	治安很好,沒有任何犯罪事件。
It's the safest place I know!	那是我所知道,最安全的地方!
The mood in "Paradise" is peaceful.	「天堂」的氣氛祥和。
Nobody ever gets angry!	從來沒有人生氣過!
They should name it "Harmony."	他們應該把當地取名爲「和諧」。
They don't have any pollution.	那裡沒有任何污染。
There is no garbage on the streets.	路上沒有垃圾。
It's the cleanest place I know.	那是我所知道,最乾淨的地方。
***Fifth**, the weather is ideal!*	第五點,天氣很理想!
It has a perfect tropical climate.	氣候是完美的熱帶性氣候。
Every day is a blue sky day!	每天都是蔚藍晴空!

15

** —————————

peaceful〔ˈpisfəl〕*adj.* 愛好和平的;平靜的
crime〔kraɪm〕*n.* 犯罪　　mood〔mud〕*n.* 氣氛
name〔nem〕*v.* 爲⋯命名　　harmony〔ˈhɑrmənɪ〕*n.* 和諧
ideal〔aɪˈdiəl〕*adj.* 理想的　　tropical〔ˈtrɑpɪkl〕*adj.* 熱帶的

15

The nights are too romantic!	夜裡真是浪漫！
It's too perfect to be true!	這裡太完美了，簡直不像真的！
It's way better than a movie.	這裡比電影裡面還好。
Every star shines just for you.	繁星只為你閃耀。
The cool night breeze relaxes you.	夜晚涼爽的微風讓你心情放鬆。
Warm waves lap at your feet.	暖暖的波浪輕拍腳底。
I hope you get the picture.	我希望你能知道。
"Paradise" is truly awesome.	「天堂」真的很棒。
But it's time to end this speech.	但是，該是我們結束這場演講的時候。
Can you guess where paradise is?	你猜得出來天堂在哪裡嗎？
Here's a clue.	給你一個線索。
"Paradise is near."	「天堂就在附近。」

***

**

romantic〔ro'mæntɪk〕*adj.* 浪漫的
way〔we〕*adv.* 遠遠地；大大地；非常
shine〔ʃaɪn〕*v.* 發光；照耀　　breeze〔briz〕*n.* 微風
lap〔læp〕*v.*（波浪）輕拍　　***get the picture*** 知道情形；明白
awesome〔'ɔsəm〕*adj.* 很好的　　clue〔klu〕*n.* 線索

It's in China.	它就在中國。
It's in the south.	它就在南方。
It's not too far from here.	它離這裡不會很遠。
It's true.	真的有這地方。
I swear to God it's true.	我向上帝發誓，這是真的。
If you're lucky, you'll find it too.	如果你夠幸運，你也會找到它。
Be nice to me.	對我好一點。
I might tell you more.	我可能會告訴你更多。
I might even take you there!	我甚至會帶你到那裡！

15

Thank you for your attention.	謝謝你們專心聽我演講。
Now please go find your paradise.	現在，請你去尋找你自己的天堂。
In your mind, in your backyard, or somewhere in China.	在你心裡，在你家後院，或是在中國的某個地方。
Thank you!	謝謝大家！

** ————————————————

swear〔swɛr〕*v.* 發誓　　backyard〔'bæk'jɑrd〕*n.* 後院

【背景説明】

1. I'm so excited to be here. (能來到這裏，我非常興奮。)

　　excite 是「情感動詞」，情感動詞的用法非常簡單，
看下面例子就知道：

> It excites me. (它使我興奮。)
> = I am excited by it. (我對它很興奮。)
> = It is exciting to me. (它令我興奮。)

　　一般及物動詞，「人」做主詞用主動，「非人」做主詞，
用被動，但情感動詞剛好相反，人做主詞時，一定要用被
動形式，但是沒有被動意義，情感動詞的過去分詞已經快
要變成純粹的形容詞了，有些已經變了，如：I'm tired.
(我很累。)這個 tired 已經變成純粹的形容詞。

　　I'm so excited to be here. 比 I'm so happy to
be here. 或 I'm so pleased to be here. 都要強烈。

2. I've got some hot news for you!
(我有最新的消息要告訴你們！)

> 　　I've got 也可説成 I got，有些美國人認爲文法不對，
> 但這就是他們常説的話。如果説成 *I have got* 就是怪怪的，
> 因爲美國人不這麼説，寫的時候，才會這樣寫。美國人説
> 的話，和他寫的會話書不一樣，所以我們讀了美國人做的
> 會話書，説話不像美國人。
>
> 【例】　A: Why are you so happy? (你爲什麼這麼高興？)
> 　　　　B: I got some good news. (我有好消息。)
>
> 　　　　(I got = I've got = I have)
> 　　　　(*I have got* 【書寫英文】)

要注意，news 這個字，是抽象名詞，不可數，我們中文
説：「我有一個消息要告訴你。」英文不能説：*I have a news
to tell you.*（誤）英文應該説：I have news to tell you. 或
I have some news to tell you. 理論上，抽象名詞不可數，
可用單位名詞來表「數」的觀念，「一個消息」在字典上是
a piece of news 或 an item of news，但是，如果你跟美
國人説：I have *a piece of news* to tell you. 這句話是沒
有錯的，但並不是美國人一般所説的話，我們要避免使用。

3. I'*m dying to* tell you about a place.
（我很想要告訴你們一個地方。）

15

die〔daɪ〕*v.* 死，I'm dying.（我要死了。）但
I'm dying to tell you about it. 完全和死無關。

be dying to do sth. 很想做某事；渴望做某事

I'*m dying to* go home.（我很想回家。）
I'*m dying to* eat something.（我很想吃東西。）
I'*m dying to* go abroad.（我很想出國。）

不要和另一個成語 *be dying for sth.*（很想要某物）
混淆，for 後面接的是名詞。

【例】 I'*m dying for* a cup of coffee.（我很想要一杯咖啡。）
I'*m dying for* a new car.（我很想要一部新車。）

4. It's a spectacular spot!

spect:acular〔spɛk'tækjələ˞〕*adj.* 壯觀的；奇觀的
look :particular

從字根上分析 spectacular 這個字，就知道是「看起來
奇特的」，就是「壯觀的；奇觀的；壯麗的；驚人的」。

這句話的字面意思是「它是一個壯觀的地點！」引申爲
「這裏的景色非常優美，非常吸引人！」

5. I wish I could live there forever. (但願我能永遠住在那裡。)

　　這句話是美國人的文化，美國人很喜歡說 I wish 之類的話，例如，美國人到了一個好的地方，他常會說 "I wish I could stay here forever." (我希望我能永遠待在這裡。)

　　當他們到了餐廳裏面，吃到好吃的東西，就會說 "I wish I could eat this every day." (我希望我每天都吃這個。) 或是說 "I could eat this all day." (我整天都可以吃這個東西。)【句中省略 I wish】

15

6. It's a magical sight. (它是個神奇的景象。)

　　magical〔ˈmædʒɪkḷ〕*adj.* 神奇的　　sight〔saɪt〕*n.* 景象

　　美國人很喜歡用 magical，當他們吃到好吃的東西時，他們常說："This is magical." (真神奇，太好吃了。)

　　這句話也可以說成：It's a magical place. (這個地方真神奇。)

7. It's like a fairy tale setting.

　　fairy〔ˈfɛrɪ〕*n.* 仙女；仙子　　*fairy tale* 童話故事
　　setting〔ˈsɛtɪŋ〕*n.* 場景；(小說、戲劇等的) 背景；
　　　(舞台的) 佈景

　　fairy 這個字的意思是「神仙；小仙女；小仙子；小精靈；小妖精」，tale 和 story 不同，tale 專指「虛構的故事」，story 也許是虛構，也許是真實的，所以，fairy tale 就是「童話故事」。setting 主要意思是「戲劇的場景」，在這裏是童話故事裏面虛構的「佈景」，是一種假的環境。所以，這句話的意思就是「這裏就像一個童話故事中的佈景。」

8. It's Shangri-La.

Shangri-La〔'ʃæŋgrɪˌla〕*n.* 香格里拉；世外桃源

出自 James Hilton 的小説 *Lost Horizon*（失落的地平線）中，假想的喜馬拉雅山山谷名，代表「理想世界」。

據説現在已經找到 James Hilton 書中所説的地方，是在中國雲南省的中甸。現在，有一家五星級連鎖飯店，名字就是 Shangri-La Hotel（香格里拉飯店）。

9. It's Utopia.

　　Utopia（烏托邦）常拿來形容一個完美的假想地，出自 Thomas More 1516 年出版的小説 *Utopia* 中描述的理想國。在小説中，「烏托邦」有 54 個城鎮，財產公有，男女老幼每日工作 6 小時，各盡所能，各取所需。

所以這裏的 It's Utopia. 是指「這是理想國。」也就是「在這裏你想要什麼，就有什麼，人人平等。」

10. It's like heaven ***here and now***!

here and now　①現在；馬上（= *at once*）

　　　　　　　　②此時此地（= *this place and this time*）

【例】 We must solve the problem ***here and now***.

（我們現在必須立刻解決這個問題。）

【*here and now = right now in this place*】

Pay attention to what I say ***here and now***.

（現在請注意聽我説。）【*here and now = now in this place*】

　　要常説 ***here and now***，要儘量説以前沒説過的成語和句子，英文才進步得快。***here and now*** 在不同的情況，有不同的解釋，只要合乎前後句意即可。

15

11. I'm crazy about it!

這句話字面的意思是「我爲它而瘋狂」，引申爲「我非常喜歡它！」(= *I like it very much!*)

當你很喜歡某個東西，或某個嗜好，你就可以用 *I'm crazy about*....

【例】*I'm crazy about* traveling. (我非常喜歡旅行。)
I'm crazy about Chinese food.
(我非常喜歡吃中國菜。)
I'm crazy about my girlfriend.
(我非常喜歡我的女朋友。)

12. They're as warmhearted as can be!

warmhearted〔'wɔrm'hɑrtɪd〕*adj.* 熱心的；親切的
(= *kind, friendly, and loving*)

as ~ as can be 非常

as warmhearted as can be 是 as warmhearted as *warmhearted* can be 的省略。

You are kind. (你很好心。)
You are helpful. (你很熱心助人。)
You are *warmhearted*. (你很熱心。)

我們中國人說到「熱心」，第一個想到的是 enthusiastic，事實上，這個字應該用在 be enthusiastic about *sth.*。
【例】He is enthusiastic about baseball.
(他熱衷於棒球。)

看到一個人很熱心，你應該說："You're kind. You're helpful. You're warmhearted."

13. I feel like I belong.

> belong〔bəˋlɔŋ〕v. 合得來；成爲集體的一份子

> 這句話字面意思是「我覺得我屬於那裏」，引申爲「我覺得自己不是外人。」
>
> 在這篇演講稿中，因爲前面説 There, I'm so at home. 所以 I feel like I belong. 後面不再接 there。
>
> 【例】 This is my kind of place. (我喜歡這裏。)
> I love it here. (我愛這裏。)
> I *belong* here. (我適合這裏。)
>
> 在美國人日常生活當中，他們很喜歡説 belong，當你到了美國人家裏面去作客，你就可以説：
>
> You're so kind. (你們眞好。)
> You treat me so well. (你們對待我這麼好。)
> I feel like I *belong*. (我覺得自己不是外人。)
>
> 【在這裏，belong 是指 belong to the family，就像家庭的一份子 (a member of the family)】

14. It's a lush green oasis! (它是一片鬱鬱蔥蔥的綠洲！)

> lush〔lʌʃ〕adj. 草木茂盛的 (= *full of plant life*)
> oasis〔oˋesɪs〕n. 綠洲

> 可以有好幾個形容詞，共同修飾一個名詞。英文中，常用同類的形容詞，來加強語氣。(形容詞的排列，詳見「文法寶典」p.190)
>
> 這句話字面的意思是「它是一個草木茂盛，綠色的綠洲」，可翻譯成「它是一個草木茂盛的綠洲。」爲什麼這樣説呢？因爲在一般沙漠中的綠洲，樹木非常稀少，如果用 lush 和 green 來強調 oasis，那在中文，我們就可以引用中文的成語「鬱ㄩˋ鬱ㄩˋ蔥ㄘㄨㄥ蔥ㄘㄨㄥ」來強調草木繁盛。
>
> 這句話也可以翻成「它是一片鬱鬱蔥蔥的綠洲！」

15

15　

15. The beaches are *picture-perfect*.（海灘風景如畫。）

picture-perfect【俗】*adj.* 非常完美的；風景如畫的
（= *having perfect conditions, executed perfectly*）

> 　查遍所有的辭典，都沒有 *picture-perfect*，除了在 Talking American 中才有解釋。*picture-perfect* 字面的意思是「好到像是在明信片、海報、圖畫中的」，引申為「非常完美」，要看句子的前後文意來翻譯。
>
> 【例】The weather is *picture-perfect* for fishing.
> 　　　（這個天氣非常適合釣魚。）
> 　　　The Yellow Stone Park is *picture-perfect*.
> 　　　（黃石公園風景如畫。）
> 　　　What a *picture-perfect* place!（這個地方風景如畫！）
>
> 　凡是你看到任何東西畫面很完美，像是在風景明信片中的，你都可以用 *picture-perfect* 來形容。picture-perfect 也可寫成 picture perfect。

16. There are *tons of* things to do.（有很多事可以做。）

ton〔tʌn〕*n.* 噸　　*tons of* 很多（= *lots of*）

　tons of 字面意思是「好幾噸的」，用以強調「很多很多」，可接可數名詞或不可數名詞。

【例】I bought *tons of* fruit for you.（我買了很多水果給你。）
　　　I have *tons of* work to do.（我有很多事要做。）
　　　She got *tons of* birthday presents.
　　　（她收到很多生日禮物。）

　　　He has *tons of* money.（他很有錢。）
　　　You need to drink *tons of* water.（你需要大量喝水。）
　　　I have *tons of* books to read.（我有很多書要唸。）

　你要像美國人一樣，常說 *tons of*，說起話來，才有美國人的味道。

17. You can swim, *hike*, or *explore*.

hike〔haɪk〕v. 遠足;健行;徒步旅行
explore〔ɪkˊsplor〕v. 探險

　　一般人弄不清楚 hike,凡是走在鄉下的小路或是走山路,都叫做 hike。一般我們中國人說「我喜歡爬山」,應該是 "*I like to go hiking.*" 如果說成 "I like to go mountain climbing." 則為「我喜歡去登山。」通常說 go mountain climbing 是指高危險、高難度的攀登,像爬喜馬拉雅山之類的。

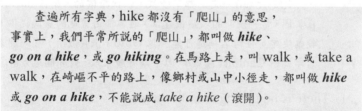

　　例: A: You look tired. (你看起來很疲倦。)
　　　　B: Yeah, I *went hiking* all day on Mt. Ali.
　　　　　 (對呀,我昨天一整天去爬阿里山。)

　又如: A: What are you going to do next week?
　　　　　 (下禮拜你要做什麼?)
　　　　B: I'm *going mountain climbing* on
　　　　　 Mt. Jade. (我要去攀登玉山。)

15

　　查遍所有字典,hike 都沒有「爬山」的意思,事實上,我們平常所說的「爬山」,都叫做 *hike*、*go on a hike*,或 *go hiking*。在馬路上走,叫 walk,或 take a walk,在崎嶇不平的路上,像鄉村或山中小徑走,都叫做 *hike* 或 *go on a hike*,不能說成 *take a hike* (滾開)。

　　美國人喜歡用 *explore* 這個字,凡是去沒去過的地方、做沒做過的事、吃沒吃過的東西,都叫 *explore*。在字典上,*explore* 主要意思是「探險」,但是在美國人思想中的 *explore*,並沒有像中國人想的「探險」那麼嚴重。*explore* 這個字,美國人幾乎天天用。

　　You can swim, *hike*, or *explore*. 可以翻成「你可以游泳、爬山,或是去沒去過的地方。」中國人所說的「爬山」,大都指 *hike*,因為古時候山上沒有路,都是爬著走的,所以中文的「爬山」是有語病的,中文把「在山上健行」,都說成「爬山」。

18. There is no crime at all. (治安很好，沒有任何犯罪事件。)

中國人說「這個地方治安很好」，美國人說 "This place has a low crime rate." 「治安」這兩個字有語病，在「辭海」上的解釋是「政治修明」，當美國人說 "The public safety is great here."（此地的公共安全、治安，一切都很好。）指很多方面，像消防、救護、執法等，各方面都做得很好。

中文： 這裏治安很差。

英文： This place has a high crime rate.
　　　 Crime is high in this place.

15

19. The mood in "Paradise" is peaceful. (「天堂」的氣氛祥和。)
= The atmosphere in "Paradise" is peaceful.

用雙引號（""）表示「所謂的～」，不是真的。

20. They should name it "Harmony."

name〔nem〕v. 為…命名　　harmony〔ˈhɑrmənɪ〕n. 和諧

凡是大家在一起，都不吵架，快快樂樂的，稱作 harmony。在美國，當一個新的城鎮被建立，通常都由當地的居民提供意見，投票決定，任何名稱都可能。像 Ohio（俄亥俄州）有一個大城，名字就叫 Canton（廣東），因早期有廣東人，對那個地方有貢獻。

21. There is no garbage on the streets.

on the streets 或 in the streets 都可以，但是美國人多用 on。這句話的意思是「在街道上沒有垃圾。」

22. It's too perfect to be true!

too…to 表「太…而不」，這句話的意思是「太完美了，不是真的！」到底是不是真的呢？要看實際情況而定。

類似的有： The news is too good to be true.
　　　　　　　（這個消息太好了，不像是真的。）

這句話的含意是，也許是真的，也許不是真的，看情況而定。

23. I hope you *get the picture.*

   get the picture 知道情形；明白（= *understand*）

   > 當你問別人懂不懂的時候，你就可以用下面其中一句話：
   >
   > ⎧ Did you ***get the picture?***（你明白了沒有？）
   > ⎨ = Did you catch my drift?（你知不知道我的意思？）
   > ⎩ = Did you get my point?（你知不知道我講什麼？）
   >
   > ⎧ = Did you get it?（你懂了嗎？）
   > ⎨ = Did I make it clear?（我說明白了沒有？）
   > ⎩ = Did I make myself understood?（我說的你了解嗎？）
   > = Do you understand?（你明白嗎？）

15

24. Here's a clue.（給你一點線索。）

   = Here's a hint.（給你一點暗示。）

   clue〔klu〕*n.* 線索；提示；暗示（= *hint*）

   美國人也常說 "I don't have a clue."（我不知道。）
   （= *I don't know.*）

25. Paradise is near.（天堂就在附近。）（= *Paradise is close.*）

26. *I swear* to God it's true.

   swear〔swɛr〕*v.* 發誓

   > 美國人講話，動不動就說 *I swear* 之類的話，例如：
   >
   > ⎧ *I swear* it's true.（我發誓是真的。）
   > ⎨ = *I swear* to God it's true.（我向上帝發誓是真的。）
   > ⎩ = *I swear* on the Bible it's true.（我手按著聖經發誓是真的。）
   >
   > ⎧ = *I swear* by my honor it's true.（我以我的名譽發誓，是真的。）
   > ⎨ = *I swear* on my reputation it's true.（我以我的名聲發誓，是真的。）
   > ⎩ = *I swear* by my life it's true.（我用我的生命發誓，是真的。）

27. I might tell you more.

   should, would, could, might 是假設法的助動詞，這句話
   是由 *If you asked me*, I might tell you. 演變而來。

【作文範例】

The Place I Like Most

Sometimes we need to take a break from our busy, fast-paced lives. At these times we try to find a place to get away from it all. We need a place where we can truly relax and forget all our troubles. *In short*, we need a paradise on earth. That is why I feel so lucky to have found my Shangri-La.

15

There are so many reasons why I love this place. *First*, the people there are so kind. They treat you like family. *Second*, the scenery is outstanding. There are majestic mountains and white beaches. It is as pretty as a postcard. *Third*, there are so many things to do. There is an activity for everyone. *Fourth*, it is so safe and peaceful. There is no crime at all, and no one ever gets angry. *Finally*, the weather is ideal. It has a perfect tropical climate. No matter what time of year you go, the sun is shining.

This paradise has so many good things to recommend it. Best of all, it is close by. It is in China, in the south, and not too far from here. I hope that you can visit it someday. I'm sure you will agree that it is one of the best places on earth.

16. *Change Is the Name of the Game*
改變是一切

Ladies and gentlemen:	各位先生，各位女士：
Please listen up.	請注意聽。
I have just three words to say:	我只要說三個字：「變、
"Change, change, change!"	變、變！」
Change to succeed.	為了成功，要改變。
Change to achieve.	為了功成名就，要改變。
Change to better your life.	為了改善生活，要改變。
Life is *change*.	人生就是要改變。
Change is life.	改變就是人生。
Learn to play "the *change* game."	要學會改變。
Here is some advice.	這裡有一些建議。
You need to know it.	你必須知道。
The older you get, the more	你年紀愈大，愈需要改變。
you must change.	

16

** ———————————————————————

listen up 注意聽　　achieve〔əˈtʃiv〕*v.* 成功；功成名就
better〔ˈbɛtɚ〕*v.* 改善　　advice〔ədˈvaɪs〕*n.* 勸告；建議

16

First, accept change.	第一，接受改變。
Change is certain.	改變是必然的。
Nothing stays the same.	沒有任何事是一成不變的。
Face the facts.	面對現實。
Accept reality.	接受現實。
Every day will bring change.	每天都會有變化。
Change is inevitable.	改變是不可避免的。
It will happen.	它終究會發生。
Get ready for it right now.	現在就要做好準備。
Second, enjoy change.	第二，要享受改變。
Have a passion for it.	要非常喜歡改變。
It can be a lot of fun.	變化是相當有趣的。

**

accept〔əkˈsɛpt〕*v.* 接受
certain〔ˈsɝtn̩〕*adj.* 確定的；必然的
reality〔rɪˈælətɪ〕*n.* 現實
inevitable〔ɪnˈɛvətəbḷ〕*adj.* 不可避免的
passion〔ˈpæʃən〕*n.* 熱情；愛好
have a passion for 熱愛

Change is exciting.	改變令人興奮。
Change is an adventure.	改變就是一種冒險。
Who knows what will happen next?	誰知道下一步會發生什麼事？
Change keeps us young.	改變能讓我們永保青春。
Change keeps us fresh.	改變能讓我們生氣蓬勃。
It's like a magic "youth pill."	它就像是神奇的「不老仙丹」。
Third, realize it's never too late to change.	第三，要知道改變是永遠不嫌晚。
Anytime is OK.	任何時間都可以。
Transform your life at any age.	在任何年齡，你都能轉變你的人生。
Don't say you're too old.	不要說你太老了不能變。
Don't be set in your ways.	不要被你的習慣給侷限住了。
The world will pass you by.	你會跟不上世界的腳步。

16

** ————————————————

adventure〔əd'vɛntʃɚ〕*n.* 冒險   fresh〔frɛʃ〕*adj.* 有精神的
magic〔'mædʒɪk〕*adj.* 神奇的   youth〔juθ〕*n.* 年輕
pill〔pɪl〕*n.* 藥丸   ***youth pill*** 不老仙丹
realize〔'riə,laɪz〕*v.* 知道；了解
transform〔træns'fɔrm〕*v.* 改變；轉變
set〔sɛt〕*v.* 設（限）   ***pass by*** 通過

Make yourself change.	讓自己改變。
Age is no excuse.	年齡不是藉口。
Adapt or get left behind.	如果不改變，就落伍了。
Ladies and gentlemen:	各位先生、各位女士：
Change with defeat.	當你遭遇挫折，你要改變。
Change with success.	當你成功時，也要改變。
If you rest, you will rust.	如果你停止改變，就會變遲鈍。
Change to learn.	改變可以增長知識。
Change to grow up.	改變就會成長。
Change for the better every day.	改變可以得到更美好的明天。
I've said enough.	我說得夠多了。
I hope you "catch my drift!"	希望你們能明白我說的話！
Change, change, change or you will fail, fail, fail.	變、變、變，不然你會一敗塗地。

16

** ————————————————

excuse〔ɪkˈskjus〕*n.* 藉口
adapt〔əˈdæpt〕*v.* 適應　　***get left behind*** 落後
defeat〔dɪˈfit〕*n.* 挫折；失敗　　rust〔rʌst〕*v.* 生銹；變遲鈍
drift〔drɪft〕*n.* 漂流（物）；要點

Change is a new start.	改變意味著全新的開始。
It's a new beginning.	改變是全新的起點。
It's a fresh lease on life.	改變會讓你過新生活。
Don't fear change.	不要畏懼改變。
Make it your ally.	讓它成爲你的好朋友。
It is a powerful tool.	它是超強利器。
Change right now.	現在立刻改變。
You owe it to yourself.	你應該這麼做。
Now go out and change the world.	現在就去改變這個世界。

16

Take care.	保重。
Enjoy the day.	祝你有美好的一天。
Let's take a water break!	讓我們休息一下！
I'll be around if you have any questions.	有問題的話，歡迎來找我，我就在這兒。

**————————————

lease〔lis〕*n.* 租約；租期　　*a fresh lease on life* 新生活
ally〔'ælaɪ,ə'laɪ〕*n.* 盟友
powerful〔'pauɚfəl〕*adj.* 強有力的　　tool〔tul〕*n.* 工具
owe it to oneself (*to do sth.*) 認爲自己應該做（某事）
break〔brek〕*n.* 休息時間　　around〔ə'raund〕*adv.* 在附近

【背景説明】

　　美國哈佛大學商學院學生畢業時，校長在畢業典禮上，曾告訴同學，企業成功的秘訣就是：

Change! Change! Change!

　　一家經營不善的公司，需要改變；經營好的公司，也需要改變。你今天得到第一，明天呢？不見得第一。要保持領先，就得求新、求變。這篇演講稿，你非背熟不可，你可以用它來勸告周圍的人。

1. Change *is the name of the game*.

> 　　這句話字面的意思是「改變是遊戲的名稱」，引申為「改變非常重要。」美國人喜歡玩 game，不管任何遊戲或比賽，像：basketball *game*（籃球賽），baseball *game*（棒球賽），football *game*（美式足球賽）。
>
> 　　*the name of the game*「比賽的名稱」，也就是「活動的名稱」。比如説，你要舉辦一個活動，最重要的就是「活動的名稱」。當你説 Change *is the name of the game*. 就表示「改變是非常重要的。」英文解釋就是 Change is very important.
>
> 其他的例子有：
>
> 　　Getting good grades *is the name of the game* for you.
> 　　（成績優異對你很重要。）
> 　　Forming good habits *is the name of the game*.
> 　　（養成好習慣很重要。）
> 　　Helping without being asked *is the name of the game*.
> 　　（主動幫助別人很重要。）
> 　　Taking the initiative *is the name of the game*.
> 　　（採取主動很重要。）
>
> 　　總之，你要常説 the name of the game，你説的英文才像美國人。

16

2. *Please listen up.*

此用法源自於美國軍隊，你如果說 Please listen. ，是請求別人聽你說；如果說 *Please listen up.* 有命令的口吻。

【比較】Please listen! (請聽我說，好不好？)

　　　　　Please listen up! (請注意聽！)【up 有加強語氣的味道】

3. Change to succeed.
   Change to achieve.
   Change to better your life.

Change *to succeed.*

在這裡，to succeed 是副詞片語修飾動詞，表「目的」，所以可以譯成「爲了成功，要改變。」這句話等於 Change in order to succeed.

16

Change *to achieve.*

在一般字典上，achieve 多當及物動詞，作「完成；實現」解。事實上，achieve 也可當不及物動詞，作「達到預期目的；如願以償；成功」解。所以，這句話要譯成「爲了功成名就，要改變。」在這句話中的 achieve，等於 succeed。

achieve 當不及物動詞的例子很多，如：

We must work hard to *achieve.*
(爲了達到目標，我們必須努力。)

To *achieve*, he works day and night.
(爲了成功，他不眠不休地工作。)

Change *to better your life.*

better 主要意思爲「較好的」，這裡當動詞用，作「改善」解，相當於 improve。這句話的意思就是「爲了改善你的生活，你要改變。」

* 不定詞片語當副詞用，修飾動詞，根據前後句意，可歸納爲：
  表示目的、理由、條件、結果、原因。(詳見文法寶典 p.413)

4. Life is change.
   Change is life.

> 　　當你碰到一成不變的人，就可以對他們說這兩句話。
> Life is change. 是 Life is about change. 的省略。
>
> 　　about 的意思，相當於 around「環繞」，也就是「人生的重點是改變。」同理，Change is life. 是 Change is about life. 的省略。字面上的意思就是「改變圍繞著人生」，也就是「人生少不了改變。」
>
> 　　這兩句話就是要鼓勵人們不要墨守成規，在中國人的思想中，很少這麼說，在美國文化中卻很重要。

5. Learn to play "the change game."

16

> 　　這句話的字面意思就是「學會玩改變的遊戲。」由於美國人的觀念中認為，不要把事情看得太嚴重，做任何事都可以像玩遊戲一樣輕鬆，所以這句話引申為「要學會改變。」
>
> 【比較】Let's change.（我們要改變。）【一般語氣】
> 　　　　Let's *play "the change game."*【語氣輕鬆，不嚴肅】
> 　　　　（我們改變吧！）
>
> 　　　　Live well.（好好過日子。）【一般語氣】
> 　　　　Let's *play "the game of life."*【語氣輕鬆】
> 　　　　（好好過日子，凡事不要看得太嚴重。）
>
> 　　　　Let's improve.（我們來改善。）【一般語氣】
> 　　　　Let's *play "the game of improvement."*【語氣輕鬆】
> 　　　　（我們來改善吧！）

6. You need to *know it*.
   = You need to know.

> 　　know 作「知道；了解」解時，可當及物和不及物動詞。
>
> 　　　　A: We need to go now.
> 　　　　B: I *know it*.（= I know.）

7. Nothing stays the same.

　　字面上的意思就是「沒有一件事會是相同的」，引申爲
「世事無常，隨時都會有變化。」美國人常說：

　　　　Seasons change. (季節在變。)
　　　　People change. (人也在變。)
　　　　Nothing stays the same. (世事無常。)

　　如果你沒有做好改變的準備，就會跟不上時代。

8. Get ready for it right now.

　　美國人的觀念中，凡事都要未雨綢繆，預先做準備。例
如，美國人計劃要休假去旅行，多半在一年前就預先籌備好
了；美國人去打仗，隨身連屍袋 (body bag) 都準備好了，
不過他們並不知道那個袋子的功用，因爲長官會跟士兵說
"You won't ever need it. Don't open it."。

　　Get ready for it right now. 句中的 Get，相當於 Be，
就是「現在就要做好準備。」

　　老師常和學生說 : You must ***get ready for*** the test.
(你要好好準備考試。)

9. It can be a lot of *fun*.

　　fun 可做名詞用，表「有趣的人 (事、物)」，可放在 be
動詞後面，做主詞補語。下列例子中的 fun，都做名詞用。

　　　He is ***fun***. (他是個有趣的人。)
　　　The story is ***fun***. (這是個有趣的故事。)
　　　We're having ***fun***. (我們現在玩得很快樂。)
　　　【fun 在此指「歡樂時光」】

　　很多人搞不清楚 fun 的原因，是因爲 fun 也可以當形容
詞用，置於名詞前。

　　　He is a ***fun*** guy. (他很有趣。)
　　　Disneyland is a ***fun*** place. (迪士尼樂園是個好玩的地方。)

16

10. Change is *an adventure*.

   adventure〔əd'vɛntʃɚ〕*n.* 冒險；特別的經歷；新的體驗

   > *adventure* 在字典上的意思是「冒險」，但英文的 adventure
   > 和中文講的「冒險」，意思上不一樣。中文的「冒險」，有正、
   > 負兩面的意思，美國人說的 adventure，多是正面的意義。所
   > 以此句可以翻成「改變是一項勇敢的行動」，當然也可以翻成
   > 「改變是一項冒險。」
   >
   > 　　但如果說成 Change is a risk. 就變成「改變有風險」，強
   > 調改變的風險很大，帶有負面含意。
   >
   > 　　美國人常說 *adventure* 這個字：
   > Life is *an adventure*.（人生就是一場特別的經歷。）
   > Traveling is *an adventure*.（旅行就是一項探險。）
   > Meeting new people is *an adventure*.
   > （認識新朋友是一項新的體驗。）
   >
   > * 在中國人的思想中，adventure 就是「冒險」，你可以把 adventure
   > 　當做「冒險」來背，但是英文裡 adventure 的含意，不像中文說
   > 　得那麼嚴重，這就是中西文化的不同。如果你老是把 adventure
   > 　當作「冒險」解，你就說不出上面的句子了。

16

11. Change keeps us fresh.
   It's like a magic "youth pill."

   > 　　fresh 主要的意思是「新鮮的」，這裡作「煥然一新」解。
   > 這句話可翻成「改變使我們生氣蓬勃。」
   >
   > 　　magic "youth pill" 就是「神奇的不老仙丹」，也可以說
   > 成 "youth elixir"，或直接說成 elixir。
   > elixir〔ɪ'lɪksɚ〕*n.* 長生不老藥

12. Transform your life at any age.
   = Change your life completely at any age.

   trans｜form〔træns'fɔrm〕*v.* 轉變（= *change the form*）
   A→B｜形式
   across

   > 　　從字根上分析就知道是形式的改變。這句話字面的意思是
   > 「不管你幾歲，你都可以改變你生活的型式。」可引申為
   > 「不管你幾歲，你都可以完全改變你的人生。」

13. Don't be set in your ways.

　　set 的意思是「設定的；固定的」，相當於 fixed，這句話字面的意思是「不要被設定在你的方法裡」，引申為「不要侷限在你固有的習慣裡。」(= *Don't be fixed in your ways.*)

　　way 作「習慣；慣例」解時，要用複數的形式。

這句話也等於 Don't be trapped by your habits.

14. The world will pass you by.

　　pass by 「經過」，這句話字面的意思是「世界將從你身旁經過」，引申為「你會跟不上世界的腳步」，也就是「你將錯過機會。」(= You'll miss your chance. You'll be left behind.)

16

15. Change *with defeat*. (當你遭遇挫折時，需要改變。)

defeat〔dɪˈfit〕*n.* 挫折；失敗

　　with defeat 為介詞片語，當副詞用，由前後文的句意可知，這裡是表時間。所以 Change with defeat. 等於 Change when you fail.

16. Change to learn.

　　不定詞片語當副詞用，修飾動詞，可以表示目的、條件、結果、理由、原因等。(詳見文法寶典 p.414) 在這裡根據前後文句意，表「結果」。

Change *to learn*. (改變可以增長知識。)

= Change ***so that*** *you can learn.*

17. If you *rest*, you will *rust*.

　　這句話 rest 和 rust 押韻，所以唸起來鏗鏘有力。

　　這句話字面意思是「如果你停止，就會生銹」，引申為「如果你故步自封，就會停滯不前。」英文解釋為 If you stand still, you'll die a slow death. 字面的意思是「如果你站著不動，你就會慢慢死掉。」引申為「如果你故步自封，就會停滯不前。」就像河流一樣，如果停止流動，就變成一灘死水，這句話也可翻成「如果你停止改變，就會變遲鈍。」

18. I hope you "catch my drift!"

drift〔drɪft〕*n.* 漂流（物）；要點

　　這句話字面的意思是「我希望你抓到我的漂流物。」之所以會有這種說法，是由於人有時講話會滔滔不絕，就像河在流動般，而水中的漂流物，就像說話的要點，因為漂流物隨波逐流，不容易捉摸，就好像話說太快時，很難抓到話中的重點，所以，美國人把 drift 引申為「要點；主旨」，因此這句話可譯為「我希望你明白我的話！」

　　在字典裡可查到 the drift 有「要點；要旨」的意思。當你不了解別人所說的話時，你可以說：

What are you trying to say? I don't *catch your drift*.
（你到底想說什麼？我不明白你的意思。）

```
┌ catch sb's drift
└ = get sb's drift

┌ = catch sb's point
└ = get sb's point

  = understand sb.  明白某人的意思
```

19. It's a fresh lease on life.

lease 就是「租約」，這句話字面的意思就是「這是人生的
新租約」，引申為「這是人生的新開始。」這句話就等於 It's
turning over a new leaf.（它讓我宛若新生，過新生活。）

a fresh lease on life 新生活（= *a new lease on life*）

看下列例子：

【例 1】　A: I've decided to get ***a fresh lease on life***.
（我決定要改頭換面，過新生活。）
B: Good for you.（太好了。）

【例 2】　A: Stop messing around.（別混了。）
B: Thanks. I need to get ***a new lease on life***.
（謝謝你。我需要洗心革面，過新生活。）

16

20. Don't fear change.
Make it your ally.

> ally〔ˈælaɪ, əˈlaɪ〕*n.* 盟友；盟邦　　這個字的發音要注意，
> 不要唸成〔ˈælɪ〕。因為 y 在字尾輕音節時，很少唸成 / aɪ /。
> 【在 Kenyon, Knott 發音字典中，這個字有兩個發音，但大多數美國人
> 都唸成〔ˈælaɪ〕。】ally 是比 friend 還要親密的朋友，可翻成
> 「盟友」（= *a person who provides help*）。
>
> Make it your ally. 字面的意思是「使它成為和你一伙的」，
> 也就是說「使它成為你的好朋友。」
>
> 小孩子在一起時，很喜歡說「我們是一國的。」英文就是
> "We are allies."

21. *You owe it to yourself*.

> 字面的意思是「你虧欠你自己」，引申為「你應該這麼做。」
> (= *You should do it. You deserve it. You are entitled to it.*)
>
> 美國人常說這句話，例如，你可以和你的朋友說：
>
> You should take a day or two off. (你應該休息一兩天。)
> *You owe it to yourself*. (你應該這麼做。)
> You deserve it. (這是你應得的。)
>
> 你看到你的好朋友，住在較差的飯店，你就可以說：
>
> Don't be so cheap. (不要那麼小氣。)
> Stay in a five-star hotel. (住五星級飯店。)
> *You owe it to yourself*. (這是你應得的。)

16

22. Now go out and *change the world*.

> 　　這句話字面的意思是「現在出去改變世界」，go out 並非
> 叫你真正出去，而是要你「採取行動，不要保持現狀」，這句
> 話引申為「現在就去改變世界。」
>
> 　　*change the world* 是美國人的口頭禪，你要常說這句話，
> 才像美國人。
>
> 　　當美國人看到有人浪費資源時，就會幽默地說：
>
> Conserve energy and *we can make the world a*
> *better place*. (節省能源，能讓世界更美好。)
>
> 　　鼓勵人的時候，你也可以說：
>
> I believe you can *change the world*.
> (我相信你可以改變世界。)

23. Take care.
Enjoy the day.
Let's take a water break!

> 中國人道別的時候，喜歡説「好好保重」，美國人也一樣，他們會説 Take care. 在這裡 Take care. 的意思就是 Be careful. Watch out.
>
> Enjoy the day. 和 Have a good day. 意思相同，就是表示「祝你有美好的一天。」，或「再見。」
>
> 到了下午的時候，你還可以説 Enjoy the rest of the day.
>
> 早上道別時，你要説 *Enjoy the day*. 其實，你一整天都可以説 *Enjoy the day*.
>
> *Let's take a water break*. 有兩個意思：
>
> ① 休息一下，喝杯水。
>   (= Let's take a break, and get some water.)
>
> ② 休息一下。(= Take a break.) 在這裡，用 water 這個字只是爲了幽默一下。
>
> 説 Let's take a water break. 時，是帶有開玩笑的口吻，water break 源自古人騎馬時，馬累了要喝水，就要停下來，讓馬匹休息一下。

16

> 一般老師説下課休息時，會有下列説法：
>
> Let's take a break. (休息一下吧。)
> Let's take a short break. (休息一下吧。)
> Let's take a ten-minute break. (休息十分鐘。)
>
> Let's take a coffee break. (休息一下，喝杯咖啡。)
> Let's take a Coke break. (休息一下，喝杯可樂。)
> Let's take a water break. (休息一下，喝杯水。)

> 在本篇演講中，take a water break 是幽默的用語，寫作文的時候，要小心，不要用錯。

【作文範例】

Change Is the Name of the Game

Life is often compared to a game and it is constantly changing. *Physically speaking*, we change from being young to being old. *Intellectually speaking*, we change from being ignorant to being well informed. Change is an inevitable part of life.

In addition to the natural changes we experience, there are all kinds of changes facing us. *For example*, we know that we have to prepare for rainy days. *Therefore*, we can change from being wasteful to being frugal. We know that we can succeed only by working hard. *As a result*, we can change from being lazy to being industrious. It is obvious, *then*, that we can change to succeed, and we can change to better our life.

In sum, it will be to our advantage to constantly remind ourselves that change is inevitable. It is good to accept change, and it is never too late to change. We should change for the better every day.

16

【中文翻譯】

改變是一切

人生常被比喻成一場遊戲,總是變化無常。就生理上來說,我們會由年輕變老。就智慧上來說,我們會由懵懂無知,變成博學多聞。改變是生命中不可避免的一部份。

除了這些生命中註定會經歷的改變,我們還要面臨各種不同的變化。舉例來說,因為我們知道要未雨綢繆,所以我們就會從浪費變成節儉。因為我們知道唯有努力才能成功,我們會由懶惰變勤快。顯然,我們可以藉由改變而成功,藉由改變來讓人生更美好。

總之,我們要不斷提醒自己,改變是必然的,這對我們必定是有所助益。接受改變是好的,改變永遠不嫌遲。為了更美好的明天,我們應該勇於求新求變。

17. *How to Make Friends*
如何交朋友

Friends, classmates, and guests:	各位朋友，同學和來賓：
I've got a treat for you.	我要告訴你們一個好消息。
You're going to learn how to	你們將會學到如何致富。
be rich.	
I won't be talking about money.	但我不是要談如何賺錢。
Forget about diamonds, gold, or land.	不要想到鑽石、黃金，或土地。
I'm talking about the wealth of	我要談的是關於友誼的
friendship.	財富。
Friends are real treasure.	朋友是眞正的財富。
Their value is priceless.	他們是無價的。
Let's talk about how to make friends.	我們來聊聊如何交朋友。
First, to make a friend, be a friend.	首先，要交朋友，先做朋友。
Be loyal.	要忠心。
Be dependable.	要可靠。

17

** —————————————————————————

guest〔gɛst〕*n.* 來賓　　treat〔trit〕*n.* 可喜的事或物；好消息
diamond〔'daɪəmənd〕*n.* 鑽石　　gold〔gold〕*n.* 黃金
wealth〔wɛlθ〕*n.* 財富　　friendship〔'frɛndʃɪp〕*n.* 友誼
treasure〔'trɛʒɚ〕*n.* 財富　　value〔'væljʊ〕*n.* 價值
priceless〔'praɪslɪs〕*adj.* 無價的
make friends 交朋友　　loyal〔'lɔjəl〕*adj.* 忠心的
dependable〔dɪ'pɛndəbḷ〕*adj.* 可靠的；值得信賴的

Never gossip.	不說閒話。
Never judge.	不評斷。
Remember a promise is a promise.	要記得遵守承諾。
***Second**, **be** selfless.*	第二，要無私。
Be generous.	要大方。
Love to share whatever you have.	要喜愛分享你所擁有的任何東西。
Do things for others.	爲他人處理事情。
Take joy in acts of kindness.	在做好事當中，你會獲得喜悅。
Sacrifice your time and help others.	犧牲你的時間，去幫助他人。
***Third**, really **care** about people.*	第三，眞誠地關心別人。
Find people fascinating.	發覺人們是很有趣的。
Be interested in them.	對他們產生興趣。
Find joy in having friends.	在結交好友中體驗樂趣。
Sincerely like people.	眞誠地喜歡人。
They will like you right back.	他們也會喜歡你。

17

** ————————————

gossip〔'ɡɑsəp〕*v.* 說閒話　　judge〔dʒʌdʒ〕*v.* 評斷
promise〔'prɑmɪs〕*n.* 承諾　　selfless〔'sɛlflɪs〕*adj.* 無私的
generous〔'dʒɛnərəs〕*adj.* 大方的　　joy〔dʒɔɪ〕*n.* 歡樂；喜悅
act〔ækt〕*n.* 行爲　　kindness〔'kaɪndnɪs〕*n.* 仁慈
sacrifice〔'sækrə,faɪs〕*v.* 犧牲　　***care about*** 關心
fascinating〔'fæsn̩,etɪŋ〕*adj.* 迷人的；有極大吸引力的
interested〔'ɪntrɪstɪd〕*adj.* 有興趣的 < *in* >
find joy in 從…中得到歡樂　　sincerely〔sɪn'sɪrlɪ〕*adv.* 眞誠地

Fourth, for God's sake, be yourself.	第四，看在老天的份上，做你自己。
Be true blue.	做一個忠貞不二的人。
Always be sincere.	永遠誠摯待人。
Be honest.	要誠實。
Don't be fake.	不要虛偽。
Never pretend to be someone you're not.	不要故意做作。
Fifth, be *fun* to be with.	第五，要當一個有趣的人。
Be full of life.	要有精神。
Laugh a lot.	時常洋溢笑容。
Be enthusiastic.	要熱心。
Greet others with a smile.	用微笑和人打招呼。
Let them know you like them.	讓他人知道你喜歡他們。
Be positive.	要積極。
Be optimistic.	要樂觀。
Enjoy being with people.	喜歡和朋友在一起。

17

** —————————————

for God's sake 看在老天的份上　　*true blue* 忠誠的
sincere〔sɪnˋsɪr〕*adj.* 真誠的　　honest〔ˋɑnɪst〕*adj.* 誠實的
fake〔fek〕*adj.* 虛偽的　　pretend〔prɪˋtɛnd〕*v.* 假裝
fun〔fʌn〕*adj.* 有趣的　　*be full of* 充滿　　life〔laɪf〕*n.* 精力
laugh〔læf〕*v.* 笑　　enthusiastic〔ɪn͵θjuzɪˋæstɪk〕*adj.* 熱心的
greet〔grit〕*v.* 和～打招呼　　positive〔ˋpɑzətɪv〕*adj.* 積極的
optimistic〔͵ɑptəˋmɪstɪk〕*adj.* 樂觀的

Sixth, make people feel important.	第六，讓別人感覺他們很重要。
Talk to them about themselves.	跟他們聊聊他們發生的事。
They will love you for it.	他們一定會因而喜歡你。
Compliment them.	稱讚他們。
Praise them.	讚美他們。
Really appreciate them.	非常重視他們。
Finally and most importantly, remember the golden rule.	最後也是最重要的是，記得這條金科玉律。
Everyone knows it.	每個人都知道。
Don't forget it.	千萬不要忘記。
Give and you shall receive.	如果你付出，你就會得到回報。
Like and you will be liked.	喜歡他人，你也會被他人所喜歡。
Treat others the way you'd like to be treated.	你要別人怎麼對待你，你就怎麼對待別人。

17

** ————————————————————

compliment (ˈkɑmpləmənt) v. 稱讚
praise (prez) v. 讚美
appreciate (əˈpriʃɪˌet) v. 重視
finally and most importantly 最後也是最重要的是
golden rule 金科玉律　　treat (trit) v. 對待

Friendship is a two-way street.	友誼是互諒互讓的關係。
If you want a friend, you must be a friend.	如果你想要有朋友，你必須先當朋友。
Trust and respect are the keys.	信任和尊重就是關鍵。
Making true friends is not easy.	交到真心的朋友並不容易。
The rewards are worth the efforts.	你的努力所獲得的報酬是值得的。
Just be true and follow my advice.	只要真誠，並遵從我的建議。
Thanks a bunch!	非常感謝各位！
You're a great group.	你們真是很棒的一群。
I'd like to be your friend!	我真想做各位的朋友！
Enjoy life.	享受生命。
Enjoy your friends.	享受和朋友在一起的時光。
Be a "super friend."	當一個「超級好朋友」。

17

**

two-way street 互諒互讓的關係　　trust〔trʌst〕*n.* 信任
respect〔rɪ'spɛkt〕*n.* 尊敬　　key〔ki〕*n.* 關鍵
reward〔rɪ'wɔrd〕*n.* 報酬　　worth〔wɝθ〕*prep.* 值得
effort〔'ɛfət〕*n.* 努力　　follow〔'fɑlo〕*v.* 遵從
advice〔əd'vaɪs〕*n.* 勸告；建議　　bunch〔bʌntʃ〕*n.* 束；捆；群
super〔'supɚ〕*adj.* 超級的；極好的

【背景說明】

這篇演講稿是一篇萬用演講稿,你隨時都可以用演講稿的內容來勸告、鼓勵別人。

1. I've got *a treat* for you.

> 這句話也可以加強語氣説成 I've got *a special treat* for you. 在句中的 treat 作「可喜的事或物」解。
>
> treat 當名詞,主要的意思為「請客」,常被引申為「好東西」,像是一個特別的禮物或好消息等。
>
> 當你對別人説 *I've got a treat for you.* 的時候,可能表示:
>
> ① 我有個特別的禮物要給你。
>   (I've got *a special gift* for you.)
>
> ② 我有個特別的東西要給你。
>   (I've got *something special* for you.)
>
> ③ 我有個好消息要告訴你。
>   (I've got *good news* for you.)
>
> 美國人在日常生活中常説到 treat (可喜的事或物) 這個字,例如:What *a treat* to be here! (在這裡真高興!)
>   = I'm very happy to be here!
>
> treat 這個字,是一般中國人不太會用的字,所以你要常用這個字,才像道地的美國人。你至少要天天説:*What a treat to be here!*

2. Their value is *priceless*. (他們是無價的。)
   = They are *invaluable*.

> priceless (無價的;極貴重的)
> = invaluable
>
> valueless (沒有價值的)
> = worthless

17

注意不要把 priceless「無價的」和 valueless「沒有價值的」混淆，這兩個字意義相反。

price｜less　從字根上分析，無法以價格來估計，即為「無
　　　　　not

價的；極貴重的」，這樣分析就容易記了。

3. *To make a friend, be a friend*.

這句話是美國人的口頭禪。To make a friend 是不定詞片語，當副詞用，意義上表條件，整句的意思是：

If you want to make a friend, you have to be a friend.

（如果你想要交朋友，你就必須先做別人的朋友。）

如果老是想叫別人請客，佔別人便宜，你就交不到朋友。

4. Never judge.

美國人的觀念裏，不該去評斷（judge）他人的好壞，他們認為只有上帝才能評斷（Only God can judge.），人是沒有資格評斷別人的。就是因為美國人喜歡評斷別人，所以父母常告誡小孩說：Never judge.

5. *A promise is a promise*.

這句話字面的意思是「諾言就是諾言」，引申為「你必須遵守諾言。」（= You have to keep a promise.）美國人很重視諾言，所以他們還常說：

Don't make any idle promises.（不要輕許諾言。）
Don't throw promises around.（不要輕許諾言。）
Live up to your word.（要遵守諾言。）

You have to keep your word.（你必須遵守諾言。）
You have to follow through on what you said.
（你必須落實你的諾言。）

17

當別人答應你一件事，但卻未完成，你就可以說下面
三句話：

Remember *a promise is a promise*.
（要記得遵守你的諾言。）
You gave your word. （你已經做出承諾了。）
I was counting on what you said.
（我原本很倚賴你說的話。）

6. Love to share *whatever you have*.

whatever you have 為名詞子句，做 share 的受詞。

【比較】Love to share *what you have*.【一般語氣】
（喜愛分享你所擁有的東西。）【what = the things that】

Love to share *whatever you have*.【加強語氣】
（喜愛分享你所擁有的任何東西。）【whatever = anything that】

這裡的 Love to share... 意思是 *You should* love to share...。

17

7. Take joy *in acts of kindness*.

acts of kindness 字面意思是「好心的行為」，其實就是
「做好事」。這整句話的字面意思是，在做好事當中
（in acts of kindness），你可以獲得喜悅（take joy）。

美國人常說 *in acts of*「在～的行為裡」，如：
Take joy *in acts of* generosity.
（慷慨大方可以獲得喜悅。）
Take pleasure *in acts of* goodness.
（做好事可以獲得快樂。）
Take pride *in acts of* humility.
（在謙卑中可以獲得驕傲。）

8. Find people fascinating. （發覺人們是有趣的。）
fascinating〔'fæsn̩,etɪŋ〕*adj.* 迷人的；有極大吸引力的

fascinating 在此為補語，用來補充說明前面的 people。

9. ***Find*** joy ***in*** having friends.（從交朋友中，得到樂趣。）
　= ***Find*** pleasure ***in*** having friends.
　= Get joy from having friends.

　　　　這句話字面的意思是「在擁有朋友中，找到樂趣」，也就
　　是「從交朋友中，得到樂趣。」要把 find joy in 當成一個成
　　語來看，等於 get joy from。

10. They will like you ***right back***.

　　　　right 爲副詞，副詞修飾副詞，是爲了加強語氣，在此作
　　「馬上；立刻」解。

　　【比較】① They will like you ***back***.（他們也會喜歡你。）
　　　　　　　They will like you ***right back***.
　　　　　　　（他們馬上就會喜歡你。）
　　　　　② I'll be ***back***.（我會回來。）
　　　　　　　I'll be ***right back***.（我馬上就回來。）
　　　　　③ Let's go ***now***.（我們現在走吧。）
　　　　　　　Let's go ***right now***.（我們現在馬上就走。）

17

11. ***For God's sake***, be yourself.

　　　　字面上的意思是「因爲上帝的緣故，做你自己」，引申爲
　　「看在上帝的份上，做你自己，要眞實地把自己呈現出來。」
　　for God's sake 是美國人的口頭禪。

　　　　⎧ ***for God's sake***（最常用）
　　　　⎪ for heaven's sake（常用）
　　　　⎨ for goodness' sake（常用）
　　　　⎩ ***for Christ's sake***（少用）

　　　　所謂「看在老天的份上」，就表示「最重要的是」，相當
　　於 above all 或 more than anything。例如：

For God's sake, don't do that again!

（拜託，不要再做那件事了！）

For God's sake, stop bothering me!

（拜託，不要再煩我了！）

For God's sake, forget it! （拜託，算了吧！）

12. *Be yourself.*

這句話字面的意思是「做你自己」，引申為「做本來的你、平常的你。」也可以說成 *Be your normal self*.

美國人也常說：

You are not yourself today. （你今天不對勁。）

You are not quite yourself today. （你今天不太對勁。）

意思就是 You are a little different today.

或是 You are acting a little strange today.

看到周遭沒自信的同學，你隨時可以說這三句話鼓勵他：

Be yourself. （做自己。）

Believe in yourself. （相信自己。）

Love yourself anyway. （愛自己。）

13. Be *true blue*.

你每天都可以和你的朋友說下面三句話：

You are a *true blue* friend.

（你是我最忠實的朋友。）

I knew I could count on you.

（我知道我可以信賴你。）

I knew you wouldn't let me down.

（我知道你不會讓我失望的。）

【比較】 a *true* friend 忠實的朋友

a *true blue* friend 最忠實的朋友

17

true 和 blue 押韻，這兩個字放在一起，讓這句話感覺起來，
既強調又幽默。You are a true blue friend. 也可加強語氣，
説成：You are a true blue friend *through thick and thin*.
（不論甘苦，你都是我忠貞不二的好朋友。）

【註】true blue 這個詞彙，源自於十七世紀蘇格蘭長老會
（Scottish Presbyterians）為對抗保王派（Royalists）
的紅色，而採用的一種不易褪色之藍色染料，後被引申
作「忠貞的；忠誠的」解，就相當於 loyal 或 faithful。

14. Be *full of life*.（要有精神。）

　　當你看到某人精神很好，容光煥發時，你就可以説：

> You are *full of life*.（你很有精神。）
> = You are *full of pep*.
> = You are *full of energy*.

> = You are *peppy*.
> = You are *energetic*.
> = You are *in high spirits*.

15. 美國人在舉例説明到「最後一點」時，常會用 at last 或 finally，
　　若是要強調「最後也是最重要的一點」時，會用 *finally and
　　most importantly*。

16. Treat others the way you'd like to be treated.

　　treat 在此做動詞，作「對待」解。這句話字面上的意義為
　　「以自己想要被對待的方式去對待別人。」

17

17. Friendship is a *two-way street*.

街道有兩種，一種叫做 one-way street「單行道」，一種叫做 two-way street「雙向道」。Friendship is *a two-way street*. 字面的意思是「友誼是雙向道」，引申爲「友誼是雙方面的；友誼是種互諒互讓的關係。」two-way street 引申爲「雙方面的」。*two-way street* 的英文解釋是 "a situation that can not or should not be handled by only one person"。

美國人常在婚禮致詞的場合中，對新人們説這些話：

Marriage is *a two-way street*.
（婚姻是雙方面的；婚姻是一種互諒互讓的關係。）
It requires give-and-take.（必須相互妥協。）
I wish both of you the greatest happiness.
（我祝你們擁有最大的幸福。）

17

18. Thanks *a bunch*!（非常感謝！）

bunch〔bʌntʃ〕*n.* 一捆；一束；一群

a bunch 原指「一捆；一束」，在日常生活中，常引申爲「很多」，或是「一群」，等於 a lot。

當你看到很多人的時候，你就説："Oh, there's *a bunch* of people over there."（噢，那裡有好多人。）

當你看到桌上有很多食物，你就可説："Oh, there's *a bunch* of food here."（噢，這裡有好多食物。）

你説話要説得像美國人，你就要常説 bunch 這個字。
當你要謝謝別人時，你就可以説：

Thanks *a bunch*!（非常感謝！）
= Thanks a lot!

【作文範例】

How to Make Friends

I remember my parents once told me how to be rich. *To my surprise*, I learned the way to wealth has nothing to do with money, diamonds, gold, or land. They told me that all I have to do is to obtain as much friendship as possible, because friends are real treasure. Their value is priceless.

As a result, I always enjoy making friends. *In fact*, I've even found out some secrets for making friends. *To begin with*, to make a friend, first be a friend. True friends never gossip nor judge others. *Second*, I love to share whatever I have and do things for others. *Actually*, I take joy in acts of kindness. *Third*, I make it a habit to laugh a lot so that people will know I like them. It's terrific to greet others with a smile. *Finally and most importantly*, I bear in mind the golden rule that I have to treat others the way I'd like to be treated. Friendship is a two-way street. Trust and respect are the keys.

To sum up, making true friends is not easy. *However*, the rewards are worth the efforts. If we can enjoy our friends and life, we'll be the richest and happiest people in the world.

17

【中文翻譯】

如何交朋友

　　我記得我父母曾經告訴我致富之道。令我驚訝的是，他們的致富之道，竟和金錢、鑽石、黃金或土地都毫無關係。他們告訴我，我只需要盡可能地獲得更多的友誼，因為朋友才是真正的財富。他們是無價的。

　　因此，我一直都很喜歡交朋友。事實上，我還甚至還找到一些交友的祕訣。首先，如果要交朋友，就必須先當個朋友。真正的好朋友，是不會說人閒話，或評斷他人。第二，我喜歡和人分享任何我所擁有的東西，我也樂於替他人處理事情。事實上，在做好事當中，我總能獲得喜悅。第三，我時常洋溢笑容，我把它當成一個習慣，這樣子人們就會知道我喜歡他們。用微笑打招呼，這感覺棒透了。最後也是最重要的是，我將這條金科玉律，銘記在心，那就是想要別人如何對待我，我就要如何對待別人。信任和尊重就是關鍵。

　　總之，交到真心的朋友並不容易。然而，努力所得到的報酬是值得的。如果我能享受和朋友在一起的美好時光，如果我能享受生命的話，我一定會是全世界最富有、最快樂的人。

17

18. Just Saying Thank You Is Not Enough
只說謝謝是不夠的

Ladies and gentlemen:
I'm glad you're here.
I've got a true story to tell.

各位先生，各位女士：
我很高興你們在這裏。
我要告訴你們一個真實的故事。

It's about a guy I know.
He had a foreign maid.
She served him for three
  years.

故事是關於一個我認識的人。
他有一位外籍女傭。
她侍候他三年。

This guy treated her well.
He gave her good pay.
He gave her a nice room to
  live in.

這個人對她很好。
他給她很好的薪水。
他給她很好的房間居住。

18

** ―――――――――――――――

glad〔glæd〕*adj.* 高興的   guy〔gaɪ〕*n.* 人；傢伙
foreign〔'fɔrɪn〕*adj.* 外國的   maid〔med〕*n.* 女傭
serve〔sɝv〕*v.* 服侍   treat〔trit〕*v.* 對待
pay〔pe〕*n.* 薪水；工資

He was sure he was a good boss.	他確信自己是一個好老闆。
On her final day, he took her to the airport.	在她要離開的最後一天,他帶她到機場。
As she was about to leave, he asked, *"Did I treat you well?"*	當她要離去的時候,他問她:「我待妳好嗎?」
To his dismay, the maid said, *"No."*	他嚇了一跳,女傭竟然說:「不好。」
"You never once said thank you to me."	「你從來沒對我說過一次謝謝。」
This guy thought she was ungrateful.	這個人覺得她不知道感激。
In reality, this guy is a kind person.	事實上,這個人是一個好人。
He is intelligent and well-educated.	他很聰明並受過良好教育。
But he seldom says thank you.	但是他很少說謝謝。

18

**———————————————

boss〔bɔs〕*n.* 老闆　　final〔'faɪn!〕*adj.* 最後的;最終的

be about to 即將　　dismay〔dɪs'me〕*n.* 驚慌

to one's dismay 令某人驚訝的是;令某人嚇一跳

ungrateful〔ʌn'gretfəl〕*adj.* 不感恩的;忘恩負義的

in reality 事實上　　intelligent〔ɪn'tɛlədʒənt〕*adj.* 聰明的

well-educated 受過良好教育的　　seldom〔'sɛldəm〕*adv.* 很少

Tragically, soon after, this guy suffered a stroke.

不幸地，不久之後，這個人中風。

Now, he can never speak again.

現在他再也不能說話。

He lost the joy of saying thank you to others.

他失去了對別人道謝的樂趣。

Saying thank you is a gift.

跟人道謝是一種恩典。

It costs nothing to say.

完全不用花錢。

It means everything to hear.

聽到道謝的話會很高興。

There is a lesson to be learned here.

從這故事可以學到一個教訓。

Never miss a chance to say "thank you."

絕對不要錯過說「謝謝」的機會。

Showing appreciation is better than giving gold.

表示感謝勝過給別人黃金。

18

Just saying thank you is not enough.

只說謝謝還不夠。

People say thank you every day.

人們每天都說謝謝。

You ***must*** really mean it.

你必須是真心的。

** ———————————

tragically〔'trædʒɪklɪ〕*adv.* 不幸地　　suffer〔'sʌfɚ〕*v.* 遭受；蒙受
stroke〔strok〕*n.* 中風　　gift〔gɪft〕*n.* 恩典；禮物
appreciation〔ə͵priʃɪ'eʃən〕*n.* 感激　　mean〔min〕*v.* 有…的意思

A thank you ***must*** come from the heart.

感謝必須發自內心。

You ***must*** say it sincerely.

你必須眞誠地說出來。

You ***must*** use body language.

你必須使用肢體語言。

Look at the person.

看著對方。

Smile.

微笑。

Nod your head.

點頭。

18

There are many other ways to say thank you.

還有許多其他的方式來表達謝意。

Just saying one single sentence is not enough.

只說單獨一個句子是不夠的。

You should say at least three sentences in a row to show your appreciation.

你應該至少連續說三個句子以上,來表示你的感謝。

** ———————————————

sincerely〔sɪn'sɪrlɪ〕*adv.* 眞誠地

body language 肢體語言　　nod〔nɑd〕*v.* 點(頭)

single〔'sɪŋgl̩〕*adj.* 單一的

at least 至少　　***in a row*** 連續地

Example one: If a stranger
  opens a door for you, say:
*Thank **you**.*
*How nice of **you**!*
You *are so thoughtful.*

第一個例子：如果有不認識
的人幫你開門，你可以說：
謝謝你。
你人真好！
你真體貼。

Or you can say:
Thanks.
You're nice.
You're very polite.

或者你可以說：
謝謝。
你真好。
你很有禮貌。

Example two: After someone
  gives you a ride, say:
Thanks for the ride.
You are a good driver.
I owe you one.

第二個例子：在某人送你一
程之後，你可以說：
謝謝你送我一程。
你很會開車。
我欠你一次人情。

I really appreciate it.
You've helped me a lot.
You've saved me a lot *of trouble.*

我真的很感激。
你幫我很多忙。
你幫我省掉很多麻煩。

18

** ————————

stranger〔'strendʒɚ〕 *n.* 陌生人；不認識的人
thoughtful〔'θɔtfəl〕 *adj.* 體貼的
polite〔pə'laɪt〕 *adj.* 有禮貌的   ride〔raɪd〕 *n.* 搭乘
give sb. a ride 讓某人搭便車   owe〔o〕 *v.* 欠
appreciate〔ə'priʃɪˌet〕 *v.* 為…表示感激   save〔sev〕 *v.* 省去

Take care.	保重。
Drive safely.	開車要注意安全。
Catch you tomorrow.	明天見。

Example three: **When someone gives you a present like a watch or a pen, *you can say:***	第三個例子：當某人送你一個禮物，像是手錶或筆，你可以說：
Thank you so much.	非常感謝你。
It's wonderful.	這個禮物太棒了。
It's what I always wanted.	這是我一直很想要的東西。

18

It's perfect.	這個禮物太完美了。
How did you know?	你怎麼知道這是我想要的東西？
It's just what I needed.	這正是我需要的東西。

You can also say:	你也可以說：
What can I say?	我能說什麼呢？
I'm speechless.	我說不出話來。
You shouldn't have.	你不應該這麼做的。

** ─────────

take care 保重　　safely〔'seflɪ〕*adv.* 安全地
wonderful〔'wʌndɚfəl〕*adj.* 美好的
perfect〔'pɝfɪkt〕*adj.* 完美的
speechless〔'spitʃlɪs〕*adj.* 說不出話的

I really don't deserve it.	我真是不敢當。
You're too good to me.	你對我太好了。
I really like this gift.	我真的很喜歡這個禮物。
It's very useful.	這東西很有用。
I was going to buy one.	我本來要去買的。
You read my mind.	你知道我在想什麼。

Example four: When in a
restaurant, say to your waiter:

第四個例子：當你在餐廳的時
候，你可以對你的服務生說：

Great *service.*	你服務得很好。
*You did a **great** job.*	你做得很好。
You're very professional.	你非常專業。

18

*Tell the cook it was **great**.*	請轉告廚師這餐飯很棒。
I really enjoyed the meal.	我真的很喜歡這一餐飯。
I'll be back again.	我還會再來光顧的。

** ————————————

deserve〔dɪˈzɝv〕*v.* 應得　　***read** one's **mind*** 知道某人在想什麼
waiter〔ˈwetɚ〕*n.* 服務生
professional〔prəˈfɛʃənḷ〕*adj.* 專業的
cook〔kʊk〕*n.* 廚師　　meal〔mil〕*n.* 一餐飯

Example five: If someone
　lends a helping hand, say:
Thank you for your kindness.
I'm indebted to you.
How can I repay you?

第五個例子：如果某人幫你
忙，你可以說：
謝謝你的好意。
我很感激你。
我該如何報答你？

You're a godsend.
I'm very grateful.
Thank you from the bottom of
　my heart.

你來得正是時候。
我非常感激。
我打從心底感謝你。

Thanks a lot.
That was nice of you.
I'm forever in your debt.

非常謝謝你。
你人真好。
我永遠感謝你。

18

** ────────────

lend a helping hand 助一臂之力（= *give a helping hand*）
kindness（ˋkaɪndnɪs）*n.* 親切；好意
indebted（ɪnˋdɛtɪd）*adj.* 感激的　　repay（rɪˋpe）*v.* 報答
godsend（ˋgɑd͵sɛnd）*n.* 意外獲得的心愛之物；天賜之物；意外的好運
grateful（ˋgretfəl）*adj.* 感激的
bottom（ˋbɑtəm）*n.* 底部　　forever（fəˋɛvə）*adv.* 永遠地
debt（dɛt）*n.* 債　　***be in*** one's ***debt*** 感謝某人

Ladies and gentlemen:
A thank you says you care.
It says you are mature and aware.
It shows you have a good education.

Now go out and practice.
Say thank you to the people
  around you.
Say thanks in many different ways.

Practice on friends, strangers,
  or any deserving people.
Remember a little bit goes a long way.
The more you thank people,
  the happier you'll be.

I'm grateful for your attention.
You've been wonderful today.
I had a good time and I hope
  you did too.

各位先生，各位女士：
一句感謝代表你在意。
這代表你成熟又懂事。
這代表你受過良好的教育。

現在就出去練習。
對你周遭的人說謝謝。

用許多不同的方式說謝謝。

練習或實踐在朋友、陌生人，
或是任何值得的人身上。
記得，一點點就很有用。
你愈感謝人，你將會愈
快樂。

我很感激你們的聆聽。
你們今天都很棒。
我很快樂，我希望你們也很
快樂。

18

**

say〔se〕v. 表示；說   care〔kɛr〕v. 在意
mature〔mə'tjur, mə'tʃur〕adj. 成熟的
aware〔ə'wɛr〕adj. 察覺到的   show〔ʃo〕v. 顯示
practice〔'præktɪs〕v. 練習；實踐   deserving〔dɪ'zɝvɪŋ〕adj. 值得的
bit〔bɪt〕n. 一點點   *go a long way* 大有用處；很管用
attention〔ə'tɛnʃən〕n. 注意   *have a good time* 過得很快樂

【背景説明】

這篇演講稿太重要了，如果你生活想過得愉快，你就得學習感恩，學會說感謝的話，在美國尤其重要，你愈會説 Thank you.，你的人生旅途就愈順利。這篇演講背完之後，你就可以隨時把演講中的故事説給別人聽。

這篇演講稿強調：

①光説 Thank you. 不夠，你必須眞誠，發自内心，而且要有肢體語言，對別人説 Thank you. 的時候，要：Look at the person.　Smile.　Nod your head. 因爲大家都説 Thank you. 你和別人説得一樣，等於没有説。

②光説一句不夠，要至少説三句以上，才表現出你的感謝之意，説愈多句愈好，「演講式英語」眞有趣，你不只在學英文，你還在學説話、學做人。

這篇文章有五個教你感謝別人的例子，這五個例子中的會話，你背起來要快、要大聲，能夠在一口氣背完，你就永遠不會忘記了。如 Example three 中的 15 句話，你要訓練自己，能在 12 秒内背完，在「一口氣英語②」中，有詳細的説明。這五個例子，背得很熟，變成直覺後，整篇演講稿才可以背得下來。

18

1. He gave her good pay.

> 這句話也可以説成 He gave her **a good salary**.
>
> 要注意 pay 之前不加冠詞 a。這句話的意思是「他給她好的薪水。」

2. As she was about to leave, he asked, *"Did I treat you well?"*

　　ask 是授與動詞，後要接間接受詞和直接受詞，但是
ask 的間接受詞可以省略。這句話也可說成：…he asked
her, *"Did I treat you well?"*

3. *To his dismay*, the maid said, "No."

　　（他嚇了一跳，女傭竟然說：「不。」）

> To his dismay 這句成語美國人常說，如：
>
> *To my dismay*, he didn't show up.
> （真嚇了我一跳，他居然沒出現。）
> *To my dismay*, she doesn't look happy.
> （真嚇了我一跳，她看起來不快樂。）
>
> dismay 的主要意思是「驚慌」，to *one's* dismay 的
> 主要意思是「令某人驚慌」，就是「嚇了某人一跳」。

18

4. This guy thought she was ungrateful.

　　這句話字面的意思是：「這個人認為她不知道感激。」也
就是：「這個人認為她不懂得感恩。」

5. Tragically, soon after, this guy suffered a stroke.

　　soon after 是 soon after *the incident* 的省略，等於
a short time after「在…之後不久」。

例：He arrived *soon after* three. （他在三點過後不久就到了。）

　　在前面句意明確時，after 後的名詞可以省略。

例：She got married last year, but *soon after*, she got
a divorce. （她去年結婚，但不久之後，她就離婚了。）

　　soon after 在這裏是 soon after *the wedding* 的省略。

美國人說「中風」的講法，和生病不同，「他中風了」，
美國人說成： ① He suffered a stroke.

② He had a stroke.

「他生病了。」的講法有：

① He suffers from illness.

② He is sick.

③ He is ill.

④ He is not well.

6. It costs nothing to say.

這句話是 It costs *you* nothing to say. 的省略。

cost 的意思是「花費」，這句話的意思是「它並不花你任何錢。」

7. It *means everything* to hear.

這句話字面上的意思是「聽到了這件事，非常有意義」，
引申為「聽到這件事很開心。」也可以說成：

It *means the world* to me to hear that.

= I'm so happy to hear that.

It *means everything* to hear. 不可說成 *It means everything to hear it.*（誤）

因為 to hear 修飾 everything，被不定詞所修飾的名詞或代名詞，
是不定詞意義上的受詞，所以，不需要再重複文法上的受詞。

18

8. Never miss a chance / to say / "thank you."

= Never miss a chance / to say thank you.

…say "thank you" 和 …say thank you 句意完全相同，
用雙引號只是為了強調 thank you 這兩個字。這句話說的時
候，要注意這兩句話的停頓不同。

9. ***I owe you*** one.

> 　　字面的意思是「我欠你一次」，引申為「我欠你一次人情。」這是表示感謝的話。當別人幫了你的忙，你就可以說 I owe you one. 句中的 one 是指 a favor。
>
> 　　也可以加強語氣說：
>
> ***I owe you*** a lot. (我欠你很多；我非常感謝你。)
> ***I owe you*** big. (我欠你很多；我很感謝你。)
> ***I owe you*** a big favor. (我欠你一個大人情。)
>
> ***I owe you*** big time. (我欠你很多；我非常感謝你。)
> ***I owe you*** so much. (我欠你非常多；我很感謝你。)
> ***I owe you*** more than words can say.
> (我欠你多到言語無法表達；感激不盡。)
>
> 　　【big time 字面的意思是「快樂時光」，I owe you big time.
> 　　「我欠你快樂時光」，引申為「我欠你很多。」】
>
> 　　講 ***I owe you***. (我虧欠你。) 之類的話，非常討好別人，每天都不要忘記說幾句，會讓你的修養變得更好，別人快樂，你也快樂。

18

10. I really appreciate it.

> ap｜preci｜ate
> ―――――――――
> to ｜price ｜ v.
>
> 　　從字根上分析，表示「估價」，引申為「重視」，再引申為「賞識」，所以受詞通常非人，**不可接人表示感激**。
>
> ***I really appreciate it***. 在美國人的思想當中，是「我非常重視這件事情。」如：I appreciate your kindness. (我很感激你的好意。)
>
> 　　為什麼中國人不會用 appreciate 這個字呢？因為中國人的思想是感激某人，而美國人是「賞識」某事。中文說「謝謝你的幫助」，英文要說成：

I *appreciate* your help.

= I *thank* you *for* your help.

要記住，appreciate 後接非人，thank 後面要先接人。

反正，要常説 I appreciate it. 或 I really appreciate it. 表示感謝。

【中翻英】 我感謝你。

I *appreciate you.* (和中文意思不符)

I appreciate it. (正)

I appreciate you. 的意思是「我很賞識你。」(= I *value you.*)

11. *Take care*.

Take care. 就是 Take care *of yourself*. 的省略。

這句話很常用，美國人在道別時常説 Take care. 就是像中文的「好好照顧自己。」意思就是「保重。」

A: I'm leaving. (我要走了。)

B: *Take care*. (保重。)

18

12. Catch you tomorrow.

這句話的字面的意思是「明天要抓你」，引申爲「明天見。」是美國人的幽默用語。你也可以説：

Catch you later. (待會兒見。)

= I'll catch you later.

或是説 I'll try to catch you later. (我會儘量想辦法去見你。) Catch you later. 也許是待會兒見，也許是明天，或一年以後見面，講這句話的意思是，希望能夠很快見到你。

13. You shouldn't have.

這句話是假設法的過去式，是 You shouldn't have *done that.* 的省略，表示你過去不該這樣做。

14. You're too good *to me*.

這句話的意思是「你對我太好了。」這裏的 to 是介系詞，不是 too~to + V. 的用法。

美國人也常說 You're too kind to me.

15. When in a restaurant, say to *your waiter*.

在美國的餐廳裡，waiter（服務生）主要是靠小費過活，在好的餐廳，一天小費有三、四百塊美金，在餐廳裡，會劃分區域服務，你坐的位子，就是那個區域的專屬 waiter 替你服務，所以美國人習慣說 *your waiter*, my waiter 之類的話。自己的醫生、律師，他們都會說 my doctor、my lawyer。

18

16. I'll be back again.（我會再回來。）
    = I'll come back again.

17. *I'm indebted to you*.

indebted 原本的意思是「對~負債的」，這句話字面的意思是「我對你負債」，表示「我很感激你。」

由於 *I'm indebted to you*. 這句話太常使用了，所以 indebted 已經變成純粹的形容詞，表示「感謝的」。

這句話也可以加長說成：

I'm indebted to you for your kindness.

（我非常感謝你的好意。）

18. *You're a godsend.*

> 字面的意思是「你是上帝派來的」，也可引申爲「你來得
> 正是時候。」
>
> > *You're a godsend.*
> > = Thank God you're here.
> > = You showed up just at the right time.
>
> 當你急需要幫助的時候，你的朋友突然出現，你就可以
> 說 *You're a godsend.*（你眞是上帝派來的；你來得正是時候。）
>
> 在字典上 godsend 的意思是「意外獲得的心愛之物」，和
> 這裡的用法不一樣，要特別注意。

19. I'm forever in your debt.

I'm in your debt. 有兩個意思：① 我欠你的債。② 我感謝你。

I'm forever in your debt. 意思是「我永遠感謝你」，在這
裡當然不是指「我永遠欠你的債」。

18

I'm in your debt. 等於 I'm indebted to you. 都表示「我
很感謝你。」

20. Practice on friends, strangers, or any deserving people.

這句話是 Practice *saying thank you* on friends, …的省
略。practice 有「練習」和「實踐」的意思，這句話的意思就
是「練習或實踐在朋友、陌生人，或是任何值得的人身上。」

21. A little bit goes a long way.

這句話的意思是「一點點就很有用。」

美國人很喜歡說 *go a long way* 這類的話，比如在落後國
家，你可以說：

Here, a little money *goes a long way*.

（在這裡一點小錢就很有用。）

【作文範例】

How to Show Your Appreciation

Saying thank you is very important. It is not only a way to express appreciation, but also an important social skill that helps people to get along better. *However*, the words "thank you" have become so commonplace that they have lost some of their meaning. Too often people say these words without any feeling. It is just a habit. *Therefore*, it is not enough to just say thank you; you must really mean it. If you really want to express your thanks, you must speak sincerely from your heart.

In addition to speaking sincerely, there are other ways to show that you truly mean what you say. One is to use body language. When you thank someone, look at him, smile and nod your head. Another is to say more than just "thank you." Try to say at least three sentences, including a compliment or a comment. *For example*, when someone gives you a gift say, "Thank you so much. It's wonderful. You have excellent taste." *Above all*, never miss a chance to say thank you, because a thank you says you care. The more you thank people, the happier you'll be.

18

【中文翻譯】

如何表達謝意

　　說謝謝是非常重要的。這不僅是一種表示感激的方式，也是一項重要的社交技巧，它可以幫助人們相處得更融洽。然而，「謝謝」這兩個字已經變成如此地普通，以致於喪失了一些意義。人們常常說這些話，不帶任何感情。說這些話只是一種習慣。因此，只說謝謝是不夠的；你必須是真心的。如果你真的想要表達你的感謝，你就必須從心中真誠地說出謝謝。

　　除了真誠地說出口之外，還有其他方式可以表現出，你是真心地說出這句話。一種是使用肢體語言。當你感謝某人時，要看著他、微笑，並點頭。另一個方法就是，不能只光說「謝謝」兩個字。試著至少說三句，包括稱讚或表達你的意見。例如，當某人送你禮物時要說：「非常感謝你。這東西太棒了。你的品味真好。」最重要的是，絕對不要錯過說謝謝的機會，因為一句謝謝表示你在意。你愈感謝別人，你將會愈快樂。

19. A Wedding Address
婚禮致詞

Mr. and Mrs. Michael Wang,
distinguished guests,
ladies and gentlemen:

王麥可夫婦，
各位貴賓，
各位先生及女士：

My name is Samuel.
I'm a good friend of both parties.
It's a great honor for me to be here
　to address you.

我叫撒姆爾。
我是雙方的好友。
能在此向你們致詞是我莫大的
榮幸。

Today is a joyous occasion.
We are here to witness the union of
　two wonderful people.
We are gathered here to celebrate the
　wedding of Michael and Sherry.

今天是個快樂的日子。
我們在此見證這對佳人的結合。

我們齊聚於此慶祝麥可和雪莉
的婚禮。

Michael, *the groom*, you are an ace.
Sherry, *the bride*, you are a gem.
You go together like ducks and
　water.

新郎，麥可，你是一流的人才。
新娘，雪莉，妳是很有價值的人。
你們在一起就像如魚得水。

19

**

distinguished〔dɪ'stɪŋgwɪʃt〕*adj.* 傑出的　　　***distinguished guests*** 貴賓
party〔'pɑrtɪ〕*n.* 一方　　honor〔'ɑnɚ〕*n.* 榮幸
address〔ə'drɛs〕*n.* 演講　*v.* 向～演講　joyous〔'dʒɔɪəs〕*adj.* 喜悅的
occasion〔ə'keʒən〕*n.* 場合　　witness〔'wɪtnɪs〕*v.* 見證
union〔'junjən〕*n.* 結合　　wedding〔'wɛdɪŋ〕*n.* 婚禮
groom〔grum〕*n.* 新郎　　ace〔es〕*n.* 一流的人才
bride〔braɪd〕*n.* 新娘　　gem〔dʒɛm〕*n.* 寶石；有價值的人

You two are compatible.	你們兩個人很相配。
You're suitable for each other.	你們彼此適合。
You belong together.	你們兩個很合適。
You two are the perfect couple.	你們倆是最完美的一對。
You're a match made in heaven.	你們是天造地設的一對。
You were made for each other.	你們是天生一對。
Now, ladies and gentlemen:	現在，各位先生及女士：
Let's raise our glasses.	讓我們舉杯。
Let's propose a toast to the newlyweds.	讓我們爲這對新人乾杯。
We wish you health.	祝你們健康。
We wish you wealth.	祝你們發財。
We wish you a bunch of children.	祝你們兒孫滿堂。
Be happy.	快快樂樂。
Enjoy your life.	享受人生。
Live long and prosper.	長壽且好運連連。
Congratulations!	恭禧你們！
Best wishes to you both!	向你們獻上我最誠摯的祝福！
May you live happily ever after!	祝你們從此過著幸福快樂的日子！

19

** ——————————————

compatible〔kəm'pætəbl̩〕*adj.* 適合的　　suitable〔'sutəbl̩〕*adj.* 適合的
belong〔bə'lɔŋ〕*v.* 屬於；適合　　couple〔'kʌpl̩〕*n.* 一對（= *match*）
be made for 完全適合　　raise〔rez〕*v.* 舉起
propose a toast to 爲～乾杯　　newlyweds〔'njulɪ‚wɛdz〕*n. pl.* 新婚夫婦
a bunch of 一群　　prosper〔'prɑspɚ〕*v.* 好運；順利；成功
best wishes 最誠摯的祝福　　*ever after* 從此

【背景説明】

　　一般美國人的習慣，通常是在早上或中午，在教堂、法院，或是在家裡，舉行婚禮。大都是晚上宴客，每個人都可以上台演講，或是被迫演講，你背了這篇演講，你就天不怕、地不怕，胸有成竹了。這篇演講稿很幽默，可以説是美國人結婚演講的公式，你一定要背熟。

1. It's a great honor for me to be here to ***address*** you.
　　address〔ə'drɛs〕*n.* 演講　*v.* 向～演講

　　　　address 當「住址」解釋時，唸成〔'ædrɛs〕，在這裡，***address*** 是作「向～演講」解（= *speak to* ），***address*** 通常用在比較正式的場合，像 The president ***addressed*** the nation.（總統向全國發表演講。）

2. Today is a joyous occasion.
　　　　　凡是升官、發財、生日、慶功宴，美國人都常説這句話。
　　joyous〔'dʒɔɪəs〕*adj.* 快樂的（= *happy* ）
　　occasion〔ə'keʒən〕*n.* 場合；特殊的時刻（= *event* = *special time* ）

19

　　　　這句話字面的意思是「今天是一個快樂的場合」，也就是「今天是一個快樂的日子。」

3. We are here to ***witness*** the union of two wonderful people.
　　witness〔'wɪtnɪs〕*v.* 見證（= *see personally* ）
　　union〔'junjən〕*n.* 結合

　　　　這句話的意思是「我們在這裡見證這對佳人的結合」，神職人員或法官也常講這句話。

4. You go together ***like ducks and water***.

> 　　　　這句話的意思是「你們在一起，就像鴨子和水一樣」，鴨子和水，鴨子喜歡在水中游，比喻二者分不開，所以這句話引申爲「你們在一起就像如魚得水。」

> 當你看到一對男女朋友，或一群志同道合的好朋友，
> 你就可以説："You go together *like ducks and water*."

在字典有一個成語，a duck to water（自然地；輕而易舉地），
不適合用在本句中。

5. *You belong together*.

這句話字面的意思是「你們適合在一起」，就是「你們兩個很合適。」你看到一對男女朋友，你就可以説：

You two are compatible.（你們兩人很相配。）
You're suitable for each other.（你們彼此很適合。）
You belong together.（你們兩個很合適。）

這些話在會話中很常用到。

6. You're a match *made in heaven*.

這句話字面的意思是「你們是在天上製造的一對」，
也就是「你們是天造地設的一對。」

19

7. You *were made for* each other.

be made for（完全適合），這個成語用得很多，比如
説：This house *is made for* you.（這棟房子很適合你。）
看到一個人，男生或女生，穿了漂亮的衣服，你就可以
説：These clothes *are made for* you.（這衣服很適合你。）

8. Let's propose a toast to the *newlyweds*.

> newlyweds（'njulɪ,wɛdz）*n.pl.* 新婚夫婦，這個字拆開
> 來爲 newly 和 wed（wɛd）*v.* 結婚（= *marry*），美國人把
> 新婚夫婦叫做「新結婚的」，newly-wedded 當變成名詞後，
> 再變成複數，即成爲 *newlyweds* 這個字，複數表示是新婚夫
> 婦兩個人。這句話的意思是「讓我們向這對新人敬酒。」

9. Live long and prosper.

prosper〔'prɑspɚ〕v. 好運；順利；成功

> 有些美國人見到人打招呼，或再見的時候，喜歡説：
> Live long and prosper. 這句話來自電視影集 "Star Trek"
> （星艦迷航記），現在，在電視廣告上，也常出現這句話。
> 任何時候都可以和好朋友説：Be happy. (快快樂樂。)
> Enjoy your life. (享受人生。) *Live long and prosper.*
> （長壽且好運連連。）

10. Best wishes to you both!

　　美國人常説 *Best wishes.* 是由 I wish you the best.
轉變而來，表示「我祝福你好運連連。」當別人生日、結
婚、搬家、換工作、告別、生病，或甚至遭遇到不幸，
你都可以説 *Best wishes.*

【例】 A: I'm looking for a new job. (我要換工作了。)
　　　 B: *Best wishes.* (祝你好運。)
　　　 A: I'm going on a trip tomorrow. (明天我要去旅行。)
　　　 B: *Best wishes.* (祝你好運。)
　　　 A: My mom is in the hospital. (我媽生病住院了。)
　　　 B: *Best wishes.* (祝她早日康復。)
　　　 A: Today is my birthday. (今天是我生日。)
　　　 B: *Best wishes.* (生日快樂。)

　　Best wishes. 可説是萬用句，不管別人説什麼，你幾乎
都可以用得到。*Best wishes* to you both! 的意思是「祝福
你們兩位！」

11. May you live happily *ever after*!

　　ever after「從此；從此以後一直」，在童話故事裡，
典型的結局是 They lived happily *ever after*. (他們從此
以後一直過著幸福快樂的日子。) 這句話的意思是「祝你
們從此過著幸福快樂的日子！」

19

【作文範例】

Wedding Congratulations

Dear Michael and Sherry,

I would like to congratulate you on your wedding. It was a joy to witness the union of two such wonderful people. Michael, you are an ace. Sherry, you are a gem. You two are so compatible that you go together like ducks and water. I am sure that you were made for each other.

I want to wish you good health, wealth and a bunch of children. May you enjoy your life together and live happily ever after.

Best wishes to you both,

Samuel

19

20. Farewell Speech by Host
送別演講

Ladies and gentlemen:　　各位先生，各位女士：
It's hard for me to say this.　　我很難把這些話說出來。
I've got a lump in my throat.　　我難過得說不出話來。

We all know Andy is about　　我們都知道安迪就要離開了。
　　to leave.
We're all sad to see him go.　　我們都捨不得看他走。
We don't want him to go.　　我們不想要他走。

He belongs here.　　他屬於這裡。
This is his home.　　這裡就是他的家。
He should stay here forever.　　他應該永遠待在這裡。

Andy is fun to be with.　　和安迪在一起很有趣。
He's a humorous guy.　　他很幽默。
He really cracks us up.　　他真的會使我們開懷大笑。

20

** ——————————————

hard〔hɑrd〕*adj.* 困難的　　lump〔lʌmp〕*n.* 塊
throat〔θrot〕*n.* 喉嚨　　belong〔bə'lɔŋ〕*v.* 屬於
humorous〔'hjumərəs〕*adj.* 幽默的　　guy〔gaɪ〕*n.* 人；傢伙
crack〔kræk〕*v.* 使破裂　　***crack sb. up*** 使某人捧腹大笑

***Andy is always helpful*.** 安迪總是樂於幫忙。
He always chips in. 他經常伸出援手。
He pulls his weight. 他盡他的本份。

***Andy is kind*.** 安迪很有愛心。
He's considerate. 他很體貼。
He really cares. 他真心關懷周圍的人。

He's like a member of the 他就像我們家裏的一份子。
 ***family*.**
He's also our friend. 他也是我們的朋友。
He's our confidant. 他是我們推心置腹的好朋友。

We work together. 我們一起工作。
We learn together. 我們一起學習。
We play together. 我們一起遊樂。

20

**　　　**

chip〔tʃɪp〕*n.* 籌碼　*v.* 下賭注
chip in 集資；共同出錢；共同幫助
weight〔wet〕*n.* 重量；重擔
pull* one's *weight 盡某人自己的本分
considerate〔kənˈsɪdərɪt〕*adj.* 體貼的
care〔kɛr〕*v.* 關懷；關心　member〔ˈmɛmbɚ〕*n.* 成員
confidant〔ˌkɑnfəˈdænt〕*n.* 知己；密友

Sometimes we have different opinions.	有時候我們意見不同。
We don't always agree.	我們不見得總是看法一致。
In the end it always works out.	但最後都能化解歧見。
Talking isn't his game.	他不善於言辭。
Listening is his middle name.	他很會傾聽別人說話。
He's a problem solver.	他很會解決問題。
We're counting our blessings.	我們要想想我們有多幸福。
He came along at the right time.	他出現得正是時候。
We were lucky to have him.	我們很幸運能有他。
Andy, we know you have to go.	安迪，我們知道你必須離開。
Your time with us is done.	你在我們這裡工作的期間已經屆滿。
All good things must come to an end.	天下沒有不散的筵席。

20

** ——————————————————

not always 不一定　　agree〔ə'gri〕*v.* 意見一致
in the end 到最後　　*work out*（問題）獲得解決
middle name 專長；個性；特點
solver〔'sɑlvɚ〕*n.* 解決問題的人
count〔kaʊnt〕*v.* 計算　　blessing〔'blɛsɪŋ〕*n.* 幸運的事
count one's blessings 想想自己有多幸運　　*come along* 出現
done〔dʌn〕*adj.* 結束的　　*come to an end* 結束
All good things must come to an end.【諺】天下沒有不散的筵席。

We all agree.	我們意見一致。
We all feel the same way.	我們都有共識。
I know I speak for everyone.	我知道我代表大家講這些話。

Keep in touch.	和我們保持聯繫。
E-mail us.	和我們通電子郵件。
Let us know how you're doing.	讓我們知道你的情況。

Pick up the phone.	拿起電話筒。
Give us a ring.	打電話給我們。
Give us a jingle.	撥電話給我們。

Andy, *you have an open invitation*.	安迪,我們隨時歡迎你。
Come back whenever you want.	不論什麼時候,想回來就回來。
You're always welcome.	我們隨時歡迎你。

20

** ─────────────────

feel the same way 有同樣的感覺　　*speak for* 代表…講話
keep in touch 保持聯繫　　e-mail〔'i,mel〕*v.* 傳電子郵件給～
pick up 拿起　　phone〔fon〕*n.* 聽筒
ring〔rɪŋ〕*n.* 鈴聲;電話(= *telephone call*)
jingle〔'dʒɪŋgl̩〕*n.* 叮噹聲;電話(= *telephone call*)
give sb. a jingle 打電話給某人(= *give sb. a ring* = *give sb. a call*)

Come for a visit.	來這裡看看我們。
Stay as long as you like.	想待多久就待多久。
The door is always open.	大門隨時都為你開著。
No one can take your place.	沒人能取代你。
No one can fill your shoes.	沒人能代替你的職位。
You're one of a kind.	你是獨一無二的。
You're irreplaceable.	你是不可取代的。
How can we do without you?	我們怎麼能沒有你？
Who will we turn to?	我們該去找誰來幫忙我們呢？
You are such a part of us.	你是我們不能缺少的一部份。
We'll all miss you.	我們都會想念你。
We'll think of you always.	我們將經常想到你。

20

**

take one's place 取代某人
fill one's shoes 接替某人的位置或工作
one of a kind 獨一無二的（ = *one-of-a-kind* = *unique* ）
irreplaceable〔͵ɪrɪ'plesəbḷ〕*adj.* 不可取代的
turn to 向～求助（ = *go to* ）

No more tears.	大家不要再流淚了。
We know you'll do well.	我們知道你將過得很好。
Our prayers go with you.	我們的祝福與你同在。
Be well.	要健康。
Stay well.	要保持健康。
Make your mark.	要轟轟烈烈地做一番大事。
A toast to Andy.	敬安迪一杯。
Bravo.	你太棒了。
Hip, hip, hooray!	萬歲，萬歲，萬萬歲！

**

tear〔tɪr〕*n.* 眼淚
do well 過得很好；表現好
prayers〔prɛrz〕*n.pl.* 祈禱；祝福
well〔wɛl〕*adj.* 健康的　　stay〔ste〕*v.* 保持
make one's mark 成名；成功
(= *become successful and influential*)
toast〔tost〕*n.* 乾杯　　bravo〔'brɑvo〕*n.* 好極了！（喝采聲）
hip〔hɪp〕*n.* 喝采、歡呼聲
hooray〔hu're〕*n.* 表高興或讚許的歡呼聲
Hip, hip, hooray! 萬歲，萬歲，萬萬歲！
(= *Hip, hip, hurrah!*)

20

【背景説明】

　　這篇演講稿太有用了。凡是你的朋友要離開，你都可以用得到。美國人的習慣和中國人一樣，當哪一個人要離開了，都會舉行一個聚會，美國人稱做 going-away party 或 farewell party。在公司，有人離職或退休，或者有人要出遠門，他們都會舉行 party，藉此機會來聚一下，聯絡感情。

1. It's ***hard*** for me to say this.

　　也可以説成：It's ***difficult*** for me to say this. *或*
It's ***not easy*** for me to say this. *這句話的意思就是*：
「我很難把話說出來。」this *是指* this talk *或* this speech。

2. I've got ***a lump*** in my throat.

> 　　這句話的字面意思是：「在我喉嚨裏有一塊東西。」
> lump〔lʌmp〕*n.* 塊，a lump *是指*「一塊東西」，*如* a lump of sugar（一塊方糖）、a lump of meat（一塊肉）、a lump of mud（一塊泥土）。
>
> 　　這句話引申爲：「我傷心得說不出話來，想要哭。」*就像中文的*「我哽咽欲泣。」
>
> 　【例】　A: That was a touching speech, wasn't it?
> 　　　　　　（剛剛那眞是感人的演說，對不對？）
> 　　　　　B: Yeah, ***I've got a lump in my throat*** now.
> 　　　　　　That was fantastic.
> 　　　　　　（對啊，我現在感動得說不出話來。那個演講眞棒。）

20

3. We're all ***sad*** to see him go.

> 　　這句話字面意思是：「看到他走，我們全都很傷心。」
> 引申爲：「我們都捨不得看他走。」在中文裏的「捨不得」，
> 翻成英文，在很多地方，都可以用 sad。

中文：我捨不得走。
英文：I feel *sad* to leave.
中文：他捨不得用錢。
英文：He is *sad* to spend his money.
中文：他捨不得離開學校。
英文：He feels *sad* to leave school.

4. He belongs here.

　　這句話字面的意思是：「他屬於這裡」，引申為「他應該待在這裡。」美國人喜歡用 belong 這個字，當他們看到一個不喜歡的人，就會說：He doesn't belong here.（他不應該待在這裡；他是多餘的。）

5. Andy is fun *to be with*.

　　不可說成：*Andy is fun to be with him.*（誤）

　　不定詞片語，在句中已經有意義上的受詞時，就不可以再有文法上的受詞，所以 with 後就不可再用 him。

　　這句話的意思就是「和安迪在一起很有趣。」也可以說成： Andy is a fun person *to be with*.

　　平常和美國人在一起的時候，你可以說：You're a fun guy. 或 You're fun to be with. 他聽了會很高興。

20

6. He really *cracks* us *up*.

　　crack 這個字的主要意思是「使破裂；使爆裂」，如：玻璃遇到熱水就會爆裂（crack）。

crack sb. up 使某人大笑【源自使某人嘴巴裂開，發出爆裂聲】（= *make sb. laugh a lot*）

　　這句話的意思就是，「他真的會使我們開懷大笑。」

7. *He always chips in.*

> chip 這個字，主要意思是「一片」，像 potato chips
> （洋芋片），當動詞時，主要意思是「把東西弄成一片一片」。
>
> chip〔tʃɪp〕*n.* 碎片；籌碼　*v.* 切為小片；用籌碼下賭注
> *chip in* 集資；湊錢【這個成語源自在撲克牌賭博時，大家用籌碼下賭注】
>
> 　　*He always chips in.* 的字面意思是「他總是把籌碼丟
> 進來」，引申為「他總是樂於幫忙。」
>
> 　　當別人幫助你的時候，你就可以説：Thank you for
> *chipping in.*（謝謝你助我一臂之力。）
>
> 　　當大家一起開車出去旅行，有人出停車費、有人出油
> 錢，有人買零食，這就是很典型的 "chip in"，英文解釋
> 就是：*share in giving money or help*（共同出錢或出力）。
>
> 【例】　A: Here is five bucks for gas.（這是五塊錢的油錢。）
> 　　　　B: Thank you for *chipping in.*（謝謝你的資助。）
>
> > 美國人一般的習慣，一起出去旅行，要付油錢時，大
> > 家會平均分攤，車子的主人通常不付，因為他擁有車，並
> > 且要開車。上面對話的意思是説：油錢如果是二十元，每
> > 人分攤了五元，這個動作就是 chip in。

8. *He pulls his weight.*

20

pull one's weight 盡某人的本分（= *do one's share*）

　　這個成語源自於「拉自己那份貨物的重量」，這句話的
字面意思是「他拉自己那一份的重量」，引申為「他盡他的
本分。」（= *He does his share. He does what he is
supposed to do.*）

　　這個成語美國人常説。當別人稱讚你的時候，你就可
以謙虛地説：I'm just *pulling my weight.*（我只是盡我的
本分。）

【例】 A: You are a hard worker. (你很認真工作。)

B: I just *pull my weight*. (我只是盡我的本分。)

你也可以加強語氣地說: I just *pull my own weight*.
(我只是盡我自己的本分。)

9. He really cares. (他真心關心別人。)

這句話是 He really cares *about people around him*. 的省略。

10. He's our *confidant*.

confidant〔͵kɑnfəˋdænt, ˋkɑnfə͵dænt〕*n.* (男性) 密友;
(男性) 知己【唸起來怪,是由於源自法文】

這個字有兩個拼法,發音相同,女性的密友,叫做
confidante。記住字尾有 e 的是女性密友。

例如,你看到你的男性的好朋友,你就可以說: You're my
confidant. (你是我的知己。) 你看到女性的好朋友,就說:
You're my *confidante*. (妳是我的好朋友。)

11. He's like a member of the family. (他像是我們家裡的一份子。)

20

美國人會把好朋友當成是家裡的一份子,美國人常說:
A man's home is his castle. (家就是城堡,不容他人侵入。)
但是,對好朋友,他們習慣把朋友帶到家裏來住,他們會說:
Please make yourself at home. (請不要拘束。) 把這裏當
做你自己家一樣,你可以隨便到冰箱拿東西吃。

你對你的好朋友,就可以說:

You're like my brother. (你像我的兄弟。)
You're like a member of the family.
(你就像是家裡的一份子。)【the family 也可說成 my family】
We're like brothers. (我們像兄弟一樣。)

12. Talking isn't *his game*.

game 的基本意思是「遊戲」，某人常玩的遊戲，就是他的專長。這句話的字面意思是「講話並不是他玩的遊戲」，引申爲「說話不是他的專長」，也就是「他不善言辭。」

【例如】 Selling cars is *my game*. (賣車是我的專長。)

　　　　 Teaching English is *his game*.(教英文是他的專長。)

13. Listening is his *middle name*.

美國人的名字有 first name、*middle name*，和 last name。last name 是他們的「姓」，放在最後一個，例如

美國的總統：George　Walker　Bush
　　　　　 first name　middle name　last name

美國人的 *middle name* 在他們家族裏面，是有意義的，通常是紀念他們認爲在他們家族重要的成員。Listening is his *middle name*. 字面的意思是「聽是他中間的名字」，也就是「聆聽是他重要的一部份」，引申爲「他擅長傾聽別人說話。」

這個慣用句的公式是：「*sth.* is *one's middle name*.」

middle name 可以引申爲「專長；個性；特點」。

【例】 Teaching is his *middle name*. (教書是他的專長。)

　　　 Generosity is his *middle name*. (慷慨是他的個性。)

　　　 (= *He is very generous*.)

　　　 Kindness is his *middle name*. (他個性很好。)

　　　 Talking is his *middle name*. (他很會講話。)

　　　 Making friends is his *middle name*. (他擅長交朋友。)

　　　 Service is that company's *middle name*.

　　　 (那家公司的特色是服務良好。)

　　　 Listening is his *middle name*. 這句話等於 Listening is his *game*. 【作「專長」解的時候，his middle name 等於 his game。】

20

14. We're *counting our blessings*.

count〔kaunt〕v. 計算 blessing〔'blɛsɪŋ〕n. ①祝福 ②幸運的事

這句話的字面意思是「我們在計算我們種種幸運的事」，引申為「我們要想想我們有多幸福。」

【例】 When you feel sad, *count your blessings*.
（當你傷心的時候，想想自己種種幸福的事。）

在這裏的 *count your blessings* 的含意是 *remember how lucky you are*。

當你的朋友在抱怨的時候，你就可以說：*Count your blessings*.（你想想看你自己有多幸福。）

又如： A: I'm so unlucky today.（我今天真倒楣。）
B: You need to *count your blessings*.
（你必須想想自己有多幸福。）

15. He *came along* at the right time.

come along 美國人常用，中國人不會說，所以我們要研究研究。come along 的意思有：

① 進展（= *develop*）
How's your English *coming along*?（你的英文進展如何？）

② 跟著（= *follow*）
You go now; I'll *come along* later.（你先走；我隨後就來。）

③ 趕快（= *hurry up*）
Come along, or we'll be late.（趕快！否則我們就要遲到了。）

④ 出現（= *appear*）
He *came along* at the right time.（他出現得正是時候。）

這句話也可說成：He came at the right time.（他來得正是時候。）

從現在起，當你說英文的時候，要常說 *come along*，你說起來才像美國人所說的話。

20

16. *Your time with us is done.*

　　　　done 和 finished 這兩個字，都表示「已經完成了；結
束了」，但是，在這個句子裏，就不能説：Your time with
us is finished. (你和我們在一起的時光已經結束。) 表示我
們已經絕交。

　　　　例如，你要把某人開除，你就可以説：

Your time with us is finished. You're fired.
(我們不再來往了，你被開除了。)
【在這裡 finished 的語氣非常不好，有厭惡的感覺。】

　　　　Your time with us is done. 這句話的意思是「你和我們
在一起的時光，已經告一段落。」並未表明你將來和我們還
來不來往。

17. All good things must come to an end.

　　　　這一句是英文諺語，字面的意思是「所有美好的事物都
有結束的時候」，引申爲「天下沒有不散的筵席。」

18. We all agree.
We all feel the same way.
I know I speak for everyone.

20

　　　　We all agree. 字面的意思是「我們意見一致」，引申爲
「我們大家都有共識；我們大家都同意。」

　　　　We all feel the same way. 這句話的意思是「我們有同
樣的感覺」，也就是「我們有共識。」和 We all agree. 意義
相同。美國人常重覆相同意義的話，來加強語氣。

　　　　I know I speak for everyone. (我知道我代表每個人講
話。) 説這句話是因爲，前面説了 We all agree. We all
feel the same way.

speak for 代表…講話；爲…辯護

【例】 I *speak for* my class. (我代表全班講話。)
I *speak for* my mother. (我代表我媽媽講話。)
My lawyer *speaks for* me. (我的律師替我辯護。)

19. E-mail us.

e-mail〔ˈiˌmel〕 v. 寄電子郵件 (= email)
E-mail〔ˈiˌmel〕 n. 電子郵件 (= Email)

在 Webster 英英字典中，e-mail 是動詞，E-mail 是名詞，但是因為這是新的字，有些人並沒有遵照這個規定。

現在的人喜歡說：E-mail me. 之類的話，這裡 e-mail 雖然是動詞，但因為是在句首，所以要大寫。他們把普通郵件戲稱做 snail mail (蝸牛郵件)。

20. Give us a ring.
Give us a jingle.

ring〔rɪŋ〕 n. 鈴聲   jingle〔ˈdʒɪŋl〕 n. 叮噹聲

ring 和 jingle 這兩個字，都是電話的響聲，現在都代表 telephone call。

美國人喜歡說 Give us a ring. 有點幽默的語氣，講 Give us a jingle. 就是更俏皮的語氣。以後，叫別人打電話給你，你就可以說：*Please give me a ring*. 或 *Please give me a jingle*. 說這兩句話，比 Please call me. 要來得輕鬆、幽默，不那麼死板。

20

21. You have *an open invitation*.

invitation〔ˌɪnvəˈteʃən〕 n. 請帖；邀請

一般的請帖 (invitation) 上面，都會註明時間，但是給人家一個沒註明時間的請帖，就叫做 *open invitation*，表示隨時都歡迎他來。

【例】 A: When can I visit you? (我什麼時候可以來看你？)
B: You can come at any time. *You have an open invitation*. (你隨時可以來。隨時都歡迎你來。)

22. No one can fill your shoes.

把鞋子穿上，美國人説：Wear your shoes.（把鞋子穿上。）或者幽默地説：Fill your shoes.（把鞋子穿上。）【塞進你的鞋子】

在這裏，No one can fill your shoes. 字面的意思是「沒有人能夠穿你的鞋子」，引申爲「沒有人能取代你的職位。」所以，在句中的 fill one's shoes，是指「接替某人的工作或職位」。講這句話是幽默的語氣，所以不説：No one can *wear* your shoes.（誤）

23. *You are one of a kind.*

即使全世界最大的英漢字典，也找不到 one of a kind，只有在 Webster 及 Collins Cobuild 英英字典上才有。

one of a kind 獨一無二的（＝*unique*）
這個片語太常用了，現在已經可以變成一個字：one-of-a-kind。

【比較】 *one of a kind* 同類的只有一個（表示「獨一無二」）
　　　　 two of a kind 同樣的有兩個（打撲克牌，兩張一樣點數）
　　　　 three of a kind 同樣的有三個（打撲克牌，三張一樣點數）
　　　　 four of a kind 同樣的有四個（打撲克牌，四張一樣點數）

two of a kind 很少用，通常用 pair 代替。

打撲克牌的時候，拿到兩張 A，你就説：I have a pair of aces.（我有兩張 A。）當你拿到了三張 A，你把牌一攤，你就説：I have three of a kind.（我有三張相同點數。）當你拿到四張 A，你就説：I have four of a kind.（我有四張相同點數。）

24. We'll think of you *always*.

這句話也可説成 We will *always* think of you.（我們將永遠想念你。）

25. You are such a part of us.

這句話字面的意思是「你是我們不能缺少的一份子」，引申爲「你對我們非常重要。」

20

> ***a part of us*** 很常用。
>
> 你看到一個人，你很喜歡他，像是你生命的一部份，
> 你就可以説：You are a part of me. (我非常愛你。)
>   = You are a part of my life.
>   【這兩句話強調字面的意思，通常對最親密的人講，
>   像你的女朋友、妻子或子女等】
>
> 你看到一個好朋友，你可以説：
>   You are a part of my family.
>   = You are a part of the family.
>   = You are a member of the family.
>   (你像是我的家人；我把你當作我的家人一樣。)
>
> 【比較】You are a part of us. 【一般語氣】
>   You are ***such*** a part of us. 【加強語氣】
>   (你是我們不能缺少的一份子；你對我們非常重要。)

26. Our prayers go with you.

   prayer ① ('pre‧ɚ) *n.* 祈禱者
       ② (prɛr) *n.* 祈禱；祝福 (通常用複數)

    這句話字面的意思是「我們的祈禱或祝福和你同在」，引
   申為「我們祝福你。」這句話的意思就是：We pray for you.
   (我們祝福你。)

20

27. Be well.
   Stay well.

> 這兩句話句意相同，well 做形容詞，是表示「健康的」。
> Be well. 要健康。(= *Be healthy*.)
> Stay well. 要保持健康。(= *Stay healthy*.)

28. Make your mark.

   mark (mɑrk) *n.* 痕跡
   make one's ***mark*** 成功；成名 (= *make it big*)

    這句話的字面意思是「使自己留有痕跡」，表示「要成功。」

美國人喜歡説幾年幾年要成功，他們習慣把他們要做的事先講出來。

【例1】 I'll ***make my mark*** in three years.

（我三年後要成功。）

【例2】 A: I want to be rich. （我想要有錢。）

B: Stop talking about it, and go ***make your mark***.

（別說了，趕快去做大事。）

29. Bravo.

bravo〔'brɑvo〕*n.* 好極了（喝采聲）

當你看到有人跳舞跳得很漂亮，唱歌唱得很好，演講講得很好，你都可以説 Bravo. 在戲院，觀眾通常一面拍手，一面喊 Bravo. Bravo. 你高興喊幾句，就喊幾句。這個字來自義大利文。在這篇演講中的 Bravo. 是指「你好極了。」，也就是「你很棒。」的意思。

30. Hip, hip, hooray!

hip〔hɪp〕*n.* 喝采歡呼聲

hooray〔hu're〕*n.* 歡呼聲（= *hurrah*）

單獨説 *Hip, hip.*（誤）沒有什麼意義，沒有人會這麼説。美國人在聚會的時候，通常手上拿著啤酒，一個人帶頭叫 Hip, hip，其他人就跟著叫 hooray! 也可以一個人連續喊：Hip, hip, hooray!（萬歲，萬歲，萬萬歲！）

hooray 這個字也可以單獨使用，如當公司達到業績，開香檳酒慶祝的時候，你就可以呼喊：Hooray! Hooray! 這個時候就可以隨便喊多少次了，不像 Hip, hip，後面只喊一聲 hooray！

20

【作文範例】

March 13th, 2022

Dear Andy,

This is a sad day for me. I know you have to leave but I don't want you to go. You are so kind, helpful, and humorous. ***More importantly***, you are like a friend of the family. We have not only worked together, but also learned and played together. You are my friend and confidant. But as they say, all good things must come to an end.

Andy, I hope you will keep in touch. Please let me know how you are doing. Just pick up the phone or send an E-mail. ***Above all***, feel free to come back whenever you want. You have an open invitation and will always be welcome.

I know you will do well in the future. My prayers go with you. Be well, stay well, and make your mark.

Yours sincerely,

Jennifer

20

APPENDIX

英語會話總整理

三句為一組，按照記憶排列，很好背。

1. 表示感謝的話總整理

(1) **Thank you.** 的歸納

1. Thank you. (謝謝你。)
   Thank you very much. (非常謝謝你。)
   I can't thank you enough. (我怎麼謝你都不夠。)

2. Thank you so much. (非常謝謝你。)
   Thank you for your help. (謝謝你的幫忙。)
   Thank you for all you've done. (謝謝你為我所做的一切。)

3. Thank you for everything. (一切都謝謝你。)
   Thank you for everything you've done for me.
   (謝謝你為我所做的一切。)
   Thank you from the bottom of my heart. (我衷心感謝你。)

(2) **Thanks.** 的歸納

1. Thanks. (謝謝。)
   Thanks a lot. (非常謝謝。)
   Thanks very much. (非常謝謝。)

2. Thanks so much. (非常感謝。)
   Thanks ever so much. (非常感謝。)
   Thanks for everything. (一切都感謝。)

   説明　so = very
   　　　ever so = very

附錄

3. Thanks a lot. (非常謝謝。)

Thanks a million. (非常謝謝。)

Thanks a billion. (超級謝謝你。)〔有點幽默的語氣〕

4. Thanks heaps. (非常感謝。)

Thanks a bunch. (非常感謝。)

Thanks a bundle. (非常感謝。)

【説明】 heap〔hip〕*n.* 一堆　　bunch〔bʌntʃ〕*n.* 一堆；一把
bundle〔'bʌndl̩〕*n.* 一把；一捆
Thanks heaps. 字面意思是「謝謝一堆」，表示「非常感
謝。」同理，Thanks a bunch. 和 Thanks a bundle. 也
是指「非常感謝。」

(3) 其他感謝的話

1. You have my thanks. (感謝你。)

You have my gratitude. (感謝你。)

You have my appreciation. (感謝你。)

2. I'm grateful. (我非常感謝。)

I'm really grateful. (我真的很感謝。)

I'm more than grateful. (我感謝得不得了。)

〔more than 作「不只…而已」解〕

3. I'm in your debt. (我感謝你。)

I'm indebted to you. (我感謝你。)

I'm forever indebted to you. (我永遠感謝你。)

【説明】 be in *one's* debt = be in debt to *sb.*「受某人恩惠」，
debt 字面意思是「債務」。
I'm in your debt. 字面的意思「我欠你的債」，引申
為「我虧欠你」，即「我感謝你。」

附錄

4. I appreciate it. (我感謝。)
   I appreciate it very much. (我非常感謝。)
   I appreciate the things you've done for me.
   (我感謝你為我所做的一切。)
   【注意：appreciate 作「感激」解時，後面不能接「人」。】

5. Obliged. (感謝。)
   Much obliged. (很感謝。)
   I'm much obliged. (我很感謝。)

6. I owe you. (我感謝你。)
   I owe you one. (我欠你一次人情。)
   I owe you a big one. (我欠你一個大人情。)

7. I owe you big. (我欠你很多人情。)
   I owe you big-time. (我欠你很多人情。)
   I owe you a lot. (我欠你很多。)
   【big-time 不可寫成 *big time*】

8. I owe you a favor. (我欠你一次人情。)
   I owe you a big favor. (我欠你一個大人情。)
   I owe you a huge favor. (我虧欠你太多了。)

　 説明　講 I owe you. 之類的話，表示「非常感激。」，美國人
　　　　最喜歡聽。

2. 回答感謝的話總整理

當別人對你說 "Thank you." 或 "Thanks." 你該如何回答？

1. You're welcome. (你別客氣。)
   You're most welcome. (你真客氣。)
   You're entirely welcome. (你太客氣了。)

　 説明　也可以加強語氣說：You're most certainly welcome.
　　　　You're welcome. 的本義是「你是受歡迎的。」引申
　　　　為「你很客氣。」

2. My pleasure. (我的榮幸。)
   It was my pleasure. (我的榮幸。)
   It was a pleasure. (眞榮幸。)

3. The pleasure was mine. (我的榮幸。)
   The pleasure was all mine. (我很榮幸。)
   The pleasure was entirely mine. (我非常樂意。)

4. My honor. (我的光榮。)
   It was my honor. (是我的光榮。)
   It was an honor. (很光榮。)

5. No problem. (沒問題。)
   No trouble. (沒問題。)
   No sweat. (沒關係。)

   說明 sweat 的主要意思是「流汗」，No sweat.「沒有流汗」，
   表示並沒有費很大的功夫，引申爲「沒關係。」用這句話
   來回答 Thank you. 表示親近。

6. Nothing. (沒什麼。)
   Nothing at all. (沒什麼。)
   It was nothing. (沒什麼。)

7. Don't mention it. (沒關係。)
   Don't worry about it. (不要放在心上。)
   No big deal. (小事一椿。)

   說明 這三句話可以一次講，加強語氣，很順，用以回答別人
   的感謝。

8. A: Thank you. (謝謝你。)
   B: Any time. (不客氣。)

   說明 Any time. 源自 At any time. 原爲 I can help you at
   any time. (我任何時候都可以幫助你。)
   Any time. 是對回答 Thank you. 的最好的回答話。

3. 打招呼總整理

除了說 How are you? 你還會說什麼？

1. How are you? (你好嗎？)
   How have you been? (你好嗎？)
   How's life been treating you? (你日子過得如何？)

   説明 How have you been? 是 How are you? 的完成式。
   也可説成：How've you been? = How you been?
   【語言的轉變，愈來愈短，由於人們愈來愈懶得講話。】
   How's life been treating you? 字面的意思是「生活
   怎麼對待你？」引申為「你日子過得如何？」這句話也可
   以只説 How's life? 以後，你跟別人打招呼，就可以
   一次説這三句了。

2. How are you doing? (你好嗎？)
   How are you getting along? (你進展如何？)
   How are things going with you? (你近況如何？)

   説明 How are you doing? 美國人常説成 How're you
   doing? 或 How you doing?
   get along 進展
   第三句可以簡化：
   How are things? (近況如何？)〔一般語氣〕
   How are things going? (近況如何？)〔加強語氣〕
   How are things going with you?〔語氣最強〕
   (你近況如何？)
   這三句話美國人都常説。
   你學會了 How *are* you doing? 你以後見到美國人，
   也要常説 How're you doing? 或者 How you doing?
   要習慣説這類的問候語。

附錄

3. How's it going? (情況如何？)
   How's everything? (一切好嗎？)
   How's everything going? (你一切情況如何？)

   説明 go 作「進展」解。

   這三句話後，都可以加上 with you，來加強語氣。

   How's it going *with you*?
   How's everything *with you*?
   How's everything going *with you*?

4. What's up? (有什麼事？)
   What's happening? (發生什麼事？)
   What's going on? (發生什麼事？)

   説明 中國人見面說：「吃飽了沒有？」、「吃過飯了沒有？」
   並非一定問吃飯的問題，而是打招呼。

   美國人見面問：What's up? What's happening?
   What's going on? 也是並非一定問「發生了什麼事？」

   現在 What's up? 有一個最新的説法和寫法是：
   Wazzup〔waz'ʌp〕?

   從今天起，你見到人，就可説：Wazzup?
   不要忘記，一次説愈多句愈好。

5. What's new? (有什麼新的事情發生？)
   What have you been doing? (你在忙些什麼？)
   What have you been up to? (你在忙些什麼？)

   説明 What's new? 和 What's up? 一樣，除了字面意思之
   外，美國人常用來打招呼，並不一定真正問你有什麼新
   的事情發生。例如：

   A: What's new? (有什麼新鮮事？)
   B: Nothing. (沒什麼。)

   A 和 B 都是在寒暄。

打招呼的時候說：*What are you doing?* 就不對了，
因爲它的意思是「你在做什麼？」可是它的完成時態，
美國人就常說。

What have you been doing? 字面意思是「你一直
在做什麼？」引申爲「你在忙些什麼？」是美國人常用
的打招呼用語。

What have you been up to?
be up to 的意思是「正在做」，這句話字面的意思是

「你正在做什麼？」引申爲「你最近在忙什麼？」

A: What have you been up to? (你在忙什麼？)
B: Same old thing. (做的都一樣。)

4. 回答打招呼總整理

別人對你說 How are you? 你該怎麼回答？

1. Fine. (好。)
   I'm fine. (我很好。)
   I'm doing just fine. (我非常好。)

   說明 I'm doing just fine. 也可說成 I'm doing fine.
   但不可說成 *I do fine.* (誤) 用現在進行式表示情感。

2. Great. (很好。)
   I'm great. (我很好。)
   I'm doing great. (我非常好。)

3. Okay. (還好。)
   I'm okay. (我還好。)
   I'm doing okay. (我還好。)

附錄

4. Dandy.
Fine and dandy.
I'm just fine and dandy.

〔説明〕 dandy〔'dændɪ〕 *adj.* 極好的（ = *very good*）
這三句話中國人少說，但美國人常說。

A: How are you?（你好嗎？）
B: ***Dandy***.（很好。）
A: How's it going?（情況如何？）
B: ***Fine and dandy***.（好、非常好。）
A: How's everything?（一切好嗎？）
B: ***I'm just fine and dandy***.（我很好。）

從現在開始，當別人跟你打招呼的時候，你就要回答
Dandy. Fine and dandy. 之類的話了。每次跟外國
人講話，要説不一樣的句子，你的英文才會進步。

5. Happy as a clam.（我很快樂。）
Couldn't be better.（好極了。）
As good as it gets.（好極了。）

〔説明〕 你有沒有看到，假日的時候，美國人坐在門口、躺在
草地上一動也不動，你看他們像什麼？像一個一個的
蛤蜊（clam）。他們懶洋洋地，一動也不動，覺得很
快樂，所以才會有這種表達法。

As good as it gets. 源自 It is as good as it can get.
（能多好就多好），表示「再好不過了」，或「好極了。」
Couldn't be better. 字面的意思是「沒辦法更好了」，
也就是「好極了。」這句話用得太普遍了。

Couldn't have been better. 是表示過去「好極了。」

【比較】A: How's life?（你好嗎？）
B: ***Couldn't be better***.（好極了。）〔現在式〕
A: How was your trip?（你的旅行如何？）
B: ***Couldn't have been better***.（好極了。）〔過去式〕

6. I can't complain. (我不能抱怨。)
No complaints. (沒什麼好抱怨的。)
I have nothing to complain about. (我沒什麼好抱怨的。)

說明 美國人最喜歡抱怨了，所以老師教小孩說：
Don't complain. (不要抱怨。)
所以，美國人常喜歡用 I can't complain. 來回答。
I 有的時候可以省略，變成 Can't complain.

A: How's life been treating you?
(你日子過得如何？)
B: *Can't complain*. (沒什麼能夠抱怨的。)

A: How have you been? (你好嗎？)
B: *No complaints*. (沒什麼好抱怨的。)

A: How are things going? (近況如何？)
B: *I have nothing to complain about*.
(我沒什麼好抱怨的。)

Can't complain. 和中國人的語言文化不同，所以中國人少說。Can't complain. 字面的意思是「不能抱怨」，引申為「沒有什麼能抱怨的」，表示「一切都很好。」

5. 表示再見的總整理

(1) 簡單再見的歸納

1. Bye. (再見。)
Bye-bye. (再見。)
Good-bye. (再見。)

2. So long. (再見。)
Farewell. (再見。)
Happy trails. (一路順風。)

當別人出遠門時，很久以後才會見到時，你可以說 So long.，可能源自 It will be *so long* before I see you again.「要過很久，我才能見到你。」

附錄

Farewell. 也是要對出遠門的人所說的話，像電影「霸王別姬」，英文片名就是 "Farewell My Concubine"。

Happy trails. 句中的 trail 主要的意思是「小道；小路」，古時候沒有現在的大馬路，所以用 trail 這種小路，當朋友要出遠門了，習慣就會說：***Happy trails.*** (一路順風。) 現在路已經變寬，從 trail 變成 road，但人們依然保持原有的語言，不說 Happy roads. (誤)。所以，當你的朋友要出遠門時，如：出國旅行、唸書，或畢業，朋友要分離時，就可以說："So long. Farewell. Happy trails."

3. Adios. 〔ˌɑdɪˈos〕(再見。)
   Hasta luego. 〔ˈɑstaˈluego〕(再見。)
   Hasta la vista. 〔ˈɑsdɑ lɑ ˈvɪsdɑ〕(再見。)

這三句話是無價之寶，你不知道要跟外國人相處多久，才會聽到這些他們圈內的話。這三句話都是西班牙語，都表示「再見。」在美國，很多地方，現在還沿用西班牙為地名，最近，眾多的墨西哥人移民美國，更造成這些話的流行。以後你和美國人說再見時，你就可以說這三句話，他們會覺得很親切。

4. Have a good day. (再見。)
   Have a nice day. (再見。)
   Have a good one. (再見。)

Have a good day. 和 Have a nice day. 只有白天可以用，而 ***Have a good one.*** 句中的 one 是指 day, morning, afternoon, evening 其中一個，因此早上、下午、晚上都可以用。

例：A: Good-bye. (再見。)
　　B: ***Have a good one.*** (再見。)

A: I'm going home. (我要回家了。)
B: ***Have a good one.*** (再見。)

A: It's getting late. I have to go. (已經很晚了。我要走了。)
B: ***Have a good one.*** (再見。)

5. **Later**. (再見。)
   See ya. (再見。)
   Ciao. (再見。)

ya〔jɑ〕*n.* 你 (= *you*)　　ciao〔tʃau〕*n.* 再見

　　Later. 是 See you later.的省略，意思是「待會見」。

See ya. 中的 ya (= you)，ya 是非常口語的講法，在一般字典上找不到，但是美國人常說，在口語中，you 都可以講成 ya，如：Thank you. 可說成 Thank **ya**.再者，Catch you later.可說成 Catch **ya** later.

　　Ciao 這個字出自於義大利文，等於英文的 Hello. 和 Good-bye.，凡是見面和再見都可以用 **Ciao**. 這個字，當別人不管跟你再見或見面時，跟你說 **Ciao**.，你也可以回答 **Ciao**.。

　　例：A: Hello! (哈囉！)
　　　　B: **Ciao**. (哈囉！)

　　　　A: I'm going. (我要走了。)
　　　　B: **Ciao**. (再見。)

6. I'll see you. (我會再見到你。)
   I'll see you soon. (我會很快再見到你。)
   I'll see you real soon. (我真的會很快再見到你。)

　　這三句話很棒，一句比一句還要強烈的想要再見到你，連續說這三句話，別人聽了會很高興。

7. See you. (再見。)
   I'll be seeing you. (我會再見到你。)
   I'll be seeing you soon. (我會很快再見到你。)

附錄

　　這三句話很棒，一句比一句有感情，說 See you.比較輕鬆，未帶感情，說 I'll be seeing you. 就有感情了，I'll be seeing you soon.更有感情。進行式和未來進行式都比較有感情，說話的句子愈長，愈有感情。

8. Catch you later. (待會兒見。)
 I'll catch you later. (我會待會兒見到你。)
 I'll try to catch you later. (我會想辦法跟你見面。)

Catch you later.比 See you later.來得幽默，因為 catch
字面的意思是「抓」，這三句話也是一句比一句有感情，你
需要常說。

9. I gotta go. (我要走了。)
 See you later, alligator. (待會見。)
 In a while, crocodile. (待會兒見。)

gotta〔'gɑtə〕【俚】(= got to)

  I gotta go.【常用】
= I got to go.【少用，不要學】
= I've got to go.【常用】
= I have got to go.【一般美國人不這麼說，喜歡咬文嚼字的人才說】
= I have to go.【常用】

alligator〔'ælə,getə〕n. 短吻鱷（產於美國及中國，體型比 crocodile 小）
crocodile〔'krɑkə,daɪl〕n. 大型的鱷魚（產於非、亞洲、美洲，嘴尖長）

alligator

crocodile

See you later, alligator. 唸起來很順口，因為 later〔'letə〕
和 alligator〔'ælə,getə〕押韻，later 的字尾和鱷魚的字尾
gator 發音相同，都唸成 /etə/。

In a while, crocodile.

in a while 不久（= *before long*）

　　In a while 是 I will see you in a while. 的省略，表示
「待會兒見。」while〔hwaɪl〕和 crocodile〔ˋkrɑkəˏdaɪl〕這
兩個字的字尾，都唸成 /aɪl/。有些美國人說：After a while,
crocodile. After a while 表示「過了一段時間」，比
In a while 時間長一點。

　　alligator 和 crocodile 都是「鱷魚」，並不是指人，只是
講著好玩，尤其是美國小孩再見時喜歡說 See you later,
alligator. In a while, crocodile. 講這些話有一點童心未
泯，開玩笑的語氣。

(2) 離開某人時

1. Take care.（保重。）
   Good to see you.（很高興看到你。）
   It was good to see you.（真是高興看到你。）

   　　　美國人很懂得去體貼別人，所以在與別人道別的時候，
   都會要對方好好地保重自己。Take care.也可說成 Take
   care of yourself.然後看到朋友時會很高興，就算要離開
   了，也要跟他說，能夠看到你是件很高興的事。

2. Nice meeting you.（很高興認識你。）
   Nice talking to you.（很高興和你說話。）
   Nice running into you.（很高興認識你。）

3. It was a pleasure meeting you.（很榮幸認識你。）
   It is a pleasure to have met you.（很榮幸認識你。）
   It's been a real pleasure.（真的很榮幸。）

6. 表示同意的總整理

(1) Yes 的歸納

1. Yes. (是。)【常用】
   Yeah. (是。)【最常用】
   Yup. (是。)【較常用】

   yeah〔jɛ,jæ,jɑ〕*adv.* (= *yes*)
   yup〔jʌp〕*adv.* (= *yes*)

   查遍所有的英漢字典，yeah 都沒有唸〔jɑ〕，可能這個字是二次大戰以後，美國人才開始使用，源自德文的 ja。

   當 yeah 作 yes 解的時候，唸成〔jɑ〕，作歡呼聲的時候，唸〔jɛ〕。

   例如：A: I won the first place. (我得到第一名。)
   　　　B: Yeah, yeah, yeah! (耶！耶！耶！)
   　　　　〔jɛ〕〔jɛ〕〔jɛ〕
   　　　　【在此的 yeah 是歡呼聲】

   又如：A: Let's go home. (回家吧。)
   　　　B: Yeah. (好。)
   　　　　〔jɑ〕

   Yup. 這個字，一般書上很少出現，可是美國人常說。

   例：A: Did you hear me? (你有沒有聽到我講的話？)
   　　B: Yup. (有啊。)

   也可以連續講兩句，來加強語氣。

   例：A: We should take a break. (我們應該休息一下。)
   　　B: Yup, yup. (好啊，好啊。)

   美國人一般認為，在講話的時候，不需要這麼拘束，以及正式。因此，當他們說 Yes 的時候，經常只會說 "Yeah"，"Yup" 則是在更隨性的情況下會說出。

附錄

2. Right. (對。)
You're right. (你是對的。)
You got it. (你是對的。)

(2) 意見一致時

1. That's true. (那是真的。)
That's right. (那是真的。)
That's for sure. (對的。)

2. I agree. (我同意。)
I agree with you 100%. (我百分之百同意你的說法。)
I couldn't agree with you more. (我完全同意。)

3. I have no problem with that. (對於那件事，我沒問題。)
I couldn't have said it better. (我無法再說得更好了。)
We see eye to eye on this. (我們意見一致。)

> eye to eye 的意思是非常的接近，表次兩對眼睛非常
> 接近地注視著對方，We see eye to eye on this. 字面上
> 的意思是「我們眼睛對眼睛來看這件事情。」引申為「我們
> 意見一致。」

(3) 表達接受的歸納

1. It's okay. (好的。)
It's fine. (好的。)
It's good enough. (夠好的。)

附錄

2. That's it. (就是那樣。)
That's the ticket. (那就是關鍵。)
That hits the spot. (那就對了。)

> That's the ticket. ticket 代表「關鍵」，所以當
> 你說 "That's the ticket." 就表示「那就是關鍵。」
>
> That's hits the spot.指的是「完全的滿足感。」
> hit 的意思是「達到」，spot 在此是指「一個人在滿意度
> 上的標準。」That's hits the spot.字面上的意思是
> 「達到我的標準。」引申為「那就對了。」

3. Never been better. (不會再更好了。)
It couldn't be better. (無法再更好了。)
It doesn't get any better than this.
(無法再比這個更好了。)

(4) 表達了解的歸納

1. I got you. (我懂了。)
Gotcha. (我懂了。)
(I) got it. (我懂了。)

> Gotcha 是 Got you.的連音。Got you, Got you
> 講快幾次，就會變成 Gotcha。這句話要多說，講話才
> 會像美國人。

附錄

2. I hear you. (我聽到了。)
I can see that. (我了解。)
I see what you mean. (我了解你的意思。)

3. I know. (我知道。)
I know what you mean. (我知道你的意思。)
I know what you're talking about. (我知道你在說什麼。)

7. 表示不同意的總整理

(1) 簡單的拒絕

1. No. (不。)
   Nope. (不。)
   No way. (不要。)

> 當美國人在很隨性說話時，表同意跟否定的時候，在字尾都喜歡加上一個 p 的音，像：Yup 或是 Nope，都是很好的例子。

2. No! (不！)
   Not a chance. (不行。)
   I don't think so. (我認為不行。)

(2) 表示不贊同的歸納

1. I don't agree. (我不同意。)
   I disagree. (我不同意。)
   I disagree completely. (我完全不同意。)

2. I don't like it. (我不喜歡。)
   I don't get it. (我不懂。)
   I don't care for it. (我不想要這樣。)

3. It's not for me. (這不是我要的。)
   It's not my style. (這不是我的想法。)
   I can't stand it. (我無法忍受。)

4. That's insane. (那不合理。)
   That's unthinkable. (那絕不可能。)
   That's out of the question. (那完全不可能。)

附錄

> That's insane. insane 是「瘋狂的」意思，所以當你聽到一個人講了會令你覺得不可思議的事情時，你就可以說 That's insane. 或 That's crazy.

8. 引起他人注意的會話歸納

(1) 引起某人注意時

1. Pardon me. (對不起。)
   Excuse me. (對不起。)
   Hello? (哈囉？)

2. Look here. (看這裡。)
   Do you hear me? (你有聽到我說的嗎？)
   Are you listening to me? (你有在聽嗎？)

3. Look at this. (看看這個。)
   Take a look at this. (來看看這個。)
   Look what we have here. (看看我們有什麼。)

(2) 邀請別人說話時

1. You got a minute? (你有空嗎？)
   Got a minute? (有空嗎？)
   I need to talk. (我需要和你說話。)

2. Can we talk? (我們可以說話嗎？)
   Can I talk to you? (我可以和你說話嗎？)
   May I have a word with you? (我可以和你說句話嗎？)

3. Let's talk. (我們來聊聊。)
   Let's chew the fat. (我們來閒聊。)
   Let's shoot the breeze. (我們來閒聊。)

   chew the fat，字面上的意思是「嚼肥肉」，為什麼叫「嚼肥肉」呢？因為肥肉會讓你在口中一直嚼，肥肉不容易嚼爛，所以會像嚼口香糖一樣，在口中一直嚼、一直動，就像在講話一樣。因此，引申為「閒聊」。

shoot the breeze 就是用閒聊來打發時間，因為 breeze 是微風，shoot 是射擊，對著風打槍，是打不著的。因此，這是很浪費時間，也是沒有意義的事情，引申為「閒聊的；浪費」時間；無意義的。」

(3) 回應別人時

1. I hear you. (我聽到了。)
   I heard you. (我已經聽到了。)
   I'm listening. (我在聽。)

2. I'm here. (我在這裡。)
   I'm still here. (我仍在這裡。)
   I'm all ears. (我耳朵全在聽。)

   耳朵是用來聽的器官，如果你全身都是耳朵，表示你什麼都聽得到，什麼都聽的進去。如果你在上課時，老師問：「你聽懂了嗎？」你可以說：I'm all ears. (我有在聽。)

9. 表示道歉的總整理

(1) 誠心的道歉

1. Sorry. (對不起。)
   So sorry. (真對不起。)
   I'm very sorry. (我非常對不起。)

2. I'm really sorry. (我真的對不起。)
   I'm terribly sorry. (我非常地對不起。)
   I'm sincerely sorry. (我由衷地對不起。)

3. I apologize. (我道歉。)
   My apologies. (我道歉。)
   You have my sincere apology. (我對你誠心的道歉。)

附錄

4. Please accept my apology. (請接受我的道歉。)
   Please accept my heartfelt apology. (請接受我由衷的道歉。)
   I offer my most sincere apology. (我獻上我最誠心的道歉。)

(2) 接受責備時

1. It's my fault. (是我的錯。)
   It's all my fault. (全是我的錯。)
   I'm fully responsible. (我完全地負責。)

2. I take the blame. (我接受責備。)
   I'm to blame. (我應該接受責備。)
   You can blame me. (你可以責備我。)

(3) 承認錯誤時

1. My mistake. (是我的錯。)
   I didn't mean it. (我不是有意的。)
   I didn't intend it that way. (我不是故意那樣做的。)

2. I shouldn't have said that. (我不應該這麼說。)
   I shouldn't have done that. (我不應該這麼做。)
   I should have asked you first. (我應該先問你。)

(4) 請求原諒時

附錄

1. Can you forgive me? (你可以原諒我嗎？)
   Can you ever forgive me? (你可以原諒我嗎？)
   Can you find it in your heart to forgive me?
   (你可以真心地原諒我嗎？)

2. I ask your forgiveness. (我請求你的原諒。)
   I beg your forgiveness. (我乞求你的原諒。)
   I ask for your mercy. (我請求你的慈悲。)

從小背「一口氣」，爭一口氣！

■ 5歲以上 開始背數字篇。
「一口氣背中文成語學英文①」
書+CD售價380元

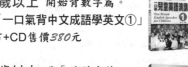
■ 小學三年級
「一口氣兒童英語演講①」
書+CD售價280元

■ 6歲以上 背「演講式英語」的「感謝父母篇」。
「演講式英語」
書附錄音QR碼售價480元

■ 小學四年級
準備國一英文考試。
「一口氣背文法」
書附錄音QR碼售價280元

■ 7歲以上
準備小一入學口試。
「問一答三英語」
書+CD售價280元

■ 小學五年級
「一口氣考試英語」
書+CD售價280元

■ 小學一年級
「一口氣背會話（上）」
書+CD售價580元

■ 小學六年級
背「演講式英語」的自我介紹、成功之道，再繼續背「一口氣背中文成語學英文①」。
「演講式英語」
書附錄音QR碼售價480元
「一口氣背中文成語學英文①」書+CD售價380元

■ 小學二年級
「一口氣背會話（下）」
書+CD售價580元

國中生必背

■ 國一 練習用所背的句子寫作文，奠定良好基礎。
「一口氣背文法」書附錄音QR碼售價280元

■ 國二 可以參加「英語演講比賽」。
「國中生英語演講①」書+CD售價280元
「國中生英語演講②」書+CD售價280元

■ 國三 增加單字量，準備銜接高中英語課程
「用會話背7000字①」
書+CD並附QR碼售價280元

演講式英語背誦記錄表

篇　　　名	口試通過日期	口 試 導 師 簽 名
1. Self-introduction	年　月　日	
2. How to Master English	年　月　日	
3. Award Ceremony Speech	年　月　日	
4. A Speech to Honor Parents	年　月　日	
5. A Speech to Honor Our Teachers	年　月　日	
6. Making an Introduction	年　月　日	
7. How to Stay Healthy	年　月　日	
8. How to Achieve Success	年　月　日	
9. Just Do It	年　月　日	
10. Happy Birthday Speech	年　月　日	
11. Why We Should Study English	年　月　日	
12. How to Be Romantic	年　月　日	
13. Don't Be Afraid to Make Mistakes	年　月　日	
14. How to Make a Fortune	年　月　日	
15. Paradise Is Waiting for You	年　月　日	
16. Change Is the Name of the Game	年　月　日	
17. How to Make Friends	年　月　日	
18. Just Saying Thank You Is Not Enough	年　月　日	
19. A Wedding Address	年　月　日	
20. Farewell Speech by Host	年　月　日	
全部 20 篇演講總複試	年　月　日	

1. 背完一篇，可至「劉毅英文教育機構」(台北市許昌街 17 號 6F)
   接受口試。通過後，可領勤學券 200 元。
2. 20 篇全部通過，可再領勤學券 1,000 元，共可領到勤學券 5,000 元。
3. 本書是無價之寶，背完終生可以使用，句子優美，有感情，任何演講都
   無法取代。

口試地點：台北市許昌街 17 號 6F　　☎ (02) 2389-5212

演講式英語
Learn English Through Speeches

附錄音 QR 碼　售價：480 元

主　　　編 / 劉　毅
發　行　所 / 學習出版有限公司　　　☎ (02) 2704-5525
郵 撥 帳 號 / 05127272 學習出版社帳戶
登　記　證 / 局版台業 2179 號
印　刷　所 / 裕強彩色印刷有限公司
台 北 門 市 / 台北市許昌街 17 號 6F　　☎ (02) 2331-4060
台灣總經銷 / 紅螞蟻圖書有限公司　　　☎ (02) 2795-3656
本公司網址 / www.learnbook.com.tw
電 子 郵 件 / learnbook@learnbook.com.tw

2022 年 1 月 1 日三版一刷
【本書改編自「劉毅演講式英語①②」】

ISBN 978-986-231-464-7